'It's Just Not Village Politics:
Westminster challenges Woodfield Magna'
- sequel to
'It's Just Not Village Cricket'

Philip Algar

Philip Algar, B.Sc. (Econ.) F.I.J., has written seven previous books. For many years, as a freelance editor and writer, he contributed regularly to UK and overseas publications on energy, economics and crisis management. He also wrote a regular and humorous column, on business topics, for a national newspaper and for a business magazine, but is now concentrating on writing books.

Philip Algar's biography of his father's life and times at sea, in peace and war 'Goodbye Old Chap' was published by Peakpublish in 2009.

IT'S JUST NOT VILLAGE POLITICS

Westminster challenges
Woodfield Magna

Philip Algar

Ken
Very best wishes,
Philip Algar.

JUMPING FISH

An imprint of Peak Platform
New Bridge, Calver
Hope Valley
Derbyshire
S32 3XT

First published by Jumping Fish 2012
Printed at svanprinters, India (www.svanprinters.com)
A CIP catalogue record for this book is available from the
British Library
ISBN: 978-1-907219-
www.peakpublish.com

Dedication

This book is dedicated to all those who fight intolerant and dictatorial authorities and companies which are determined to continue with their own selfish plans to the detriment of the local people whose lives will be disrupted

Acknowledgements

I must thank all those people in companies and government who, because of their failings and eccentricities, unwittingly, gave me so much amusement and who prompted me to write this book.

Chapter 1

It was a Friday evening in mid May, on the eve of the FA Cup final, in Woodfield Magna. That is not to imply that what was once regarded as one of the main football matches in the August-May season was to be played in the Ottershire village. The fixture was to be fulfilled in Cardiff, because Wembley, the usual venue, had been booked for an international gathering of morris dancers. This was a planning mistake by the "authorities" but the dancers now contended that the soft turf, re-laid every quarter for the last two years, might be too dangerous for their delicate movements. As a result, the stadium, now known affectionately as "Dome 2", would be empty on the crucial day. In time-honoured tradition, those responsible for the fiasco claimed that, "lessons had been learnt", thus obviating any need for anyone to lose their job. No, all this was to confirm that it was mid May in WM. Even the fiercely independent Woodfieldians accepted that it was also May in the rest of the country, wherever that was.

The small and sleepy village, which had been by-passed by history, was surrounded by steep hills, which were criss-crossed by lazy meandering brooks which collected the rainfall and oozed down the slopes towards the village. En route, they joined the Beckett, an overambitious stream, which occasionally flooded a very small and run-down caravan site, just to show that it could, although it rarely caused any damage. It was not a malicious stream and did not like adverse publicity. Indeed, any malevolent intentions that it might have had would have been thwarted by horizontal ridge ploughing in the fields and many robust hedges. The few shops, the church, garage and some of the cottages were in the centre of the village, around the square, which was but yards, or even metres, apparently, according to the few younger residents, from green fields, woods and hills which, until recently, had escaped the attention of avaricious builders and jealous urban politicians.

The number of trees around the village was diminishing each year. Quarterly inspections from the appropriate branch of the Health and Safety Executive, liaising closely with 12 other quangos which had oddly survived the government cull and which were "working locally for you in the national interest", determined that, in the future, for the first time in centuries, one might fall. This could kill a human being. According to the quango-co-ordinating £200,000 a year chief executive, this would deny the victim some basic human rights over what he tersely described as "a prolonged and indeterminate period of time going forward". The HSE view had been formulated by an erstwhile member of the financial community. It was widely believed that he had been given the job as Trees, Bushes and Hedges tsar as he used to work for a hedge fund. Predictably, he maintained that previous history was no guide to future performance.

Clearly, one of our fundamental rights, graciously and generously bestowed by the wise but unelected men and women in Brussels, is to be free from the prospect of being felled by tumbling trees. Doubtless, it is only a matter of time before trees are granted the rights to remain upright and then quangos, led by generously paid erstwhile politicians, will have to be created to determine the relative rights of trees and humans in an "ongoing conflict of interest situation".

Unfortunately, one official tree-feller, who had had only 15 years' experience, had been injured during the spring's lopping operations and his management took revenge by toppling two more trees than had been planned and issuing a serious warning about the dangers of tree-climbing by unskilled and inexperienced people.

Geoff Wood, aged 78, middle-aged by WM standards, was pontificating in the pub which, had it been a tree, would

2

doubtless have been demolished years ago. As now, he was usually preoccupied with such weighty matters as whether dogs, which lived next door to each other, when walking around the village, greeted the relevant fellow canines as neighbours. Alternatively, did they just greet each other as dogs, irrespective of whether they had previously met? He speculated that, if one dog was a neighbour but the other one was unaware of this, an embarrassing misunderstanding could occur.

However, the "tree issue", as he called it, in line with politicians who now discussed not problems, but issues, as well as "tough decisions", had exercised Geoff who had argued in the Duck and Orange, some weeks ago, that, given this attitude, it would only be a matter of time before the church steeple would have to be demolished. Tellingly, he knew of one that had collapsed some years ago, although he could nor recall where, which had narrowly missed a group of pensioners attending a funeral. Fortunately, as he put it, the steeple fell on the coffin, and, as he confided, would have killed the occupant if he had not, "fortunately" already been dead. It missed all the live people who were revived swiftly by the earlier-than-planned beginning of the wake.

This possibility, that the steeple might fall, not that somebody might be hurt, worried the lemon shandy-sipping Reverend Arthur George Nostic, whose usual congregation would double if his five sons attended. On hearing the story, he had vowed, immediately, to launch an appeal for the restoration of the whole church. Local subscriptions in the first month, totalled £3.43, two Euros, doubtless generously donated by two locals who, bravely, had ventured to foreign parts for a holiday, a small picture of Doris Day and a plastic coin from a child's game. Senior church financial authorities, themselves sincere agnostics, saw the appeal from one of their kind and immediately granted a large sum, in excess of what was required, which enabled all the repairs to be done. This surplus was used to remove and replace the centuries-old cobblestone path to the church, at the behest of the HSE, lest an accident occur for the first time ever, and to provide a scout hut. The Reverend Nostic conceded to an inquisitive local newspaper reporter that there was no scout troop in the area, and, indeed, few young people of the right age, but argued that it was wise to be prepared.

This Friday evening, the weather was fine, as it always was just before the FA Cup final. As usual, irrespective of the weather, conversation and drink were flowing in the Duck and Orange, managed by Ted Howard and his raven-haired, attractive wife, Imelda, who had given up her career in a shoe shop in the Philippines. After Ted had visited that part of the world, on what he still insisted was a holiday, she had been imported for various duties and had become an instant favourite with the males of the village.

The soporific weather had discouraged too much physical activity that evening, although some energetic members of the local village cricket club were occupied in cutting the grass or painting the pavilion. A minority were practising hard for their next fixture, in the bizarre belief that it might improve the team's prospects for achieving what some football managers call a "result". They would soon find their way to the pub for a pint or three before strolling, lolling and swaying home down the country lanes.

There was seldom any disagreement on the complex issues debated in the pub and, in a tribute to the power of democratic discussion, by late evening, everyone agreed with everyone else. The locals, who spent many happy hours discussing weather, having experienced it all their lives, did not expect the current spell of fine weather to last. Immediately the FA Cup final was concluded, what was called by the weather forecasters "unseasonably cold and wet" weather usually approached the UK as the cricket season began in earnest. It was strange that such weather was apparently unusual, argued one intellectual drinker. "After all, he contended, "it's the same every year". His friend speculated on the language used by forecasters. He did not understand how showers were "organised" and he wanted to know who did the organising. "If we knew that, we could perhaps have a word and organise the rainfall for overnight or when the English cricket team were on the brink of defeat." A stalwart member of the village

4

side suggested that, given the lack of talent and resolve often shown by the national side, the summers would always be wet.

"Precisely, just as they are now", piped up Eric Nospin, a member of the village team. He wanted to know why forecasters saw listeners "heading back" to Lords, after a truly important shipping forecast, usually broadcast at a crucial moment in the game, and showers "heading" to the west and time "heading" into the afternoon. Nobody else had picked up this new and common habit and looked at Eric in bemused fashion. He pointed out that the good weather would doubtless return in about four weeks, when the footballers returned to training and to participate in umpteen meaningless friendly matches. Why, he wanted to know, when managers moaned about how many matches were played each season, did they add to the number with all these so-called friendlies played around the world? The consensus response was that the answer was money.

Egbert Mannion, who had overcome his shyness after being ostracised at school for what some young pupils believed was an odd name, said that he was looking forward to watching the cup final the following day, between a Middle Eastern state and Russia. Enthusiasts of the once noble game, accustomed to the fact that the match took place between two domestic clubs, thus guaranteeing an English or Welsh victory, gave a collective and derisory snort, worthy of a hungry pig being offered a pork sandwich, and demanded an immediate explanation. This was posed in what can best be described as a simple question, admirable in its brevity, relevance and timing. "What do you mean?"

"Well," Egbert began, suddenly aware that most of the inmates of the Duck and Orange were staring at him and had collectively stopped drinking, in itself a rare phenomenon. "It used to be between English clubs but now they are owned by Middle Eastern and Russian types who then try to buy success by purchasing overseas players. Tomorrow's teams will probably only include one or two Brits. How many of you can name a single player who will be on the pitch tomorrow? And we wonder why we don't win the world cup with our overpaid, pampered and uninspired prima donna players."

By Egbert's standards, this was quite a speech and it attracted several approving nods and grunts. Indeed, some even went so far as to say that they would not be watching the game, even although it was to be televised, for the last time, by the BBC. Auntie had spent furiously, lavishing expensive presents on artists of little talent in an effort to persuade them to desert their current employers, and now had insufficient funds to televise a national and popular sporting event. International tiddlywinks and underwater swimming had replaced football at peak viewing times but, doubtless to the surprise of senior corporation executives, audiences had vanished with the speed of an athlete on drugs. Additionally, the demand for bottled water had cost the corporation some £400,000 in the previous year, so, understandably, given the need to spend on such necessities, there was no more money to devote to televising football. One slender hope remained for the game's supporters. A legal expert was building a case to be presented to Brussels. His view was that the absence of football on terrestrial television constituted a breach of human rights. The court had already been sitting for more than a year and a decision was confidently expected within another 18 months.

Another group of patrons were discussing some events in the news. From their general demeanour, it was clear that they held authority in little short of contempt. Apparently, one London paper had claimed that police had "shot a dead woman" and a spokesperson from the HSE had volunteered the thought that a cemetery could be a death trap. A retired footballer claimed that his erstwhile club was staring down the barrel of a wooden spoon. A member of a charity argued that an umbrella organisation should be set up to help flood victims and a tennis player, for once conceding that she had not played well, argued that, nevertheless, a win was a win, except when it was not in which case it was not a win.

Newspapers always like giving the age of people, whether or not it is of relevance to the story, so it should be mentioned that Steven Brown-Hassett, a resident of Sydney, Australia, aged 28, was on holiday. That much information would be totally irrelevant but for the fact that young Steven, as he was affectionately known in Woodfield Magna, was in the Duck and Orange and was listening attentively to the debate. He had been brought up in WM but had moved to the colony in his early teens when his parents decided to return to Australia. Undeterred by their lack of relevant experience and knowledge of business but inspired by some idiots who had appeared on a television programme, they had bought a hotel outside Sydney. Apparently, the district chosen had been on the threshold of a major development, but this had not happened and it was only when the hotel began to hold very discreet orgies, advertised as "significant networking opportunities" that business perked up. Now the parents had sold their business and moved to the country. Steven's mother had retired but his father, trading on, and, indeed, cashing in on his contacts from his previous job, was enjoying a successful new career as a politician.

Steven was pleased to see so many of the residents who remembered him. It seemed that people just did not die in Woodfield Magna or in the neighbouring village of Halston Friary whose residents also patronised the Duck and Orange. Steven's host at the pub was grey-haired Godfrey Murray, until recently, the ageing wicketkeeper for the local team.

"Well Godders, old chap," he asked, adopting what he thought was the correct form of address in England, having listened to one of the apparently aristocratic cricket commentators who often seemed less interested in the cricket than the habits of pigeons and buses, and whose ambition was to see a pigeon on a bus, "what's being happening in this sleepy little backwater of a village whilst my back was turned for a few years?"

Godfrey paused, looked a little forlornly at his empty glass and sighed just long enough to suggest that not all was as it should be in the matter of personal beer supplies. Steven noted the gesture, apologised for not replenishing his old friend's stock of the amber liquid and headed for the bar with minimal delay and what passed for alacrity. The task completed, he

7

returned to his seat and eagerly anticipated hearing what was what, and for that matter, what had been what, and, if it were not stretching a point, what might be what in the future.

He prompted Godfrey.

"I gather that there's been a bit of a row about a cricket match, played for money, possible corruption by a local builder and some problems with local councillors over what some newspapers claimed was bribery. It was all to do with building some new houses, wasn't it?"

Godfrey nodded, wondering where to begin on the story that had propelled Woodfield Magna onto the front pages of the national newspapers.

"Yes, you're right. A local builder, Brian Parker, wanted to put up some new houses in the village but his problem was that it was almost impossible to get planning approval. What's more, most of us locals didn't want any new houses as we thought that would spoil the character of this fine old village and, anyway, none of us could afford the so-called affordable houses that were planned. However, nobody listened to us, of course. That's the way that democracy works in this country now. When a new development is proposed, the politicians spend more time concerned with the welfare of insects than listening to us, and the insects don't even have a vote. Only last week, the government set up what they called a new nation-wide, blue-skies thinking group, headed by an insect tsar, paid a salary of £100,000 for a two day week, to find out why some beetles are dying out and why the English are afraid of spiders. Not only are they all mad, but they are killing our language.

Anyway, Parker also wanted publicity for the village as nobody had heard of us and he hadn't got the money to spend on massive advertising."

Steven interrupted. "But I've seen some new big houses just outside the village."

Godfrey resumed.

"Hold on, my young antipodean friend, that comes much later. Parker decided to offer a prize of £50,000 to the village that won a cricket match. The money would be spent on local developments and he also promised £25,000 to the winning club and £1,500 to each member of the winning squad. The umpires were to be rewarded well, as well."

Steven interrupted again. "And this match was between WM and Nutley?"

"Yes. All this attracted so much publicity that probably every adult in the country now knows where our beautiful village is so Parker had no need to advertise. We had television crews down here just before, during and after the match and, of course, as the match took place in the silly season, when many journalists are on holiday, we had massive coverage in the daily papers as editors decided that what was happening here was much more newsworthy and easier to cover than the troubles in the Middle East and even divorces between so-called celebrities."

"It's the same at home in Oz. It's very difficult to get what I call real news. Anyway, I've got a question. Surely, there was a chance that we would lose the game and then the money would not come to Woodfield and, anyway, why would even winning the match guarantee that, for the first time for ages, planning approval would be granted?"

"Good questions, young sir, but let me finish. Certainly, the publicity that we had would have cost millions if bought on the open market but it all came free, of course, thanks to the money that was on offer which made the story newsworthy. You're right. How could Parker, who, incidentally was president of the village cricket club, have ensured that we won the match? Only then could he initiate the second part of his grand plan. That was simple. He invited a young fast bowler, on the county books, to play for us and, in return, he would organise a new house for him, even though no new houses

9

were planned in the area. He knew that this bowler could win the game for us.

Fred Statham took the field when one of our regulars supposedly injured his ankle. There was some doubt about the severity of the injury. Those who felt, judging by his writhing and bellowing, that, at the least one leg, and possibly more, would have to be amputated, probably on the field, were reassured when, just a few hours later, they saw him jogging to the pub in the next village. Some locals even praised him for his acting ability which, according to some devotees, was even better than seen on some television soaps made in Australia.

Active substitutes were allowed and Fred won the game for us. However, Parker reckoned without the experienced cricket commentators who identified young Statham and pointed out that one of the rules of this odd match was that all participants had to live within the village or its boundaries. Statham didn't so the game was awarded to Nutley and Woodfield didn't get a single penny."

"So what's all this stuff about corruption?"

"Parker had told the local authority that he was planning to make a large donation to the winning village and that the responsibility of allocating the cash would rest on a new standing ad-hoc committee which would include four members of the local council. They would each be paid £10,000, a huge sum for what most of us regarded as very little work. Although, I suppose, to put it into context, that's the sort of money our MPs claimed a year or two back for cleaning out their fishponds and moats and providing upmarket and affordable housing for their ducks. Apparently clean ponds are essential if an MP is to do his job effectively. Imagine a decision, on, say, whether we go to war again with a Middle Eastern country and during the crucial debate in the House, a member suddenly begins to worry not about whether some rogue state can attack this country in five minutes but about the cleanliness of his fish pond and what his neighbours might say. How on earth can he concentrate on the debate? Poor fellow, he can't and it's no wonder that so many members voted in favour of attacking Iraq. Clean fishponds, clearly, are key to an informed democracy. Sorry, I seem to have diverted myself. What was I saying?"

Steven jogged his memory.

Suitably jogged, Godfrey resumed.

"Ah, yes. Parker then told the planning committee that he would be submitting an application for planning approval for a new housing estate in the near future."

Steven whistled in amazement. "So it was an on-going nudge-nudge wink-wink situation?"

Godfrey was not at all happy at this abuse of language but dealt with Steven's next question of whether Parker was arrested.

"No, the whole of our justice system has a problem or two. There is a shortage of money and nobody wants to prosecute a case unless the accused is obviously guilty. After all, holding a long and expensive trial which results in an acquittal makes those prosecuting look silly and, of course, there's always the question of the expense. I suspect that some of our trials, costing millions, are some of the most costly in the world. It's gratifying that we lead the world in something. Then, of course, even if the accused is found guilty, there is the problem of what to do with him. Our jails are already full, despite letting many criminals out very early into their sentence although more vacancies are created by the large number of prisoners who escape every year. That said, we still don't have enough cells so you can imagine that it's not considered to be wise to charge anyone with anything, unless it's really important. Parker was not. And there's another point. Some expert lawyers are arguing that, under the legislation relating to human rights, it is illegal to imprison anyone. So the authorities are playing it safe and not jailing so many people in case they are sued by the criminals. Even when they are inside, some criminals have sued the government, successfully, for failing to provide coffee at an acceptable temperature.

"To be fair to the authorities in the Parker affair, they really thought about it and there was a wide-ranging and detailed in-depth analysis of all the issues. It took them nearly the two years since Parker made the offer and cost millions of pounds. Anyway, it would have been a waste of time as Parker had disappeared and it would have been silly to waste more resources and money looking for him."

At this point, Godfrey sneered and uttered a loud and unambiguous "pah" which indicated his contempt for what passed as justice. Indeed, he felt so strongly that he allowed himself a second "pah" and one had the feeling that a third was seriously considered and rejected only at the last moment.

"One leading politician, a retired lawyer, selflessly and temporarily forsaking the time he usually devoted to fiddling his expenses on his substantial home, denounced the authorities for being more interested in saving money and reputation than risking losing cases in the courts." Godfrey added, perhaps unnecessarily, that the MP's background and work tended to diminish the impact of his allegation.

"But, as the more objective observers of the Woodfieldgate saga had to concede, Parker and his chums had been very careful and it might well have been difficult to sustain a prosecution. Some of those who wrote to the newspapers argued that it was a series of coincidences, that, together, had given the wrong impression. Troubled of Lower Middlegate, who is to letter writing what conceit is to international tennis players, even suggested that the media had exaggerated the whole affair and had decided that their target was declared guilty even although no legal proceedings had been or were about to be taken. Some correspondents questioned the role of the media in all this. 'Surely, they represent the ugly face of capitalism?'"

"What about Parker?"
"As I said, he's vanished and nobody seems to know where he is. He has, reportedly, been seen in Port Moresby, in Papua New Guinea, Monrovia and at a circus on the outskirts of

Eastbourne. Overall, since the fateful cricket match that we won and lost, the village has slowly returned to normal, although there are a few more tourists who plucked up the courage to drive down the narrow country lanes, so we've built a new car park. We locals can park there for nothing but we charge others £4.00 per hour. That tends to deter visitors. Those who do walk more than 400 yards from the car park, and they are in a small minority, don't show much interest in us and I think that they see us as inmates in a museum."

Godfrey paused to sip some more beer and his young friend followed his example, before asking what had happened to the plans to build a new estate.

"As I said before, I've seen some new houses just outside the village."

"Yes, after the rumpus had died down, and a new planning committee had been created, official approval was given to a company nobody had ever heard of, based in Archester, nothing to do with the disgraced Parker. As you may have seen, I think they've got planning permission for 12 of the big houses but they're also required, as part of the contract, to construct 25 "affordable" houses on the other side of the village, in the Northfield area. You'll remember that's about half way up the steep hill, some distance from any of the existing homes. Frankly we're all opposed to this and we hope that they will never be built. It was bad enough when we had to put up with all that dust and noise when they were building the first of the so-called executive houses and they haven't finished them and now there's the recession, so I suppose they'll abandon the project for the present, just leaving a mess."

"If the new houses are affordable, why are you all so hostile? Don't you need more people living here if the village is to survive?"

"Yes, but it won't be local people. That's the point. The government has no idea of what is affordable to us. Our income on average is at least 20 per cent down on that achieved in nearby towns. When someone dies here, their

13

home is often passed on to the offspring. That's why the population number seldom goes above 1,000. Mainly, we're all happy with that and we all know each other. We don't want the noise and mess of more building unless the homes are at sensible prices and what's most important, is that many, if not all, of the new houses will only be used as second homes. Already, a few homes in the area are owned by people who come here only at weekends, usually only during the summer, and their houses are empty for the rest of the year. They contribute nothing to village life but push property prices above what we simple locals can afford.

"We want to keep the village, broadly, as it is, but we do need some homes that we locals and others like us can really afford. If we can't afford them, we don't want them. Do you know that some children who were brought up here can't afford to come back? It's all because of those second homes. Any more-expensive building would change the local character but we'll lose the battle and Woodfield Magna will be changed for ever, for the worse. That's what these faceless, unelected and ignorant idiots in local and central government, call progress. I'm thinking of joining the protest group, which is quite a strong one, and I'd like to write something which we could call Magna Carter. On second thoughts we might ask Will, you remember him, to front the campaign, although he's in the States at the moment. Then he could sign the Magna Carter protest as Will Carter." As Godfrey spelt out this idea, he knew it sounded silly, very silly, but he'd started, so he finished.

"It's even worse. The number of young children in the area has declined so that some children from outlying villages have to be bussed in and even the local vicar is now responsible for three parishes, although it's not too demanding as I understand that the total average congregation is about 30 and the authorities have given him a second-hand bike with a very impressive bell. I just hope that our Post Office manages to survive as nearly 500 were closed in the last year across Britain. Then there's the village store. It's suffering from the lack of passing traffic and that's ironic because we don't want

14

too many visitors. About 4,000 village stores in rural areas closed in the last 12 months. It's all very tricky."

"You really think that these other new houses will be built?"

Godfrey sighed again, not this time to indicate that his glass was empty but because it was all so frustrating. He shrugged his shoulders and said, "It seems inevitable but they will be the wrong kind of houses".

"Anyway, Steven, I gather that you'll be in Woodfield for the summer, staying with Mike Redding and his family, so I expect that you'll see what happens in the village yourself. He seems to be the unofficial leader of the village and I think he has more influence on what happens than the council. He's been chairman of the cricket club for some years now and, since he retired about a year ago, he's been busy getting involved with so many committees.

"Incidentally, I heard a rumour the other day…"

Here he stopped to mop up some beer spilled near him by Nathaniel West, a retired banker, who immediately apologised and bought Godfrey and Steven pints before sitting down alongside them where the former introduced the latter. Gone was the opportunity for Steven to find out what was rumoured.

Chapter 2

After some years of living together in the village, which upset some of the more mature residents, Hilary Cook, a television gardener, married Charlotte Bush, 25, a television cook. The local residents, hearing the announcement of the pending nuptials, had braced themselves for the inevitable publicity which would plague Woodfield Magna. Charlie, as she was known, was an attractive young blonde and most agreed that the 38 year old, self-centred balding Hilary Cook was lucky to have such a permanent partner. Those who did not know the couple struggled to recall that Charlie was the female and Hilary the male. To make matters worse, the cook was called Bush and the gardener was called Cook.

It had been suggested before their wedding that it would have been a good idea to drop the Bush part, as it reminded the politically aware of one of the least popular American presidents, notwithstanding the keen competition for the title. The so-called celebrities had considered this idea seriously after their lecture tour in California attracted such small audiences that the trip failed to cover costs. Indeed, the only positive factor was that Charlie, appearing on local television chat shows frequently, denying that she was related to the president, was able to market her latest cook book and undertake some modelling work which eventually led to her being invited on to a jury to judge dancers in a national and televised competition. Hilary had been invited to appear on a number of television programmes in the mistaken belief that,"she" was an English chef and had been conspicuously less successful.

Charlie thought that if she became just a Cook, it would be good publicity as she could then claim to be a Cook by name and a cook by profession. Indeed, the prospect of being a cook and a Cook had played a tiny part in her seeking out Hilary, although, inexplicably to many, she was now deeply in love with the gardener, or so she told the celebrity magazines in which she appeared about every other month.

Her publicity agent argued against dropping the Bush, pointing out that Cook was a very common name, whereas Cook-Bush or, for he was an imaginative man who justified his high earnings, Bush-Cook was unique, and, if it were not, it should be. Charlie, unhappy with this, pointed out that the former name sounded like an odd instruction in a recipe that might appeal to vegetarians but agreed that both names had to be retained. Her husband shared many characteristics and odd ideas with the erstwhile American president and wanted to become a Bush. After a discussion that raged in the celebrity magazines for some weeks, and a vote on what the readers thought more sensible, the name chosen was Bush-Cook. Indeed, the frenzy was such that the prime minister, speaking in Parliament, even offered his own opinion on what was, apparently, "a tough decision". More people voted for the name than voted in the previous local elections across the country.

It was rumoured that at least one elderly and undiscerning local resident had become excited when she heard that the pair were to be married in the local church by the Reverend Arthur George Nostic. The fuss created by television coverage of the nuptials was soon forgotten and Woodfield Magna resumed normal service, although it remained interested in the battle between two publications on which of them had exclusive photographic rights. As one astute local resident summed it up, "All they do is garden and cook, and that's just what me and the wife do".

The government, determined to show the rural community that it cared deeply about village life, following some poor local election results, had organised a detailed national survey of crime in the countryside. There was no apparent reason for this initiative but, of course, that did not matter. What did matter was that it seemed a good idea in terms of public relations because everyone was worried about crime. Where better to start than in the countryside where little crime occurred? This analysis was to be carried out each quarter and was hailed as a bold if overdue initiative by the Association of Social Statisticians, ASS. This group had been so concerned about increasing unemployment for number crunchers that it had commissioned its own detailed enquiry into why so many figures experts were facing unemployment.

There was virtually no crime in Woodfield Magna which was top in the first of the quarterly surveys. Apparently no offence of any kind had been committed in the village in the last three months. This worried Rob Swagg, 27, prematurely avuncular in appearance yet frequently puerile in his sense of humour, albeit that it had been hidden for some time. He was the local policeman who was responsible for law and order in Woodfield and in the surrounding villages. He was delighted that he had nothing to do, apart, of course, from filling in numerous and multicoloured forms, indicating how he spent his time but he had always been imaginative and this was, as the current cliché contended, "No problem".

However, if this offensive absence of offences was continued and, worst of all, publicised, he might be moved to somewhere where he had not only to work but had someone breathing down his neck and generally bossing him around. He shuddered at the prospect. He knew from watching numerous crime series on television that all senior policemen were stupid, out of touch with the real world and played golf, which he did not. Rob regarded himself as bright and, apart from the golf defect, ambitious.

The results of the first survey were released on a slack news day. Editors, tired of covering stories about petulant footballers bravely struggling on £120,000 a week, divorced "celebrities" and computer discs containing confidential information being lost by government officials, turned enthusiastically to the new crime survey. Hordes of what might, loosely, still be called Fleet Street's best, descended on Woodfield Magna, determined to find out why the locals were so well behaved. At first, all was well. It seemed that the locals were God-fearing and rather old-fashioned "folk", or "guys", depending on which paper was conducting interviews with the locals, who did not want to be ostracised by fellow Woodfieldians for breaking the law. What the reporters failed to perceive that there was little worth stealing in the village, the lanes were too narrow to drive speedily away from a crime and that nobody irritated anyone else with very tall conifers. Boundary disputes just never happened. All that, of course, was true but there was another factor: most people just could not be bothered.

As the representatives of the tabloids eagerly sought new angles but were frustrated, their own behaviour deteriorated to levels seldom, if ever, associated with the media, well, not in Ottershire. Some Woodfieldians were penned inside their cottages as the reporters sought interviews, knocking lustily and continuously on their elderly front doors. This could not be tolerated and the villagers reacted strongly and in such a way that the visiting photographers had one of their most enjoyable and commercially successful days since members of the government had been pelted with the appropriately coloured paint by frustrated environmentalists.

Before the last reporter had retreated, the crime rate had soared as several intrusive media personnel, seeking interviews, were attacked by local farm workers with pitchforks. One penetrated a member of the fourth estate in an area that forced him to write his copy from a standing position for several days. Another was photographed by a colleague with an egg dripping down his expensive anorak and a third found that his car tyres, unlike the UK economy, had experienced deflation. Scribes from one of the more odious newspapers, appropriately, were pelted with manure and some of the female journalists had to seek shelter in the local garage after which they wrote snide pieces about "allegedly fully grown rural men" as if they were a different form of Homo sapiens, who enjoyed pics of semi-clad girls that were plastered on the walls. Such photographs, of course, would never be found on the walls of urban garages which, doubtless, carried extracts from Plato's Republic. Unselfishly, the newspaper in question, keen to assist readers to come to an informed judgement, in line with its editorial stance on all matters, devoted two whole pages, in full colour, to reproducing the shameful pics. For some days, the local garage experienced a temporary but welcome increase in business. Some city types, tired of Plato, came to WM for modest supplies of petrol.

The manure thrower, reluctantly arrested by Police Constable Rob Swagg, was subsequently charged under anti-terrorist legislation, but was found not guilty. The case lasted a week and cost the taxpayer several thousands of pounds.

This spate of lawlessness propelled Woodfield Magna to the bottom of the next survey and some journalists, who had not been to the village before, then made the journey to find out why the crime rate had soared. On this occasion, the locals, to a man and woman, refused to say anything and the coverage was predictably bland and unimaginative, whilst some papers attributed the rise and fall to a statistical quirk. The new group of journalists, their colleagues from the previous encounter having cowardly decided against a return trip, were not the only visitors to the village. The Society of Working Psychologists, concerned about increasing unemployment of its members, commissioned a detailed study, backed by some government funding, a generous award from Brussels and money from the National Lottery, to find out why a peaceful village had managed to plunge from the top to the bottom of the rural crime survey in so short a time. Their analysis was expected to be completed in the next 18 months and the predicted outcome was expected to be that it was just a statistical quirk. There was a lot of it about.

As normality returned to Woodfield Magna, Rob Swagg was becoming increasingly worried. After the battle with the media, peace had been restored and no offences had been committed in any of his villages, although there was some trouble in the primary school. Fighting had broken out after a visiting speaker told the toddlers that it was wrong for boys to hit girls and for husbands to hit their wives. Apparently, one five year old boy had disrupted proceedings by asking how many wives a husband could have and could you hit just one if you had two. He thought that his father had only one but he was not entirely sure as he'd seen his dad holding hands with one of his "aunties" when he looked through the pub window. Then, with no apparent warning, the boys, who would never have dreamt of attacking the girls, at least not until they were told that they could not, indulged in some serious fisticuffs with representatives of the fair sex. Rob did not make any arrests as the worst offender was just seven years old but writing up the fracas and filling in the necessary forms took him nearly two weeks.

There was a limit to the number of schools and societies where he could deliver lectures on crime prevention, the importance of parking cars legally and the evils of hurling manure at visitors, which, he maintained, could lead to the decay of society. This hurling business, hitherto an unknown occupation in the village, but clearly an acceptable pursuit, as it had been seen on television, immediately appealed to the children who tramped over the fields after school in the search for ammunition and targets.

If nothing changed, Rob knew that he could soon find himself working in London, dealing with violent criminals, high on drugs and low on morals, whose first act of the day would be to choose which knife to carry rather than determining which pair of trousers to wear. He shuddered at the thought of returning to the capital as well as putting the importance of selecting a knife ahead of choosing trousers. He just didn't know much about knives although he was fully briefed on the matter of trousers, and where practical, favoured the use of scissors to cut things. As he was donning his bags, he recalled a recent news item. Apparently, one of his colleagues in another part of the country had claimed that it took him 30 minutes a day to don and to shed his uniform. He was compensated by being awarded an extra week's holiday each year. Rob continued to muse. He had seen an advertisement for "trousers that move with you". How reassuring. What if you crossed the road at a busy junction and found that by the time that you reached the other side, your trousers had opted to remain in the original position?

Perhaps Rob could ensure that, to prevent his being transferred, he could ingratiate himself with the local community, generate local sympathy, indulge his love of gardening and simultaneously assist local charities. Rob was a keen gardener and, having so much spare time, he had decided to build up his relationship with the locals so that, if he were drafted to a city, there would be such an outcry that his superiors, and how he hated that word, would be deterred from posting him. One comforting and silly thought was that delays in the post would have enabled him to spend a few more weeks in WM.

Apart from his own modest garden, he had also cultivated the local newspaper, *The Woodfield and District News*, and had gone out with the editor, before she became the fashion editor of a London environmental magazine. He was not interested in sustaining the same kind of relationship with her successor, the bearded Sam Noel, who was known in the office as Knowall and always wore light brown shoes with a dark suit, or, and this must have been done deliberately to annoy, black shoes with a brown suit.

Rob had been impressed with a national scheme whereby local residents opened their gardens after being approved by well-informed officials who had to be sure that the garden was suitable, especially on matters relating to health and safety. The entry fees were given to a charity. Rob wanted to improve on that. He had been president of the local gardening club for some time and his idea was based on the national scheme. He had outlined his thoughts to the committee last winter, when they were planning the following year's activities, and it received unanimous support. It was simple: about 12 gardens in the area, including some belonging to the old but larger houses on the edge of the village, would be open on different dates, some twice, during the summer. Visitors could pay on the day or take out a season ticket, which would entitle them to go to all the gardens. The local paper gave the project its full support and acted as a centre for correspondence and the issuing of tickets.

Sam had authorised an immediate contribution to the fund and would award a prize to the owners of the garden that won most votes from readers. Children were also invited to enter a competition and to write 500 words about the garden that they liked best. The prize for the winner was £50. A camera manufacturer offered an award of £250 for the best photograph but a suggestion that another prize be available for the owner of the least-liked garden was rejected. The reward for the owners of the best garden, apart from the publicity, was to be a visit to the Chelsea Flower show in the following year. They were also to be introduced to some well-known gardening celebrities, some of whom, allegedly, could utter an entire sentence without using the words brilliant, fantastic or naturalistic. Hundreds of season tickets were sold, in advance, in Woodfield Magna, in many of the surrounding villages and in Archester. Rob had become very popular and the local hospice, located between WM and Archester, would be the recipient of a substantial sum.

The first garden would be exposed to public gaze in early June and the owners, Mr and Mrs Arthur Smythe, retired civil servants, had built up their garden during their compulsory periods of sick leave. Now they spent many happy hours, well, many hours, deadheading flowers, mowing the lawns and, in princely fashion, giving some plants a good talking to and warning them that any failure to bloom at the right time would have serious, unpleasant but unspecified consequences. They, that is the Smythes, not the plants, always made sure that they had sufficient duplicates lest a disaster befell them and their cacti prospered thanks to generous supplies of cold tea.

Other civic-minded groups were preparing for the summer round of communal festivities but all had, wisely, taken out insurance against rain as the forecasters had predicted a long hot summer. Given the new and very strict rules imposed on public gatherings, prompted by the Health and Safety Authority and the new anti-terrorist legislation, additional insurance, against no less than 67 detailed potential incidents, including arson and devastation of gardens by wild animals, had to be taken out and the costs were such that, for some villages, their local events might never be staged again, after this summer.

The village fete, to be held in the field adjoining the primary school, was troubling the organisers who were becoming very concerned that they could not find someone famous prepared to open the festivities. The Bush-Cooks had done this for some years and it was time to find someone else.

Life in the cricket club had returned to normal in the season after the great debacle in which Nutley had been adjudged the winners after Brian Parker had ensured victory for the local team by fielding an illegal player. Now, although it was less than two years since that game had made national news, the team looked very different and there was hope that a successful year was in prospect. Will Carter, the club's leading batsman in the historic season and who had scored a fine but futile century in the key match with Nutley, was now working in America and several other members of that team had retired.

Godfrey Murray, the elderly wicket keeper who had shunned the use of his hands when keeping, an innovation that, oddly, had not been followed by the professionals, ended his links with the game to spend more time with his family. George Stevenson, who had regularly announced his impending retirement from the game, had actually stopped playing. Malcolm Smith, who had faked an injury in the crucial game, to allow Fred Statham, the county cricketer, to take the field and "win" the prize game, had been vilified and had now gone to Canada to work as a lumberjack. Apparently he wanted to fulfil an ambition forged by watching hours of Monty Python repeats on television. Fortunately for the club, one of the new residents in the new large houses that had been completed, was not only a keen cricketer but anxious to become involved in local activities. His presence at the end of the previous season and the beginning of this session had ensured that the club had enjoyed some success.

The annual art show in the primary school, when amateur artists from five nearby villages displayed their works, was scheduled for mid June. For the last four years, the show, which always managed to raise money for the school, had been opened by a local but little-known man. Allegedly, he was renowned in artistic circles and sold his work in London for vast sums. Woodfieldians were convinced that he was an expert: nobody understood a word that he mumbled when opening the show and he always wore a beret, fancy spotted cravat, smock, and corduroy trousers, daubed lightly with paint thus proving that he was, indeed a painter. Only the cynics observed that, apart from the beret, cravat and smock, that was how they looked after decorating their homes.

Some members of the organising committee felt that it was time to find someone else to undertake the task of declaring the show open. The guest had become increasingly superior when commenting on the exhibits and last year was close to openly criticising a painting by John Gaitskell, a popular local man, who had attempted to portray the village's torment, after the cricket match, by painting a large black circle, like a cricket ball, with a pound sign in the middle, all of which was streaked with red on the right and interjection marks on the left. The guest speaker's criticism attracted the attention of local television and the resulting publicity resulted in Gaitskell selling the work. A London gallery, sponsored by a dog food manufacturer, gave him £100,000 for the painting which "so vividly and with so much creative imagination, so concisely encapsulates the ongoing struggles and issues of our time".

There had been another problem facing the village: the primary school had come close to being shut permanently as there were so few pupils, despite children being bussed in from surrounding villages. Given these consistent rumours, a declining number of Woodfieldians patronised the show each year and they also argued that the school had no need for new funds. However, numbers had been augmented by three children from the new houses and local villages contributed another 17 which meant that there were now about 60 infants in attendance. This was also welcome news for the organising committee and the local builders, who had responded enthusiastically to the invitation to build new toilets to accommodate the greater number of children. Some of the previous facilities had been demolished to allow for the construction of a small television studio where the infants could begin to prepare for media studies courses at university. It was unfortunate that the absence of funds meant that there was no money for equipment so the room remained unused.

Mike Redding was keen on organising a twinning relationship with a Belgian village, Hercule-sur-Poirot, and had already set up an organising committee. A logo, designed by a local student, was of an umbrella, spats and grey cells, had been rejected as incomprehensible and this had caused a major split on the committee, with some members resigning in a collective huff.

Indeed, the demand for committee members in the village was becoming intense and as few were prepared to help organise events, some locals were very busy. It was the old story, true of so many voluntary organisations: 80 per cent of the work was done by just 20 per cent of the members, who seemed to enjoy walking around the village, armed with a clipboard and looking serious. Nevertheless, one reason for the apathy shown by the majority was that they were not really interested in gardening clubs, open days, the fete, the art show or twinning with a village in a country that, like its own nationals, would have difficulty finding it on a map of Europe. They just wanted to live their lives in peace, free from the activities of well-meaning busybodies but if it helped anyone, they were prepared, in the immortal words of one local, to "toddle along and show willing". That said, more than toddling was required.

Meanwhile, the biggest challenge to the village was the construction of the so-called affordable homes. If building proceeded, that was something against which the whole village could unite. It was going to be a busy summer in Woodfield Magna.

Chapter 3

Despite the great housing problem, all the social events planned for the village during the first few weeks of summer were overshadowed by developments relating to the Post Office and the primary school. The former owed everything to central government stupidity and the latter to the frightening advance of political correctness, embraced and encouraged by the same idiots in office. As some Woodfieldians noted, in language that had to be admired for its accuracy and eloquence, both these problems had been "dumped on us by those expense-grabbing, ill-informed, pompous know-all, know nothings up in Westminster, with nothing else to do." In a word, the Woodfieldians were unhappy and rated their parliamentarians as less trustworthy than estate agents facing bankruptcy. Even the house-building project, another London-imposed problem for the villagers, was relegated in the ranking of community concerns.

The Post Office, like so many in the rural areas around the country, was not just somewhere where the locals bought stamps, collected their pensions and drew money. That, of course, overlooks the two occasions last year when it had been asked to find some foreign currency for holidays abroad. It was the centre of the local community where the villagers met to exchange gossip as well as to use the facilities. It did not occupy a great space, much of the original area being devoted to the sale of cards, stationary, books about cooking, brushes for cleaning the inside of radiators and, inexplicably, electric toothbrushes.

Central government, concerned about the quality of life in rural communities, and alarmed by the rising crime rates in the villages, as shown by what had happened in Woodfield Magna only a few months before, had set up a Royal Commission to study rural crime in more detail. It was expected to report within five years. Rural crime, of course, to those who knew nothing, was a major problem and much more important than rising unemployment, high petrol prices, a very poor transport infrastructure, a lack of genuinely affordable new homes and only distant medical facilities. Throwing manure at innocent journalists, for example, merely trying to do their jobs, indicated a rotten society that needed treatment.

Showing an acute understanding of rural areas and their difficulties, based on the work of highly-paid consultants based in London, who decided against visiting the countryside, on the grounds that it smelt and the animals were noisy, the government had decided that, henceforth, or even sooner, all Post Offices and other outlets were to be banned from selling postage stamps. Instead, the administration was to grant an exclusive licence to two supermarket chains, one of which, coincidentally, had tried, unsuccessfully, to set up shop in Woodfield Magna. Allegedly, the money from the sale of the franchise to sell stamps was to be used to modernise the whole Post Office network, but, of course, as critics pointed out, after various other key functions had been passed to some commercial groups, there was not much left for the Post Offices. One analyst suggested that all this was like pushing up fares on country railway lines to levels that could not be afforded by intending passengers and then the line could be closed because of a lack of custom and the land sold on to, for example, supermarkets. One national newspaper suggested that the ghost of Richard Beeching was now haunting the Post Offices.

The nearest outlet where stamps could be purchased was in Archester, nine miles away, but, for those in the village without their own transport, it might as well have been on the moon. Some of those who lived in the new houses, but who worked in the city, had volunteered to buy stamps in bulk but the new government regulations, rushed through Parliament, specifically forbade such transactions, imposing a maximum number of stamps that could be bought in any one day and making it illegal to sell stamps on to a third party. Gifts were also outlawed although nobody was able to say how the law could be implemented. The issue had been debated fully in Parliament, at least by current standards. Some members said that the five minutes granted to the second reading of the bill had provoked some of the richest oratory they had ever heard in the House.

It was astonishing, that, given the frequent hostility towards some supermarkets, two chains had signed an agreement with the government by which they would have the exclusive right to sell stamps. However, there were some advantages of the new law, according to the junior minister in the Commons who would not have looked out of place in a Big Brother programme. Reading his script with some difficulty and mispronouncing a Latin phrase, he claimed that, "the number of unemployed, *ceteris paribus,* will be reduced". This was greeted by widespread cheering from his equally stupid colleagues, many of whom, carelessly not having studied Latin, if ever, for at least many decades, thought that *ceteris paribus* was yet another new way of calculating and lowering the number of unemployed. Clearly, they favoured *ceteris paribus* and were keen to have more of it. One of our main post-war problems, clearly, very clearly, was an insufficient supply of the stuff. One member came close to asking where the UK ranked in Europe on *ceteris paribus* but he did say that the current administration's stance on the subject made the Opposition look foolish and inadequate and that their policy was flawed.

The minister, albeit with a discernible lack of obvious commitment, muttered to an eventually acquiescent House of Commons that wanted to announce the creation of a new organisation, the Stamp legislation uniformed Group (SLUG), so he did. That's what ministers can do. The new slugs would be easily identified by their new, bright red uniforms, similar to those that used to be worn by postmen, which, he was pleased to say, would be made in the UK which "gives the lie to the Opposition's repeated and ill-informed claims that we have no manufacturing capacity in this country". Presumably, if only more nations employed slugs, the UK manufacturing sector would be flourishing. He was less clear on what their role was or how the system would operate but the nature of their colourful uniforms drew appreciative comments from the government back benches, which had hitherto been mainly quiet, showing nothing of their usual boisterous, unthinking support for whatever the government, which knew best, deemed to be good for the country. Some even had misgivings about what was about to be launched but, hopeful of being made junior ministers, remained silent.

Impressively, the first prosecution occurred on the second day of the new regime when an elderly pensioner tried to buy 51 first class and 50 second class stamps for his friends in a retirement home. Following an expensive trial, the case succeeded, largely because the maximum total number of stamps that could be bought on any one day was 100. A government spokesman helpfully pointed out that the legislation allowed for the maximum number to rise, to an unspecified number, unspecified thus far, at Easter and Christmas and festivals supported by others "who contributed so much to our rich and diversified culture". Determining the maximum numbers would be a tough decision but it was a characteristic of this government, unlike the Opposition, that they did take tough decisions.

It had been contended that there was no evidence that the pensioner, 85, intended to sell the stamps on or give them away, which were serious offences. However, a weakness in his case, swiftly detected by the government's top team of 15 QCs, was that arthritis had prevented his writing letters for the last 20 years. The warden at the home testified that the accused was a generous and kindly person who, at least under the old legislation, would have given a total stranger his last postage stamp. He would never have broken the law, even the "insane, impractical and unjustified law that the Westminster cretins have introduced". This was regarded as contempt of court and he was only released when he wrote out 500 times "I must not criticise the government or Members of Parliament who know what's best for us". Pleas that he did not know of any such MPs meant that he then had to write out the inane comment 700 times and was given a five year jail term, suspended for two years. The pensioner was sentenced to prison for 30 days but it was suspended for 15 years when it was realised that there were no cells available.

There was a widespread national outcry at this absurd ban and the fact that an old-aged pensioner had been "dragged through the courts in so cruel and heartless a way", according to the most popular tabloid, increased the sense of national outrage. The media concentrated on the impact on the post offices, virtually ignoring the other outlets, on the grounds that selling stamps was a small part of their business.

Mike Redding organised transport from Woodfield Magna and surrounding villages so that about 100 residents could go to the capital to join in the biggest national demonstration since the one prompted by the government's decision to impose new taxes on windows and to ban the consumption of sausages unless they were made in the European Union. Many of those from Woodfield Magna, people, not sausages, had either never been to London or had not been since it became an ugly, dirty and over-crowded city that smelt of onions, the tax on which had been relaxed in an effort to revive the economy. That said, some of the younger element wandered away from the protest and sampled the delights of clubs which had not yet reached the village and which would never have attracted any repeat custom from the elderly inhabitants, for medical if not moral reasons. The young males were readily identified on the return trip by their smug smiles that lasted for most of the return journey but which vanished as the coaches crossed the county boundary into reality and Ottershire.

All the leading newspaper editors covered the London protest and had promised total support for a sustained campaign. The BBC nominated one of their most senior correspondents to cover the story, flying him back from Afghanistan, and ITV, impressed by the turnout of the protest in London, brought two former newscasters out of retirement to bring viewers the latest news. One of the tabloids' early initiatives was to print posters. Before long, thousands of homes, across the country, had these posters in their windows, much to the satisfaction of the makers of Sellotape.

Media coverage was huge, continuing and powerful and it seemed inevitable that the government would have to scrap the new legislation and beat another retreat on one of their key ideas. The campaign leaders, who included key figures from the church, who had hitherto been totally unknown, exhorted everyone to boycott the two supermarket chains that now had a monopoly for selling stamps. Indeed, on Thought for the Day, on BBC Radio Four, a leading cleric told an anxious nation that it was everyone's duty to boycott these "wicked, unthinking and greedy" stores. That, apparently, would be the advice he would have given to his aged grandmother, if she had not been confined to her own home for seven years. He was sued and, because of pressure on the court system, the case was to be heard four years into the future but, in the meantime, showing the gravity of his alleged offence, he was given an initial police caution. Such warnings were usually restricted to cases of grievous bodily harm but one advantage was that he acquired a weekly column in a national newspaper.

At the end of the first week of the national campaign, after the legislation took effect, there had been conflicting accounts from the supermarkets, the government and the police. Campaign organisers claimed that millions had protested across the country: the police estimate was that about 150,000 had taken to the streets. "That's only a little more than go to see Man United, a sneering and snide senior policeman claimed, thus showing his ignorance of football before maintaining that the biased media had, apparently, created the whole problem. The supermarkets maintained that business overall had been brisk although those distributing leaflets of protest outside these emporia, had seen few customers.

Confronted with this "massive and unjustified rebellion", as it was described by an unelected minister from the Lords, speaking from one of his homes in the West Indies, where

32

moats were unknown, the government increased the penalties for illegal dealing in stamps.

In Woodfield Magna, anger was palpable. Some of the residents told the local paper that they were "bloody mad". So, when the local and aptly-named MP, Mr Ian M. Simple, one of the administration's leading cronies, attempted to justify the decision at a meeting in the village hall, it was hardly surprising that his words provoked more anger. Within a few minutes of the beginning of his poor, pathetic, pointless peroration, an elderly cabbage left its erstwhile owner and headed at speed towards the fool. The critic, for his cabbage-throwing had indicated that he was such, shouted out "here's a cabbage for a human cabbage". Admittedly, it was not the most succinct of slogans but regional television, tipped off that some veggie throwing could take place, captured the incident on film and, within hours, it had attracted several million hits on YouTube, from around the world.

Hurling cabbages was always good television. Visually, it was much more effective than, for example, throwing carrots or green beans or hurling grapes, whether green or black, frankly, would not have made good television. Peas, too, were no use: even in they were still in a pod, they lacked the gravitas and weight of a good cabbage. However, projecting these particular veggies could have been developed into various reality shows. For example, teams of celebrity cooks could compete against ordinary families and, before long, as the popularity of cabbages grew, elderly and otherwise unemployed celebrities could preside over shows in which other celebrities could guess the weight of the vegetable.

Experts agreed that, although the slogan might have been pithier, the vegetable hurling was admirable and the intended victim had ducked only at the last moment. A spokesperson for the Associated World Food (Untainted) Limited, (AWFUL) confirmed that the cabbage had not been produced organically. The voiceover to the television story compared the incident to that which occurred at a press conference in Iraq when an irate scribe threw a shoe at President Bush as the shoe-thrower believed that the Bush approach to his own country was not entirely flawless.

Rob Swagg had felt that it was his duty to attend the meeting. Being a conscientious chap, and keen to make an arrest, in his own career interests, he also thought it was his duty to arrest the cabbage thrower for breaking the peace and causing a disturbance. Some angry members of the audience thought that the wrong person had been arrested and that it should have been the Simple MP. On the recommendation of his superior, Rob also charged cabbage man under the prevention of terrorism act. After much adverse publicity, the case failed and the long-suffering magistrate condemned all who had been involved in bringing the case which "not only casts doubt on their judgement but propels the entire judicial into disrepute. We who work in the cause of justice are becoming increasingly upset by the cavalier way in which absurd cases are brought to court and by the complete absence of common sense. We also deplore the casual way in which counter-terrorism legislation is being used in a misguided way with little or no regard for relevance or justice."

If this conduct continued, he warned that the UK would become a laughing stock and in an aside, overheard because he had not removed his television microphone, he added "that is if we are not already". He was later required to resign for bringing the judicial system into disrepute. Subsequently, he wrote a stinging essay for one of the tabloids and was immediately asked by each of the three main political parties to be one of their candidates at the next General Election.

A junior minister, already fated to have a short career, was then deputed by his craven senior colleagues to face the media. Looking as distraught as a bus driver who could not recall where he had left his double-decker, and despite being confronted by one of the BBC's most supine but highly-paid interviewers, he managed to make the worst of a bad job.

We have consulted widely and it is clear, very clear, from all our research that Post Offices have become parasites preying on the public purse and that stamps had to be sold in the supermarkets, where, unlike the situation in the Post Offices, real competition reigns. According to our analysis, virtually everyone is within five miles of a supermarket. If this signals the end of the Post Office in rural areas, so be it. There's a price to pay for living in remote areas and people are not forced to live in obscure villages. It's their choice and it's not the fault of the government if these tiny Post Offices cannot pay their way. We are acting on behalf of the tax payer and we cannot continue to subsidise them, I mean the Post Offices.

Of course, this absurd and patronising waffle ignored the fact that the government had effectively killed the Post Offices by preventing them from selling stamps and, earlier, removing other crucial aspects of their activities which, in the past, had enabled them to survive comfortably. However, no ambitious government minister was likely to break tradition by heeding facts or following his or her own beliefs so the situation deteriorated.

The prime minister, Harry Whitehead, was debating with himself, which boded ill for the outcome, that he ought to appear on television to explain that his colleague, in whom he had total trust, which he made clear, very clear, had been misquoted when he seemed to be condemning and even ridiculing those who lived in the country. The PM, nearly as daft as his colleague, forgot that the whole of the minister's rant, from beginning to end, had been seen, live, on television so the old excuse, of being quoted out of context, which, at once, shifted blame from the guilty speaker to the innocent media, vanished.

As the pressure mounted, the prime minister decided to speak to the nation on the postage stamp affair, despite the advice of his expensive consultants. Using up one of the party's allocated broadcasts, at short notice, he decided to argue that being in government meant taking tough decisions. It was unfortunate that he recorded the broadcast in early afternoon, forgetting that it would not be aired before 10.30 in the evening. His highly-paid media advisers, costly posers all, whose advice that the PM should not do the broadcast had been rejected with minimal discussion, "forgot" this and also failed to point out that their revered leader seemed to be a little obsessed with one word. All this was noted in the quality press, prompting serious discussion about the quality of the prime minister's advisers and their cost to the public which now amounted to millions of pounds a year. The BBC staff, preoccupied with the need to defend the license system, unfortunately forgot to mention, when the broadcast was over, that, "this was recorded earlier today".

Good day to you all. I hope that the sun is shining wherever you are, as it is here, in London, the great capital of our great country. We deserve some good weather, don't we? Incidentally, I've heard it said that the capital smells of onions. I'm here to tell you that that is just not true.

At this point, some political activists wondered why a ministerial broadcast was, apparently, about to be used to reject the notion that London smelt of onions. Doubtless millions of potential visitors, who might hear or read about the broadcast, were not even aware of the allegation. However, those foreigners who had cancelled a vacation in London, concerned about the smell, would doubtless now make new arrangements, fortified by the prime minister's words. Clearly, very clearly, the problem must have been eliminated as the country's political leader was apparently in the studio to offer the desired assurance.

He continued and, with typical and admirable directness immediately announced why he was about to address the nation. Apparently, it had nothing to do with onions.

I want to talk to you today about our decision to remove the license to sell stamps from the loss-making postal network and other outlets and transfer it to two supermarket chains. Incidentally, I would like here to pay tribute to their public spirit and, if you knew how much they are charging this government, your government, for the service, I think that you would applaud the free market system. I know I do. Their gesture allows us to close more Post Offices and, after proper redundancies have been paid, we shall all benefit as public expenditure is reduced.

36

I understand that some of you may not agree with this decision. That is your right, but you're wrong. I'm told that 90 per cent of you, of us, live within five miles of one of the selected supermarkets and, if your home is further away than that, it must seem tough but we live in a world where our daily lives can seem tough.

To do what we've done, was it tough? Yes, it was tough. Yes, it was a tough decision and one that I, I mean we, believed, passionately, that we could not avoid. I cannot be accused of ducking tough decisions, especially when such decisions have to be taken. Even my political opponents know that I take tough decisions, for the British people, when they expect me to take tough decisions. I know you do.

All my life, I have taken tough decisions. I developed the habit when I was young and my father, who seldom gave advice to anyone, and who, sadly, seemed to dislike me, although he was always very fond of my brother, said, 'never be afraid to take tough decisions, son'. That was the last time I ever saw him. He ran away with the local barmaid. I recall thinking, all those years ago, and how such words come to haunt us in later life, that that must have been a tough decision, although the barmaid was very pretty and my mother had a face like an unscrubbed potato and used to play rugby for the local club's women section until she was well into her fifties. She was a fine forward and I know that the men were afraid of playing against her. I know I was.

I'm not a quitter and I don't believe that I would have got where I am today by shying away from doing what is necessary for the benefit of my party, I mean country. We have to acknowledge that the world is changing and we must change with it unless we want to be left behind when the train leaves the station. On behalf of you all, I have bought a ticket for this nation and I don't intend to ask for a refund. I do intend to be on that train with you all. Together, we must make the journey, you and me, united in our desire to do what is best for our great nation. That's what you want and I know that I do too.

I know that, when tough decisions have to be taken, and I and my colleagues have just taken one, yes, it was tough, I really do know that from the abuse, sorry, comment in the media that not everyone will benefit. In this instance, many Post Offices all over the country will close and thus will no longer be a burden on the national accounts which means your wallet and, indeed, handbag, as we must not forget the ladies or, indeed, those gentlemen who favour carrying bags. I know I do. That said, whether we live in the city, in the country, in the suburbs, in houses, bungalows or even caravans, which I believe some of my fellow citizens favour, we all use supermarkets. I know I do.

I know that tomorrow, many of you will take part in yet more protests around the country. That is fine and I welcome it. It shows that we in this long-established democracy can show our dissent without the fear of being filmed by a policeman or hit on the head by a truncheon, except when it is justified, and we certainly can trust our policemen and women to film us or to use their truncheons only when justified. I know I do. That makes me proud and I'm sure that when you demonstrate tomorrow, there will be no violence, certainly from you, although I cannot be held responsible for what the police may do and I know that they are predicting violence.

Thank you for listening to me and I hope that you all have a good afternoon and that the sun continues to shine, as it is here.

As one of the BBC's main producers hissed quietly to a colleague. "We've known for years that he doesn't know what day it is and now the great British populace has confirmation that he doesn't know what time of day it is either."

The speech had immediate repercussions at the highest level. Someone who had worked with many different prime ministers, having watched the performance, turned to her husband. "Philip, if you can hear me over the corgis' incessant noise, what do our dogs and the prime minister have in common?" The Duke, suddenly remembering that he was sitting down, unclasped his hands which had been behind his

38

back, admitted that he did not know, and deciding to play this game, asked "OK Maj, what do our dogs and the prime minister have in common?"

"They're all barking."

Ministerial colleagues decided, at breath-taking speed, at least for politicians, that the PM, after this performance, had to go away for an enforced holiday within a few days. Before he went, they would tell him that he had to resign and they, his loyal cabinet colleagues, would confirm, when he was on the plane, away from the media, that he had resigned on grounds of ill health and that he had agreed that his Post Office plan had to be cancelled. In that way, he would take all the blame. However, unfortunately, the plan to oust the PM was to take some time, as some of his craven critics backed away from taking the fateful decision so the government suffered more sustained criticism for a few days before the PM was due to fly off to foreign climes, supposedly, on official but unspecified business.

Fortunately, the day after the PM's broadcast, was fine all over the country, which, according to some participants, suggested that this was Mother Nature's way of showing solidarity with the millions who, again, congregated in more massive protests in the all the main cities in England and Wales. Millions of Chinese-made plastic badges, square in shape, resembling a stamp, and bearing the slogan "Stamp It Out, Save the PO" had been available for sale from all Post Offices, throughout the country for the last few weeks. The demand was so great that the overall group saw an immediate and significant improvement in its finances. Northern Ireland and Scotland refused to back the Westminster regime and announced that they would print and issue their own stamps which would continue to be available in all Post Offices. However, the Scots, in yet another effort to embarrass Westminster, made the plastic badge freely available throughout the UK.

The number of protesters was boosted by those who supported a wide variety of other causes and the marchers were eagerly joined by thousands who had a grouse against the government. Many hundreds of students, who, since all examinations had been made significantly easier, wanted to go to university, especially as jobs were now so scarce and the government had hinted at a big reduction in fees, joined the throngs. They were angry that there were insufficient places available in what was laughably called higher education. However so many were virtually illiterate that they were having difficulty in speaking coherently to the media, littering their comments with a plentiful supply of "you knows" and their employment of adjectives was confined to amazing, brilliant and fantastic. Their placards contained many spelling mistakes, although that was in line with the prevailing academic view that spelling and grammar were no longer important. Academic staff, too, were revolting: they opposed the further lowering of academic standards and carried banners bearing the succinct message:

SAY NO TO INTELLECTUAL RIFF RAFF

The government, concerned about the increasing "disease of obesity" as the Health Minister called it, had appointed a Slim tsar, in the bony but not bonny shape of a young matchstick-like severely undernourished fashion model. Coincidentally, the Lowrie-like girl was addressing the crowds in Trafalgar Square at the time of the stamps protest although the failure of the public address system led to some misunderstandings of what she might be saying. It was widely thought that she was making an appeal on behalf of those overseas who were suffering from malnutrition, rather than pointing out the dangers of over-eating or consuming the wrong foods. Rumours of a new tax on the fat, promoted exclusively by a tabloid newspaper keen to increase circulation, had encouraged a massive attendance of those who felt at risk and they waddled along with the crowds. One commentator described this part of the protest march as the weightiest ever seen.

Woodfieldians were angry, very angry. They lived nine miles from the nearest stamp-selling supermarket, had no reliable, regular and inexpensive transport to the city and had been labelled second class citizens by the government. Furthermore, few of them had a computer, so were denied using email as a substitute and even those who did own a machine complained that the speed was very poor because of a lack of investment in the necessary infrastructure. In a word, the new government policy seemed to be directed specifically against Woodfield and the village's representatives on protest marches were voluble, articulate and very critical of the administration. Government ministers, watching them from the safety of their offices, noted the striking nature of the banners carried by the good citizens of Woodfield and the powerful interviews they gave to the media.

The government, or to be more accurate, the prime minister's odious spokesman, seemingly reluctant to admit the appalling stamp error but fearful of having to retreat, argued that there had been fewer protesters than had participated in protests against the Council Tax and the Iraq War, thus neatly drawing attention to two other insane decisions. The number of arrests in the street protests had not been very high and the majority of those who had been taken away had been blocking the entrance to Downing Street and shouting "stamp it out" so noisily that, according to an ear witness, members of the Cabinet were unable to think clearly. This remark prompted many excellent cartoons and political commentators wondered what had been preventing them from thinking clearly before.

In Trafalgar Square, the renowned scene of many spectacular gatherings at crucial stages in the country's history, such as the winning of the Ashes against Australia in 2005 and the announcement that the UK would host the 2012 Olympics, four men had been arrested for taking photographs of a policeman trying to take their photographs. Their production of press passes counted for nothing and they were taken into custody under anti-terrorist legislation. Another protester, shouting "stamp it out" was arrested for smoking in the street and a woman was warned about the "potentially dangerous use of an umbrella". One policeman was taken by a public-spirited citizen in a citizen's arrest for swearing at a young girl. That said, the overall sentiment amongst the police, many of whom, apparently, frequently bought stamps, seemed to favour the public and several games of football were played in the parks between the police and the protesters, prompting historians to recall similar contests during the General Strike in the Twenties, although, as they helpfully pointed out, the personnel were different.

Inspired by consistent support from not just the newspapers but the whole media, the boycott of the two supermarket chains developed very satisfactorily for another day or two, to the advantage of their competitors. Some enterprising chains, which had failed in the tendering bid for the stamp sale contract, converted the situation to their advantage by sticking large notices in their windows:

We support your Post Office: We do **NOT** *sell stamps.*

As the number of letters sent declined, partly because people could not reach the sales outlets and partly because of the public's desire to boycott the relevant supermarkets, fewer and fewer letters were sent. The already precarious financial position of the Post Office deteriorated further and a major London sorting office was the first to declare redundancies. Other sites were forced to close, at least temporarily, including one near Archester, and those who had been dismissed or who were working only part-time, soon joined the protesters. Two prominent members of the Cabinet, postmen in their earlier lives, found their sympathies divided. Many of their colleagues, confronted by the spectacle of so many so-called working class members without work, began to plan their futures outside politics.

As the protests continued, fewer and fewer customers passed through the supermarket doors. One chain withdrew its application for another 800 outlets across the UK as the time was not "propitious". Even the much-publicised corner shops enjoyed a considerable increase in business as did those not based on a corner of a street. Meanwhile, the senior Trades Union officials had demanded a discussion at number 10 Downing Street. At a session that reminded participants of the old days, when beer and sandwiches were served, largely because beer and sandwiches were served now, the union executives began to mumble something about calling out millions of other workers, on the railways and buses, and they hinted that colleagues in the oil refineries would be prepared to down tools. One snide comment from a minister that few of them actually carried tools did not improve the atmosphere.

After three days, more redundancies and short-time working were announced in the Post Offices and depots across the country. In the head offices of the two supermarket chains, members of the boards discussed the severe decline in their businesses. The boycott was working and these men, for women were rarely found at director levels, fearful of hitting their pretty little heads on glass ceilings, were worried that the public would not return, even when the dispute was settled. "I think, gentlemen, that we must bite the bullet and tell Downing Street that we shall not be selling stamps any more." This was agreed later that afternoon by the board of the other supermarket and, together, both chains sent an ambassador to the prime minister.

Astonishingly, despite the chaos and pain, he told them that the decision could not be reversed. Post Offices, as such, would never again be allowed to sell stamps and, if the supermarkets refused to sell stamps, they would be sued for breach of contract. The country just could not afford these expensive changes of policy. However he had a possible solution. In future, all Post Offices would be re-branded as Communications Centres and thus would be permitted to sell stamps, after being licensed by the supermarkets as franchisees. This news, according to an analyst, was welcomed by the Society for Re-branding and New Names, although he was not sure whether the group had changed its name.

The prime minister claimed that the exercise had been costed by experts in such matters, which was a lie. It was contended that the project would cost the country millions of pounds but the government pointed out that many individuals, who would otherwise be unemployed, would be involved full time for many months, as would their colleagues in the printing and many other sectors.

Later, at Heathrow, just before he was to leave, at last, for foreign climes, the PM was giving a brief television interview to an attractive but very dim-witted blonde whom he fancied. He was pondering offering her a seat in the Lords, although he was not sure if she was a lady. Suddenly, history was about to be made. History is like that: it sneaks up on you, without warning. Before you know what's happening, the moment has passed and, years later, people ask you where were you when such and such or this or even that, happened. People really should be warned when history is about to be made and then they can compose themselves, look at their watches, check the date and generally warn their brains that something important is about to happen. Above all, they can leave the bathroom to avoid embarrassment when asked where they were at the crucial time.

The forecast that history was about to be made was proven correct. Two of his senior colleagues, frustrated that the PM still had not announced his resignation, and unwilling to sustain any more political damage, approached him as he was heading for the departure gate. Unaware that the cameras and microphones were still live, they told him that he had lost their support, he had to cancel the stamp policy and resign immediately as this was the wish of the rest of the cabinet. One of the colleagues, a doctor and another, who for PR purposes, was a former postman, took the PM by the elbows, and he was able to offer his erstwhile colleagues one each, and escorted him into the pages of history.

A brief statement from 10 Downing Street was issued within minutes of the coup. This implied that it had been planned some time in advance, because press releases usually take days to obtain clearance. Lawyers, as a matter of principle, ponder statements for not less than three days, to justify their expensive existence. Each involved party makes changes and, if the procedure is completed, the final version is usually very similar to the first draft but everyone feels better for having been involved.

After contributing so significantly to national life for so long, Prime Minister Harry Whitehead, who has resigned, is exhausted after taking so many tough decisions over the years.

He is to take a long vacation in the West Indies with his family. All his colleagues thank him for what he has done to (sic) *the country and wish him a speedy recovery. Meanwhile, the former prime minister's plan to deny Post Offices the right to sell stamps has been cancelled, with immediate effect, and the necessary legislation will be annulled within the next few days.*

Five weeks later, the former prime minister, now easily distinguishable from his loyal subjects, and, indeed, from his disloyal subjects, for the sun had not shone in the UK on anyone, regardless of their allegiance, returned from his holiday in the West Indies. He told reporters at the airport that he was "refreshed, fit and well and ready to take all the tough decisions that, as prime minister, I have to take for the country".

It was left to the political editor of the BBC, aware that he had a world scoop, to break the news. "But Mr Whitehead you were effectively forced to resign, in front of the television cameras at Heathrow, before you went away. After the great stamp fiasco, your colleagues insisted, that, as the architect of the disastrous stamp policy, you had to resign. Then, according to your press officer, you went to the West Indies for a long rest. Now, your old long-time adversary and now friend, Lord Hartle, or Mr Hartle as he is after the emergency legislation was rushed through Parliament, is the prime minister."

At this news, the countenance of the former prime minister turned from brown to black to red before he denounced "**Mr**" Hartle in language that should have been banned until long after the 9.00 o'clock watershed. Apparently, the men were not close friends and the former prime minister, now a man of many colours, was led away, shaking his fist and making expressing doubts about Mr Hartle's parentage. Another moment in history had come and gone and, doubtless, some people were in the bathroom when it happened.

Chapter 4

The Woodfield Magna primary school headmaster was William Knapp-Green, an ugly, odious, smug and self-satisfied unpleasant middle-aged sadistic bully of the kind that dominated schools a few decades ago. His curved nose suggested that he had been a bird of prey in his previous life and that the transition, physical and mental, to being a human had been less than a total success. One could not help feeling that, if he had become angry, he could be appeased, briefly, with a nut or two or, preferably, a modest piece of human flesh. Flouting current practice, he favoured wearing a black gown and when in a hurry, it billowed out around him, creating the impression that he was about to take off, having detected some small animal for his next meal.

Knapp-Green had taken a decision that was to be discussed nationally and, once again, Woodfield was dragged on to the pages of the nation's newspapers. Last Christmas, just before the school concert, he had banned all cameras at school functions, lest the resulting photographs or footage found their way into dubious hands. Some parents had disobeyed and as soon as this was discovered, the concert was terminated abruptly, to the obvious anger of the uncomprehending and tearful children as Knapp-Green denounced the parents vigorously. Parents who had defied the ban were then severely criticised by those who were enjoying watching their offspring perform and a major rumpus ensued with adults conducting themselves in a manner reminiscent of their misbehaviour in the playground years before. Indeed, it was surprising that they were not all placed on detention.

Audio recordings had been allowed and Knapp-Green was prepared to sell photographs that he himself had taken, to parents and other relatives, on proof of identity.

In an interview with the local paper he had argued that allowing the use of cameras could encourage paedophiles and that could scar children for life. "For as long as I'm entrusted with the care of these children I'll do whatever I have to do to ensure their safety and welfare." Inevitably, the story reached some parts of the national media on a slack news day and comment was mixed. Some columnists, lauding his "common sense", praised his "brave stand in these difficult times when nobody is safe and when we must protect our children from day-to-day dangers and from these monsters".

Some newspapers revealed the absurdity of another of his recent decisions. Photographs showed children wearing goggles and safety helmets whilst playing conkers. Others captioned their coverage with the pithy label "Bonkers on conkers" and condemned his action unreservedly, pointing out that no incident had ever occurred to the children at the school in over 100 years.

Knapp-Green had participated in some local radio programmes from time to time, to discuss educational matters. Having been largely ignored by his parents, who did not like birds of prey, he really enjoyed the experience of being the centre of attention, even if the audience was minuscule. He had acquired more publicity when he suspended a teacher who had put a friendly arm around a child who had tumbled over on the tarmac-covered playground. Whilst the headmaster was concerned that the children did not suffer permanent psychological damage from the fall, it was even more important that teachers with possibly "incorrect and inappropriate tendencies" were not given carte blanche to "fondle children in a demonstration of friendliness, real or feigned".

Now the stupid bird of prey had plunged to new levels. The school's version of sports day would not include any competitive events, as defeat for the toddlers could be demoralising. Furthermore, he would not allow the day's events to be watched by anyone from outside as it was impossible to guarantee that some of the spectators might not be parents but people of malevolent intent. This decision, of course, was to protect the children and he apologised to those parents who were "normal decent men and women", implying, somehow, that they were in a minority.

The odious Knapp-Green, who was unmarried and who lived with his older brother, had been asked to participate in a debate, televised regionally, on his decision to ban parents from sports day. Without any prior thought, and without asking who else might be involved, he confirmed he would be in the Archester studio at least 30 minutes before the live broadcast was due to begin. His self-esteem rose even more when he was told that a chauffeur-driven Mercedes would call for him. He did not realise that this was to permit the television company to know precisely where he was as the timing of the programme approached: it was not because he was perceived to be important. He knew that the local authorities were becoming concerned by his behaviour so it was important for him, the school and the village to give a good performance which would ensure his continued employment. He intended to do just that.

Jane Parker had divorced Brian Parker, deemed by the press of being "guilty of inappropriate behaviour on many issues", soon after "Woodfieldgate", and subsequently sold her story for £50,000 to a tabloid paper. After a significant make-over she had become a physically different female and within six months of the divorce had begun a new career as an independent adviser and commentator on educational matters. She had appeared on television twice, discussing aspects of primary education for which she was well suited, having previously been a teacher at the local primary school in Tipton Poppleford Major.

Before parting from Brian Parker, she had incurred authority's wrath for commenting to the local newspaper about "the impact of insane attacks of truly daft political correctness permeating our educational system" and she warned about the "insidious and seemingly remorseless march of political correctness and the demise of common sense, without which we will all become caged parrots, only allowed to squawk allowable phrases at a government-determined time".

Her outspoken opposition to the nonsense had prompted an invitation to join a pressure group which was "resolutely and unambiguously opposed to the pernicious nonsense being perpetrated in our schools". When the number of children of primary school age declined in and around the local villages, those remaining were diverted to Woodfield Magna. The authorities were pleased to have an excuse to declare Jane redundant.

This was the opponent who was to challenge Knapp-Green on his banning of parents at the school sports day. He really should have asked who else was to be on the programme before deciding to appear himself but his misplaced self-confidence and arrogance, resulting from years of being able to dominate small children, had not been seriously challenged by adults. The televised live discussion would present no problems.

Ron Palmer, 64, dignified and addicted to wearing sports jackets and corduroy trousers, was interested in the history of Scottish table tennis and was a keen morris dancer, not that that is relevant but that is the sort of information cited by newspapers. He had become leader of the local council after the Brian Parker affair, the commercial one, not the one Brian had with Will Carter's wife. He had been a senior executive with a printing company in Archester and had moved to one of the older large houses, on the edge of the village, some years before. It was known as Camellia House although the main attraction was lilac. As any gardener, budding, or in the Bush-Cook category knows, camellias are less than keen on the alkaline soil that characterised this garden.

He had retired last year to spend more time in his garden and on council matters. Previously, he had shown little interest in local affairs but became so incensed at Parker's apparently corrupt efforts to change the village, for his own commercial interests, that he joined the council. Now, as all those associated with the affair had resigned or been voted out of office, he had been perceived as the best man to lead the local authority into a more tranquil era. He was about to sit down to a cooked breakfast.

In those long-since departed years of innocent childhood, when the sun shone every day and Father Christmas was an annual visitor, he had been told by his mother and grandmother that if he ventured out without "a good hot breakfast inside you," his survival to lunch time, in effect, could not be guaranteed. Clearly, just looking at a good hot breakfast was inadequate. It had to be ingested. Yes, consumption was the key as it was in determining the overall state of the national economy.

All this had exercised the very young Ron. Did this mean that those who died during the day always snuffed it after breakfast? Indeed, was their demise a direct consequence of failing to eat the much-publicised hot breakfast? Alternately, did eating the specified meal guarantee survival to lunch time? Initially the very young Ron was worried: what if he was ill or was away where hot breakfasts were not served? Did such situations qualify for exemption? In due course, he heard the phrase "continental breakfast" and, on learning that this implied only cold food, asked why anyone was still alive in Europe, which, he understood, was where most of the continental breakfasts were consumed. He was told not to be so silly, which was the usual response when he sought information or had detected a flaw in "grown-up" logic. Perhaps it was just English people who would fall over by lunch time if they spurned a hot breakfast? How did his fellow countrymen differ from foreigners and what happened to the aliens who followed their own bizarre consumption habits when visiting the UK? It was all very baffling.

It was time to set up an experiment. On the very first day of the trial, as his fellow infants arrived at primary school, he discovered that the majority had consumed just a cereal and toast. Eagerly, he anticipated lunch time: he did not expect any of his chums to keel over, as he assumed that their breakfast habits had been pursued in the past and they had lived, but it would be interesting. Lunchtime came and went and everyone was still standing, except those who had returned to sit down in the classroom, obediently, awaiting the beginning of the afternoon session. He then realised that families were capable of outrageous guile but, shrewdly, he decided against challenging the existence of Father Christmas about whom he had some serious doubts. However, the idea of having good breakfasts had persisted throughout his life. The mature man shook himself out of his pointless reverie and returned from his early primary school days.

Usually, the mail arrived around mid day or even later, as the post office sought to modernise and become more efficient, but today, as he was preparing to tackle an enticing plate of two fried eggs and bacon, for which his ardour had not diminished over the years, he heard the flap of the letter box. He waited for a moment, but, as no one collected the mail, hardly surprising as his wife had gone out, he ambled into the hall, bent low, wondered if there was anything else he could do whilst he was closer to the floor, and picked up the communications that had just arrived. They appeared to be the usual rubbish. There were pleas for money from some worthy charities and from some less worthy. If Ron had money to spare, which he did, although he always considered himself to be only moderately well off, he would not have chosen to give any to the Society for the Preservation of Grey Squirrels. Any spare cash, after contributing to groups keen to assist humans, would have been devoted to a society that was keen on the Greys' total eradication and he would have been very generous towards any society that guaranteed to rid his garden of rabbits.

Another letter told him that he had won a two week holiday in Florida, which was surprising as he had not even entered the relevant competition. A leaflet from a drugs company promised him long-lasting relief from pains that he did not have and a credit card bill caused him to look twice but it seemed right. A routine statement from the bank contained depressing news as did a circular from his financial adviser. The value of his investments had fallen again in the last quarter and, as he perused the statement, he noticed that the fee, for telling him in detail how badly he was doing, had gone up dramatically. The accompanying letter assured him that even in a falling market it was essential not to panic and it was wise to use the expertise of a company that had been active for over three years. He noted that this confession meant that the organisation lacked the experience of doing business during an economic downturn.

Someone whose photograph suggested that he had only recently left school, and whose knowledge of financial topics was probably confined to matters relating to pocket money, claimed in the sales "literature" that a loss was only a loss when a weak share was sold. Ron's main grouse was that he had taken the company's advice and bought shares in a bank that was now close to being bankrupt. He had subsequently bought more shares in the failing organisation, albeit in his role of tax payer as the government purchased the bank. These consultants were not now entitled to give him any advice and when he had the time he would dispense with their services although, doubtless, there was a fee for that too. The next time he wrote to them he would include an invoice for his time.

He and "a partner" were invited to a meeting in Archester when some of the group's senior advisers, presumably coves in their late teens, would be presenting a one-hour seminar on "How to survive the recession and make your shares work for you". Apparently, this was an important event and, as an existing client, he qualified for the special fee of "only £75 for you and a partner and this includes refreshments". One way of surviving the recession, manifestly, was to speak for an hour, on how to survive the recession, and to charge a big fee. The lure of refreshments and the prospect of being lectured by someone with minimal experience, for a large fee, somehow did not appeal.

Ron flicked through other sales pamphlets, which informed him how he could acquire "essential pills for the more mature man who wants to enjoy ALL that life has to offer: YES, that means you", which he thought must involve a huge number of pills as their impact, apparently, covered "all that life has to offer". He had always wanted to be a good snooker player. Would consumption of these pills allow him to achieve that ambition? Would they help him to become a famous bagpipe

52

player? What about clog dancing? When he had time, he would write a letter to the sales director, asking him. Writing silly letters to silly people was one of Ron's hobbies. It was fun seeing their daft replies.

Other rubbish exhorted him to buy solar heating systems that would "soon reduce those hefty bills you hate". He did a quick sum which suggested that he would break even in about 25 years. All this was torn up, in preparation for being placed in the appropriately coloured recycling box after addresses had been removed for shredding. Then Ron saw, at the bottom of the pile, a more formal and expensive-looking envelope, printed in ornate fashion with a powerful and colourful logo alongside the franking. It was, of course, from a government ministry in London.

He opened it carefully, fearing the worst. For some time, he and his fellow councillors, well supported at meetings by the local residents, had opposed the central government proposal that the hotel on the outskirts of the village should be converted into a "half-way" home for young offenders from the big cities. They would be eligible to stay when they had served most of their truncated sentences and were deemed suitable for rehabilitation.

As an admirably astute, if factually inaccurate editorial in the local paper, *The Woodfield and District News* had noted when the suggestion had first been made public:

What about OUR rights?

One of the many problems faced by society today is that crime rates are going up fast but that fewer and fewer offenders are being caught, which is hardly surprising because most of our police are busy in their offices, filling in forms, for the government to manipulate the figures to their advantage. Those louts and tripehounds who are caught receive light sentences and are then let out prematurely, partly because the prisons are full and partly because a weak government is afraid of upsetting Brussels and the so-called human rights brigade that feeds there off the gravy train that

53

we finance. These unelected and unwanted bureaucrats, more concerned by the rights of the criminals than of their victims, may invoke "basic human rights" but it is society that always pays the price.

Now, we in Woodfield Magna and the surrounding villages may well pay the price of the weak and misguided namby-pamby liberals who not only favour the early release of those who break the law but who then expect us all to foot the bill for the so-called rehabilitation of these young thugs who have terrorised entire communities. The Ministry of "Justice" has recently admitted that, over the last two years, criminals on probation are committing one murder and one rape each week. Knowing their liking for doctoring the statistics, that is doubtless an under-estimate. Do we want these young criminals, for that is what they are, however we describe them, in our community?

The government-imposed "proposal" that the elderly hotel, the Country Priory on the edge of Woodfield Magna, should be used as a "half-way" house for the rehabilitation of these young thugs is an insult to democracy and local villagers should be fearful. Why have the local people not been properly consulted before these young lawless hooligans are released into our midst? If this is an example of democracy in action, it is patently obvious why turnout at European, national and local elections, is so low. Your views simply do not matter.

It is clear that this bizarre decision, to inflict young law-breakers on our beautiful region, is about to be imposed on us by faceless politicians who have never bothered even to visit our attractive village. This arrogant government, which hates the countryside and its way of life, should remember that we still have the vote and shall do all we can to inflict a humiliating defeat on them at the next election, when they have the courage to call it.

Ron had thought that parts of this were extreme but he sympathised with the underlying sentiments. The point about democratic discussion was valid. His efforts and those of the council, not to mention the stance of the villagers, had been totally ignored. He opened the letter, shunning the eggs and bacon, which indicated the gravity with which he viewed the likely contents, and began reading.

Half-way house project

I am writing to you in your capacity on the local council. You will be aware of the minister's decision to consider the compulsory acquisition of the Country Priory Hotel on the outskirts of Woodfield Magna. Now, after a full and exhaustive internal study, which took into account the reservations of your council and some representations from local residents, as well as other key issues, it has been decided to proceed, urgently, with the project.

Work will begin almost immediately on the renovation of the hotel to make it suitable as a "half way house" for young people who have broken the law and who need to be returned to society after a suitable rehabilitation period in a pleasant rural context. We anticipate that the work, which will cost just under £10 million, will begin promptly, as there is no appeal against the minister's decision. It is our hope that this restoration work will create significant economic opportunities for the local community.

At present, it is envisaged that up to 40 young offenders will be housed at any one time. I am sure that you will agree that, rather than compelling these juveniles to remain for long periods in jail, thus allowing them to become hardened criminals, it is wise to give them the opportunity of being re-integrated into society where they can make a real contribution. I know that you and your colleagues will support this ground-breaking venture and the minister thanks you for your valuable co-operation.

Ron snarled and, although nobody was present to hear his immediate analysis, said, "lying patronising fascist louts", before pushing his uneaten breakfast to one side. Such were the implications of the communication that he did not even notice that his breakfast was cold and, quite definitely, not inside him but still on the plate. He sighed deeply and just then his wife returned from wherever she had been, which always happens when people come back from somewhere. "Mary, come and see this. Here's some more evidence that the world has gone mad and the lunatics will soon be in our backyard. We embarrassed the government with the WM cricket scandal and our sudden so-called crime wave and I bet this decision was speeded up because of the great publicity our people helped to stir up over the stamp saga, and contributed to the removal of that idiot prime minister. Now they're taking their revenge and I bet that this is not the end of it."

A few days later, the government's intentions were confirmed on the front page of the local newspaper. One reader, keen to advance his career, studied the article and rejoiced.

Meanwhile, in an Archester television studio, two people of firm views were about to engage in a live debate. The presenter, Jeremy, was beginning his introduction.

"The headmaster of a primary school in Woodfield Magna in Ottershire, William Knapp-Green, recently banned parents from attending his school's sports day on the grounds that the event might attract adults who might molest the children. This was but one of his controversial decisions which have stunned the nation lately. He's with us in the studio.

"We also have with us Jane Parker, who had substantial experience as a primary schoolteacher in rural villages before becoming an independent educational adviser. Welcome to you both.

"Mr Knapp-Green. Let's begin with you and let's just take two of your controversial decisions to start with.

"You checked all the pencils that your children brought to school and deliberately broke the sharper points."

Yes, good morning, I did that because I thought that a sharp pencil could be used as a weapon.

56

"Has there been any incident involving a sharp pencil at your school?"

No, but I read somewhere that the Haitch and Safety Executive had recommended this course of action.

Jane Parker shuddered at the word Haitch and yet another example of HSE imbecility.

The presenter continued.

"You have stopped all competitive sports and even some games at your school. Why? Of course, some schools ban boxing for example, on grounds of safety, but you deliberately set fire to your school's supplies of snakes and ladders which really upset the children. Destroying these games couldn't be on grounds of safety, can it? Apparently, some children then thought that it was acceptable to burn what they disliked, including some expensive school books. Then you had to find more money to offset the loss and some parents, who resented being asked for funds, wanted you to be fired, if you will forgive the pun. You were given an official reprimand. So why did you ban competitive games?"

Yes, that's right. I regret setting fire to the games in front of the children, which was to make a point, although I must emphasise, in my own defence, that it was in the playground. I wouldn't have started a fire in the school and that fact was certainly overlooked by the media, probably deliberately as it might have spoiled their story. But, there've been no fires for some months, not since the shed in our field was set alight by a minority of the children. It was just unfortunate that fuel was stored there and, of course, these young arsonists, I mean pupils, did not know that. They said that they thought that was where I kept their school reports.

However, we must look on the bright side: typically, the media exaggerated the incident, nobody was hurt and all the pupils now realise how dangerous it is to play with matches, indoors or outdoors, so there's a happy ending. The only loser was the insurance company and I'm sure they can afford it.

"I suspect that not everyone would agree with that summary, especially the comment on insurance companies, but what about your ban on competitive games?"

I recall vividly how and unwanted I felt when I was at school as I never managed to play any games well. All my schools revered those students who were good at games whilst according little respect to those few of us who were academically better than those who were able to kick or hit a ball a long way, which has always seemed a pointless exercise to me. I just don't understand why some so-called adults, many of them who cannot even speak coherently, are paid £100,000 a week or more to kick a ball.

Frequently, I was the only child who was left out of teams chosen by my classroom colleagues. I even used to lose at board games where no skill was required. My self-esteem plunged and stayed low for months and this has influenced my whole life. I just felt left out, because I was left out, so I vowed that, as far as possible, I would never allow my children to feel that pain that I carry with me to this day.

Do you have a family?

No, I'm single but I'm responsible for many young infants and I don't want them to grow up like me.

Jane Parker?

Yes, good morning. I'm sure that we can all agree that we don't want children growing up like Mr Knapp-Green.

The headmaster smiled wanly and tried, unsuccessfully to fend off a blush that seemed to begin in his feet and then surge though his body to his televised face. Knapp-Green was beginning to feel that he had already lost this battle even although it had hardly begun. He really should have asked who else would be involved with the programme. Jane not only had

58

experience as a primary school teacher but her new public life meant that she knew the format of a debate and was skilled in her responses. She was also looking attractive and demure and bore little resemblance to the mouse-like Mrs Parker he had known vaguely some years before. Even if she had once considered him an acquaintance, it was obvious that she was not going to spare him. He was now the enemy and he must concentrate.

Jane continued with her response.

In my opinion, it would be an even sicker society than we already have if everyone shared this gentleman's crazy obsession with political correctness and a pathological and pathetic passion with health and safety. But does Mr Knapp-Green, who, I understand, has never worked outside the primary school sector, so has never been employed in a grown-up environment, realise that adult life is all about the experience that is acquired by facing challenges, some of which we shall overcome whilst we succumb to others? Some criminologists maintain that one reason for juvenile crime is that some teenagers never had to accept a reverse, which would have enabled them to adjust to the real world. Instead, they grew up thinking that they were entitled to pursue whatever they wanted without regard for the rest of society and by using force if necessary. We need more competitive sports and games, not fewer and, incidentally, we need a government that maintains sports fields, rather than allowing them to be used for building huge ugly blocks of flats that Stalin would have approved of. All headmasters should be actively opposing the government's crazy policy of selling off sports fields and it's no wonder so many of our children are too fat.

There's another thing. Mr Knapp-Green is in love with jargon. On one occasion, I gather that he told a parent that his child occasionally suffered from oppositional defiant disorder. The parent was distraught until he realised that, from time to time, his child was just disobedient.

Jane, pleased that she had exercised so many hobby horses in so brief a comment, had not been too sure whether to end her sentence about Stalin correctly, or to finish it with the appropriate preposition. It was probably better to be ungrammatical. She was also unsure about the claim she attributed to criminologists. She seemed to recall reading it somewhere, and aware that she could make one more jibe, staring at Knapp-Green intently, as if to accuse him directly of causing much crime across the land, she added:

In some ways, I believe that this woolly thinking embraced by this headmaster is one factor why we have so much crime today.

Jeremy moved on, blithely ignoring Knapp-Green's attempt to deny that he was personally and directly responsible for national crime rates, the closure of many playing fields and an increase in the number of obese children.

"Mr Knapp-Green, let's now talk about your ban on parents from attending your school's "sports day".

A nervous Knapp-Green fidgeted before offering his response. He looked as confused as a farmer suddenly confronted by a hitherto docile sheep declining to be sheered.

Well, like all of us, I'm well aware that the number of child molesters is increasing and that we must all do whatever we can to ensure the continued safety of our children. I know we're all worried about the paedophiles now living in our midst. As a headmaster, I must accept my responsibility to ensure the safety of our children and that's why I banned all visitors, not just parents, and that's an important point, Jeremy, that your colleagues in the media have carelessly overlooked, again. The ban applies to everyone, not just parents.

The presenter, ignoring the new jibe against the media and convinced that Knapp-Green would hang himself as the interview continued, turned to Jane.

"Isn't that a reasonable position?"

Jane hardly knew where to begin but she did with a minimal delay.

First of all, there is no evidence that the number of paedophiles is increasing. We must be careful to distinguish between the number of molesters and media exaggeration which sometimes reaches hysterical proportions and scares many parents, entirely unnecessarily. Some people can't distinguish between paedophiles and paediatricians and, as you know, Jeremy, this has caused problems as ignorant vigilantes have taken matters into their own hands. I maintain that this decision to ban all parents is a massive and totally unjustified over-reaction. Some children ride bikes to school and many fall off, many more than ever attract child molesters, so should we ban cycling? Children fall over in playgrounds so should we stop them from playing? Occasionally, a conker hits a child during a game. Should we ban all conkers and chop down the horse chestnut trees? When will this nonsense stop?

Knapp-Green intervened with a sickly and patronising sneer.

Yes, but any bruise or cut sustained in a playground soon heals. Being accosted by a paedophile scars a child for life.

Jane resumed, tartly.

There are many other examples of real risk to children but we don't do anything about it because children must be encouraged to be children and we, as teachers or parents, must prepare them for the outside world where nasty things do happen. What I maintain, and let me stress this, is that the risk of molesters attending a primary school open day, when the parents are present, as well as staff, is absurd.

Jeremy had an observation.

61

"Yes, but cycling to school and its attendant risks, is surely rather different to exposing young children to the possible behaviour of paedophiles, Jane Parker?"

Yes, of course it is but what evidence is there that any of these children have ever been exposed to paedophiles? I know the local villages well and those who attended sports days were just friends and parents. What reason is there to suppose that twisted, evil and sick people would turn up? Mr Knapp-Green, by his ban on parents attending sports day, let me repeat, a massive over-reaction, has merely drawn attention to the potential for those who prey on small children. I fear that his ludicrous and disproportionate decision may be copied across the country as he has drawn attention to a potential problem that did not exist before he exercised his misjudgement and in so doing, he has probably frightened thousands of children and worried thousands of parents who had previously regarded head teachers with some respect. .

"Mr Knapp-Green, your decision to ban visitors, even parents, was it based on any undesirable behaviour, ever, in all the years you have been at the school?"

No, but society changes and it's wrong to delay any action until after an incident had happened. That's one of the main problems in this country. We ignore potential problems, when they're minor and then, when they develop into something big, we're at a loss on how to deal with them and give up. That applies to so much now and it angers me and, I'm sure many right-thinking and sensible people who are fed up with government inaction on so many issues.

Jeremy ignored this tirade, further evidence that this odious, smug, sleek-haired bird would hang himself, and asked "would it not have been possible, given your views, to allow just parents who could have been required to collect passes at the school in advance?"

We're not a massive bureaucracy and that would have taken too much time.

62

Jane intervened and was told that they were now about 60 children at the school.

So you couldn't organise passes for those parents who wanted to attend? The number would not have been great as the event was held on a Wednesday. Anyway, your excuse about having sufficient time to organise is nonsense because, as you well know, the Parents Association offered to do all the necessary work themselves.

Jeremy, interested in Jane's last remark, wanted to know why the parents' offer had not been accepted.

I'm the headmaster and I feel that I must be in charge and take full responsibility for all that happens. If I'd delegated the all-important issue of safety and something went wrong, I would have felt awful.

"Jane Parker, you were surprised at this decision and you were quoted as saying that this was madness."

Yes, I did and most thinking people feel that this is not just a bad decision but one that harms the children, who wonder why their mummies and daddies are not there.

Jane had deliberately chosen this language for addition impact.

I believe that there's not a single school in the whole of the UK that has banned parents from sports day. Why does Mr Knapp-Green, responsible for a small country school, think that he is right and everyone else is wrong?

Mr Knapp-Green?

I think that I have already covered this point but it was not just the prospect of the children being exposed to child molesters that made me take what I still regard as a very wise decision.

Jeremy wanted to know more.

63

I also wanted to minimise the possibility of a child being kidnapped.

Before Jeremy was able to seek further enlightenment, Jane burst into speech.

This is one of the daftest ideas I have heard even from this absurd apostle of political correctness and warped psychology. Does this man really believe that, with a sensible system of parental passes and teachers around the small field, looking after the children, that a kidnap could be carried out? He's being watching too many US television crime programmes. It's time that he rejoined the real world, although I'm beginning to wonder if he has ever been there.

Mr Knapp-Green, have any kidnappings taken place ever at schools in this country?

None, as far as I know but we all see the dramatic footage from the States where it seems that some disaster overtakes a school almost every day and we all know that what happens in America soon happens here. I'm only surprised, and, of course, pleased that, at the moment, we don't have more armed lunatics breaking into our schools.

Jane Parker, I assume that you haven't been convinced by what you've heard?

I certainly have not and I think that there are other things that I should point out. For example, last Christmas, Mr Knapp-Green prohibited parents from taking photographs of their children when they were performing in the school concert. Again, it was supposedly to protect the children from those who collect such photographs for their warped pleasure.

Mr Knapp-Green, is this correct?

Yes.

Jane pounced.

64

If we even accept your reason, can you explain why you yourself took photographs, which were sent to the local newspaper and were made available to any intending purchasers, parent or otherwise, without any checks on their background?

Jeremy wanted to know if this was true. Knapp-Green, well aware that he was being soundly defeated, was floundering as his next response confirmed.

Yes, but I must tell you that my decisions on banning parents from the sports day and cameras from the concert, in the interests of the children, have been backed by a leading member of the local council.

Jane could hardly wait to add another crucial comment.

Yes, that council member is your brother, isn't it?

Knapp-Green nodded and Jane resumed.

He lives with you doesn't he?

She managed to make this sound highly suspicious.

Jeremy attempted a summary.

"Mr Knapp-Green, you have banned parents from taking photographs at the school concert, lest the pictures fall into the hands of paedophiles but you took photographs yourself and have effectively sold them to anyone who wanted them. You have also prevented parents from attending sports day, in case paedophiles might molest the children or that a child may be kidnapped and you have banned competitive games on the basis that the losers will have low self-esteem. Yet you cannot provide any evidence that paedophiles or kidnappers have operated in schools in this country and, apparently, the Parents Association offered to ensure that only genuine spectators would be allowed to attend the sports day but you declined their offer.

"Jane Parker, you maintain that these actions are excessive and that there is no evidence to justify these decisions and that children must be allowed to confront difficulties and dangers to prepare them for adult life."

Jane was determined to have the last word.

Precisely. I must also add that I totally condemn this headmaster's decision that teachers must not put an affectionate arm around an infant who has fallen over. When I was a primary school teacher, I resented being considered a sex maniac because I showed some sympathy towards a small child in distress. We must fight all this nonsense before it's too late and is perceived as normal and acceptable behaviour. If we don't we shall have even more adults who are just not able to adjust to the modern and real world and we shall pay for that.

"Thank you, William Knapp-Green and Jane Parker but we must leave it there."

Chapter 5

The remodelling of the local hotel, now to be fitted out as a "half-way" house for juvenile offenders, moved at a faster pace than usually seen in the building trade in Britain, mainly because it was being carried out by Poles and Romanians. No local workers were involved which aroused local ire as there were many good men unemployed across the region. Many media commentators decided that this decision to proceed with a home for young criminals was the government's childish revenge on Woodfield after the Parker affair and for the village's articulate opposition to the stamp policy. As Ron Palmer had noted, another factor was that WM had effectively ridiculed the authorities over crime statistics.

The locals thought that the new building was superior and more luxurious than the commercial hotel that it replaced. They were right. It was re-fitted with no apparent regard for cost and the size of the tax-payers' wallets. The new building boasted a swimming pool, a tennis court and a rifle range which one local authority official bravely described as a potentially silly idea. Allegedly, the MP who had claimed the most for expenses for internal design of his second home had been consulted. This prompted a senior police officer, on the verge of retirement, to suggest that burglars should be encouraged to join the force. An investigation by one of the so-called popular papers revealed that this had already happened in the north of England. Locals questioned the need for the half-way house to have a large lake and three ornate aviaries and a comment from one local, at the Duck and Orange, who observed that it was a good way to do bird, met with stony gazes.

Sir Montmorency Cheetham, formerly a local Member of Parliament and tainted by close links with the Parker affair, was a critic of the half-way house. He had a complexion that resembled a badly ironed prune and, although this is irrelevant it is worth mentioning as this feature was used remorselessly by cartoonists. He was now the chief executive of a quango, charged with investigating corruption at local and national levels. He was paid £80,000 a year for a two day week but, in an effort to divert criticism of his new salary, he pointed out that several heads of the 800 quangos in the country received significantly more than £100,000 a year. He was required to produce a report in five years but had managed to find time to invoke the Freedom of Information Act to find out that the annual cost per inmate at The Grange, as it was now to be called, was more than £200,000. He had commented flippantly on local television that it would have been cheaper to send the youngsters to the West Indies, on an escorted holiday, for two months. He had made the suggestion in jest but the gullible junior minister, charged with the rehabilitation for prisoners, accepted the idea and praised his former colleague for such an innovative idea.

Twenty youths had gone to Jamaica whilst their new home was being significantly upgraded from the level deemed suitable for commercial guests to a level deemed suitable for those who had broken the law. Inexplicably, the crime rate in Jamaica suddenly soared but officials rejected "absurd and seriously flawed" suggestions that the young Brits were responsible for this and argued that it was but a statistical quirk, showing that it's not just in the UK that such things happen, and that data for only two months could be unreliable. The second party of convicts were sent to Tasmania, the Jamaican authorities having rejected another group lest another statistical quirk be created. Curiously, the crime on that island happened to rise whilst the young crims were there. This, too, was obviously an odd coincidence although an alert official might have noticed that they youngsters left the island with significantly more suitcases they had carried when they arrived yet they had rarely been seen in the local shops.

Now these young convicts were to spend not less than six months in Woodfield Magna, busily re-adjusting to what the judicial system perceived as the real world. It was unfortunate that the young criminals had little knowledge of this world but they did appreciate the freedom that they were allowed and vowed to take full advantage of official generosity.

The senior prisons minister, the pompous, self-righteous Hugo Barr, whose head was shaped like a rugby ball, resembled a startled mouse with a moustache but his aversion to cats was surely not the result of his odd facial features. He was to open the new home. He regaled his audience of local residents, county and central government officials and, of course, the media, with his customary lack of panache. However, the competition to guess the number of clichés used by the minister was won by one of the four representatives of the national media who claimed, modestly, that he had sat through Barr's performances in London, so he knew what to expect.

There was one incident before the cynical journalists made their way home. Some of the inmates, looking smart for the occasion in their government-purchased suits, an idea borrowed from the Iranian regime who had given some misguided British sailors new outfits, had been models of good behaviour, apart from laughing loudly at one particularly silly remark made by Barr in his opening speech.

Rob Swagg, attending in his official capacity as both the most senior and junior representative of Her Majesty's Constabulary, was summoned by the civil servant, one Chevington Bullson-Walker. Given a name like that it was just as well that there was only one. CBW, red-faced, waist-coated and wearing a button hole, and, indeed a suit that was probably even more expensive than those worn by the inmates, after many years well-paid work in the Civil Service, had become responsible for carrying the minister's briefcase and his own laptop to and from the official car. Given responsibilities of this nature, it is surely reasonable that such gifted individuals receive official recognition from their friends in the shape of a medal or two, a knighthood and a generous pension.

After the opening, redface whispered confidentially in Rob's ear. "This must not become common knowledge, but I think my laptop has been stolen. It's particularly important because it holds the minister's schedule and his next speech and some of his private and confidential emails." Then, showing his breeding and seniority, he said that he was "more than a little concerned because it could cause a spot of bother". He added that, in his view, it was a "bally nuisance".

Rob PC, that's police constable, not political correctness, had experienced hearing difficulties since, some years ago, he had dived into a cold river to rescue a dog, which was a superior swimmer to Rob and which bit him as he tried to pull the animal back to the shore. He, Rob, not the dog, which was not even present at The Grange, so could not have shown any interest, although his inability to speak would have counted against him, was forced to ask the civil servant to repeat the message.

"You think that the minister's laptop has been stolen?" he said out loud just as one of the visiting national tabloid scribes was walking past. Rob was shushed lustily by the official who lost no time in whispering, too quietly for the journalist to hear, that it was his, not the minister's. He then added, unwittingly increasing the volume, "it would be disastrous if the journalists knew about this. The minister has banked his reputation on this scheme and is keen to offset all the bad publicity he received when he sent these young lawless thugs to the West Indies and to Tasmania. The point is that these louts, who never will have any idea on how to be reasonable members of society, ought to be locked up in jail and we should throw away the key. I know that the Cabinet has been split on how to treat young criminals and this could easily cost the minister his job. If you will forgive a pun, they are not behind Barr's ideas. Please, please, old chap, do what you can to find it as soon as you can. There's a good fellow."

Rob, delighted to be employed at last, told the official that he could leave the problem with him and that he could be trusted to "resolve the matter expeditiously". To make sure that the civil servant understood, and to give him confidence, he assured him, in the manner of an ice cream salesman accepting coins for one of his delicacies, that it would be "no problem". "I'll initiate an immediate search of the premises and I'm sure that we'll soon find it. These thugs are so thick, I expect we'll find one of them using it in his room, sorry, I should have said suite."

Meanwhile, the tabloid journalist had managed to hear most of the conversation and what he had not heard could easily be conjured up. He glanced at his watch and suddenly realised that the deadline for filing copy was but minutes away. He opened his own laptop and began keying in his story.

PC Rob Swagg, totally convinced that one of the new inmates must have stolen the laptop, found the manager of the half-way house, Dick Goodfellow, and together they conducted a careful but speedy search. They had finished about a third of their task, or it may have been just 30 per cent, when Chevington Bullson-Walker, panting hard, found them. "Frightfully sorry, gentlemen, but it's dashed good news. The laptop was not stolen: I suddenly remembered that I'd checked the bally thing in at reception. Hope I haven't caused too much trouble. Thanks awfully anyway and cheerio".

Rob's morale sank. His one chance of fame had vanished and, worst of all, he had already been made to look foolish in front of these young criminals. He feared the worst in future as it was clear that he had not trusted them as was apparent in the following day's edition of *The Daily Clarion*.

Prisons Minister Hugo Barr faces sack after laptop theft

Yesterday was an important day for Prisons Minister Hugo Barr. He was opening The Grange, a half-way house for young convicts in the Ottershire village of Woodfield Magna. Within hours, his laptop computer was stolen, apparently by one of the inmates of the newly restored building for which the taxpayer has stumped up nearly £10 million, to ensure that the 40 young convicts were given a chance to be rehabilitated in a style that, unless they become successful criminals, they will never experience again.

Already in trouble for sending young criminals on holidays to the West Indies and to Tasmania, paid for by the public, which resulted in crime epidemics in previously peaceful areas, the minister's career may well be ended by this latest incident, as Barr's expensive and failing policies are unpopular with his government colleagues and senior civil servants, who are not behind Barr. They favour more young crims being put behind bars. Those who demand a more understanding attitude to young offenders will be outraged by this latest incident to an incident-prone minister and one source speculated that this theft could mean the early closure of the home.

The laptop held the minister's diary, his next speech and what were described as "some highly confidential and private emails". One of his many senior civil servants, also present at the opening, is a fierce critic of his minister's liberal policies. He has called the young inmates of The Grange "lawless thugs" and "young louts" and believes that they should be locked up in prison and the key thrown away. The local police seem to agree: the most senior officer on the case expressed confidence that the laptop would soon be recovered as "these thugs are so thick, I expect we'll find one of them using it in his room, sorry, I should have said suite".

After this, in the first few days of The Grange, all was well and, because the computer had never been stolen, peace prevailed. It was fortunate that few Woodfieldians read the offending tabloid which usually placed the divorces of shattered and gob-smacked celebrities ahead of any global news. This was partly because the editor had but a scanty knowledge of overseas, which was, as he put it in a memorable phrase "a long way away" and, as he argued, British readers want to hear about British people, not some foreigners, living in a country they could not find on a map.

The inmates appeared to be settling in and those who were seen in the village were polite and seemingly determined to make a good impression.

The Smythes, too who were due to open their garden shortly, for charity, were also determined to make a good impression and spared no effort to eliminate weeds, keep the lawn to bowling-green heights and to ensure that they had all the facilities to provide visitors with copious supplies of sandwiches, cake, tea, coffee and ice cream. The weather, too, entered into the spirit of the occasion and, a few days later, the sun looked down favourably, causing some visitors to seek shelter from the unaccustomed heat. The Smythes, aware of just how hot the house could become, left doors and windows open. The squirrels, already familiar with the location of the kitchen, having seen Mr Smythe look for food for them on a worktop, decided to save him the trouble and sat obediently on the marble work top, awaiting the return of their benefactor. The combined efforts of several squirrels and a local stray dog later had caused what Mr Smythe described as a "absolute mayhem" and, as he confided to his next of kin, it was "absolutely dreadful, dear, absolutely dreadful".

An amazing total of about 300 people ambled around the garden, asking sensible and stupid questions, praising some of the blooms and munching the home-made cake before succumbing to cups of tea, taken under the awnings the Smythes had thoughtfully provided. The day was a great success and, if the other gardens also attracted similar interest, the local hospice would do well. Rob Swagg was very pleased with the way that the day had gone and hoped that similar success would attend the other openings.

The performance of William Knapp-Green on television had not been well received in Woodfield Magna. Letters to the local paper described his performance as "ill-thought out, inept, rambling and showed that he was unsuitable to be in charge of our children". Many called for his resignation, for bringing the village into public disrepute and for showing such ignorance about the needs of young children. Some parents announced that they would be withdrawing their offspring for as long as Knapp-Green was in charge. However, for the local paper, just one week later, it was his latest idea on how to ensure safety for the children that drew most criticism.

Local headmaster suspended after shock tv programme and security sensation

William Knapp-Green, the headmaster of Woodfield Magna primary school for the last five years, has recently acquired a national reputation for advancing controversial ideas. He made an attempt to justify them to a television audience last week and, in so doing, prompted dozens of emails and letters to this paper, demanding that he resign.

He has banned competitive sports and games, as he does not want young children to feel the humiliation he experienced by being a loser when he was young. He barred parents from taking photographs during the Christmas concert, in case they fell into molesters' hands, and has denied parents access to the school field on "sports day", when, in the absence of competitive games, the children run together so there are no winners or losers. The ban on spectators was because he claimed that the school could not guarantee the safety of the children from paedophiles or potential kidnappers.

His views were comprehensively demolished by Jane Parker, now living and working in London, but who was previously a primary school teacher in Tipton Poppleford Major. She pointed out that the prospect of paedophiles and kidnappers being "successful" in the village were extremely unlikely and the headmaster's ban on parents taking photographs was difficult to sustain as he took pics himself for sale to anyone who wanted copies.

Dramatic new security proposals

However, it is his latest idea on security, as revealed exclusively in our midweek edition, that has aroused the greatest fury. Knapp-Green wants expensive, new high-security gates and security cameras mounted on the walls. A guard, inside the school, would monitor all comings and going

74

and visitors would have to pass under a security arch of the type seen at airports. Finally, the tops of all the walls would be covered with barbed wire.

The governors of the school consulted child psychologists and convened a special meeting when this paper revealed Knapp-Green's latest ideas and, having given him a personal hearing, granted him immediate leave on medical grounds. Their statement said that his ideas were totally unacceptable and, if implemented, would effectively put the children in what was like a prisoner of war camp. One governor, an eminent and qualified psychologist, who demanded anonymity, told us that, "the man is completely potty and definitely one slice short of a sandwich".

Knapp-Green has been given some time to allow him to recover from "recent events" which had left him tired and emotional, having talked about his past so openly on both radio and television. He was not expected to return to any form of work for some months and his next post will not be in Woodfield Magna. It is also doubtful if he will find another job in teaching. Knapp-Green is also a qualified carpenter and his red-haired sister, Elizabeth, 59, a former picture framer, said that the family expected him to carve out a new career. In the meantime, Ms Julia Foxworthy, a shapely and single 38 year old blonde has been appointed as Knapp-Green's successor.

Chapter 6

Life in Woodfield Magna proceeded quietly after the theft that never was although there was some excitement after the great road diversion scheme had been perpetrated. Person or persons unknown had copied standard road signs indicating that roads were closed or showing the direction of a diversion and distributed the signs, during the night, to great effect around the narrow thoroughfares of the village and surrounding area. The result was that many villagers and their visitors, as well as tourists, on the Saturday morning, found that all lanes and roads led to the village square. The resulting traffic chaos took several hours to disentangle but at least it was welcome local publicity for Rob Swagg, who sorted out the traffic expertly, according to the local newspaper.

Youthful and energetic Jack Scoop, who now lived in one of the new and relatively large houses in the village, had been a junior employee of Ratty, Ratty and Fiddler, a big PR company in London. He was working out his notice, dismissed because of alleged incompetence and, more seriously, after an enquiry into the loss of thousands of paper clips, when he had stumbled on the Parker affair. RR&F had represented Brian Parker, who had set up the infamous cricket match and sought to secure planning permission via what could best be called dubious methods. Then Jack, in conjunction, with his brother, Ivor, had been able to feed his favourite tabloid, where Ivor happened to be employed, with some interesting stories and had eventually been sufficiently successful to set up his own PR business in Archester.

Although Ivor Scoop's paper had pics and the story about all roads leading to the village square, nobody detected the hand of his brother in the affair. Rob Swagg was puzzled as it was in early April when the tabloid had earlier carried several pics of lanes around the village, with every home apparently for sale, to judge by the signs carefully inserted by a clever photographer. He never found enough evidence to confront Jack Scoop.

One Friday morning, locals exercising their canine friends saw something that made them, to a man or woman, agog. It may well have been the same for the dogs, although you don't know when they are agog. They don't comment or pull faces, possibly because they know that a bulldog did and its appearance became permanent. That's the trouble with dogs, you just don't know what they are thinking. Crafty brutes. Some of them even bite valiant policemen when saving them from cold rivers. Others have been known to bite postmen but Royal Mail, concerned about their employees' safety, managed to reduce the number of incidents dramatically by restricting deliveries to just one every other day to houses where dogs were registered, in accordance with the legislation recently introduced by the government. This was so successful that the policy of one delivery a day was extended across the whole country. One recent rumpus had been caused when a computer disc, containing information on all the registered dogs, went missing in the Battersea area.

What had prompted the humans' attention was the sight of large construction vehicles moving into what had previously been an unused field, just outside the village. In the absence of fact, rumour prospered. Was it to be the new housing estate of new affordable homes? Nothing had been heard about this which was suspicious but the widespread view was that the new houses were to be built to the north of the village, some distance from this field. After the Parkergate affair, there was no confidence in the more important local authority but nobody knew whether planning permission had been sought for anything in the village. The general view, which might subsequently proved wrong, was that planning permission had not yet been granted.

Had the venue for the village fete been changed? One of the more perceptive Woodfieldians wondered why the fete would require bulldozers, small diggers, some timber, a large number of bricks and lorry loads of glass and, of course, there was the not inconsiderable matter of cost. Another suggestion was that a permanent hard base was to be constructed for the itinerant circus that visited the village from time to time but that seemed an expensive project for an area that was used only for a few days a year. Anyway, now that animals were banned from participating in the circus, it was doubtful if it would ever return. Humans, dressed as animals, running up slopes and diving through flaming hoops somehow was not as exciting as watching dogs perform, even if their costumes were uncannily life-like.

Discussion then centred on who owned the field. Nobody knew. Some thought that it might have belonged to the infamous Brian Parker but it was suggested, perhaps wrongly, that he would never dare show his face in the village again. One old-timer pointed out that they should not rule out the possibility that someone might be acting on his behalf and doing something to the village in revenge for his humiliation. He had tried to deceive the village once and he might well try it again. Gloom fell on the assembled group as heavily as a wet blanket on a clothes horse.

Others claimed that the field had been bought by an oil company which was about to begin drilling in the village but this was immediately denied by a spokesperson for the oil company, Lawrence Thomas Percival-Bradworthy, who happened to live locally and was out exercising his own canine quadruped on his day off as he had worked late every evening that week. Generously, he took the opportunity to give a 20 minute lecture on the basics of oil and gas exploration, spending some time on the planning procedures and stressing the care taken by the company on environmental matters and pointing out the political, economic and financial consequences of relying on overseas oil. This worried some of his fast dwindling audience, who understood nothing of what he had said and still wondered whether his employers were considering applying again for permission to drill in the nearby hills. Neither he nor they were trusted.

The Bush-Cooks pushed gently through the throng to see what was happening and seemed about to go into the field before changing their minds. Did they know who owned the field? They obliged with a literal and accurate response. "Yes" was the answer but they obviously did not hear the inevitable follow-up remark as they drove off. "Well, then, just a minute, hold on, come on, tell us who it is, for heaven's sake".

The organisers of the annual fete were encountering problems. The usual people would be manning, womanning, personning the usual stalls but the main challenge, as it was every year, was to find a famous person to open the event and draw the crowds. A Bush or a Cook, or, on one glorious and very memorable occasion, both, had obliged for some years but the general feeling was that it was about time to find someone new. It was also agreed that the committee should not even ask the chef and gardener for help but the trouble was that nobody on the committee knew anyone who knew anyone who was famous. The only possible candidate was an obscure weather forecaster who lived in Tipton Poppleford Major. He only appeared on the late evening slot on regional news, when most Woodfieldians were in bed. It was agreed that he had no pulling power, as the joint chairman of the committee, Mike Redding, put it. He was responsible for advanced planning but Alf Fox would soon take over as Mike had to go abroad on business for a few months.

Amelia Fashing-Farnsby, for whom pearl necklaces had been invented, suddenly announced that she had been thinking. This drew the predictable and puerile response and she paused before revealing the product of her cerebral efforts. "Why don't we ask Jane, Parker's wife, who, I gather divorced the louse and was on the box the other day, making that headmaster of the local school, you know the man, I mean, the chap who looks like a bad-tempered eagle who wants to turn the school into Colditz, look like the idiot he is. She really gave him a pasting and I think it was partly through her performance that he's been suspended or fired or whatever it was. Anyway, I think that the village saw Jane as the innocent victim and would welcome her back."

Mike Redding stroked his chin in a way that, somehow, suggested he, too, had been caught up in this fashion for thinking and, keen to capitalise on this trend to pensive behaviour, asked what others thought. Hugh Bush, no relation of any other Bushes, had a view. "I'm sure that she would be welcomed back because I think that most of us saw her, as Amelia just said, as the innocent victim. But it's just possible that she may have come across someone who is, what do the young people say, an A list celebrity. She's an attractive lady now and it would be good if she could come with a household name. At least she's been on television once. Two for the price of one".

Mike muttered, pompously and unnecessarily, that money could not change hands as the whole purpose of the fete was to raise money for the local branch of Age UK, which meant most of those in the village. Grunts around the table indicated that all regarded this as a good idea. Suitably encouraged, Hugh said that an approach to Jane should be very carefully worded as, "Ideally, we want her to find someone for us, without being upset that we haven't asked her as the main personality". Mike confirmed that he had heard what Hugh had said, and, being tired, shamelessly used a cliché or two saying that he would take his ideas on board going forward.

Later, a jubilant Mike was able to tell his committee that Jane had responded very positively and that she and a very well-known famous face, a journalist friend of a friend who, fortuitously, lived in the same street, would, all being well, be happy to accept the invitation. The committee wanted to know the identity of the owner of the famous face but the chairman was unable to assist. He did not know but he trusted Jane and was confident that all would be well. Hugh mentioned, in what was intended to be a helpful aside, that they must know before too long, to include the name in all the publicity.

The organisers of the Village Art Show were encountering similar problems on the celebrity front. Nobody on the committee had any ideas and as this event was the first in the summer, there was great concern. "What we need is some lateral thinking", opined the committee chairman. His fellow committee members, not entirely sure what lateral thinking was but who assumed that it must be good, all nodded vigorously. "Yes, chairman", said one, "that is precisely what we need, and as much of it as possible. We must not stint ourselves", and not sure if this commodity was expensive, thoughtfully added "on behalf of the community". Unsurprisingly, like her colleagues, ignorant of the concept, she then stopped, leaving the chairman stranded, keen to show the outcome of any lateral thinking but he was lacking in ideas.

Fred Payntor, who ran the nearest art shop, promised to see if any of his contacts could oblige. Darkly, he hinted that someone in the world of art owed him a favour. Some two weeks later, he was able to confirm that Sir George Castle, a very well-known art collector, would be happy to open the proceedings. This was not entirely true: Sir George had agreed only under acute pressure. Apparently, although it was a secret, Fred, many years ago, before opening his art shop, had been Sir George's chauffeur and on one occasion persuaded a local magistrate that he, and not a drunken Sir George, had been at the wheel of the latter's Rolls Royce when it demolished a hedge and inflicted some damage on a local bus shelter, which subsequently caught fire.

The Art Show committee, having previously allowed free admission, had decided that it was time to charge. After a panel of a sub-committee had reported to the main committee, via the liaison group, it was decided, with some vigorous dissensions and several abstentions, that tickets should be sold at £2.50 each with no concessions for senior citizens. This was because about 95 per cent of those attending were in this age group. Although an Archester supermarket had given bottles of wine and orange juice, it was implied on the ticket that the entrance fee was to cover the cost of a glass of wine and a nibble. The locals had always regarded the Art show as a free show and did not respond favourably to the imposition of an admission charge. Regrettably, many of the exhibits were

81

those that had failed to sell from previous shows. To add to the lack of support, people were bored by the pretentious and pompous man who was allegedly an artist and spoke, each year, in a patronising and supercilious way and nobody had heard of Sir George although they were impressed at the thought that they would be addressed, on the night, by a knight.

Sir George, unhappy at the way in which he had been inveigled into speaking, was not enjoying his visit to Woodfield Magna. He had justified his efforts by the thought that his words of wisdom, about how contemporary artists were conspicuous for their barren imagination and who were encouraged in their incompetence by ignorant and pretentious patrons and vacuous critics and journalists, would stimulate debate. For such an important event, the media, he was sure, would be present.

They were not. Bravely, notwithstanding the lack of the media and, for that matter, most of the villagers, he droned on. "We live at a time when the mediocre is judged by the ignorant as 'brilliant', 'fantastic' or 'awesome' which merely shows that there is a pervasive bankruptcy in the use of language, as well as in art. So-called artists offer collages, possibly of drift wood, or a broken chair from their lounge and have the impertinence to call this art. Some spill a pot of paint on a carpet and then believe that they have created something wonderful. I think what they've created is only a mess but ignorant and unthinking critics, keen to be identified with such talentless little twerps, laud what the perpetrators of this nonsense regard as their work. Society has little time for the genuinely talented: the speedy delivery of fame, for its own empty promise, is all that is sought by the young, most of whom crave celebrity through television, often as, God help us, cooks and gardeners."

He did not know that the Bush-Cooks were present. Indeed, they constituted a tenth of the audience, excluding several dogs whose interest in art, fame and society were such that they all fell asleep in the first five minutes of the knightly rant. The Bush-Cooks left, reducing his audience to just 18. As Sir

George manfully continued to the end of his well-rehearsed speech, he recalled that his car had been damaged earlier when parked near The Grange. He had heard that some 40 young criminals were now living, as he told the dwindling audience, "in the lap of luxury, at your expense and mine, and one of them has scratched my Rolls". He wanted to know whether this was the kind of society we wanted. The few remaining members of his audience made a mental note that, when they acquired a Rolls, they would not leave it near The Grange.

Straying far from his brief, he suggested that this incident was a direct consequence of our society's pathetically weak stance on crime and punishment. Only eight people had remained to listen to these final comments. Apart from the committee members, there were then but three people and four dogs, none of whom had served on the committee, and whose posture suggested that they were dog-tired.

Word soon reached an enthusiastic Rob Swagg that another crime had occurred in his patch. It was unfortunate that the missing laptop had been mislaid by a careless civil servant but it would only be a matter of time before some of the miscreants misbehaved. Now was his opportunity. Sir George was clearly a little more than peeved at what had happened to his car, judging by his apoplectic countenance and it would not do Rob any harm to apprehend the criminal swiftly. He was sure that Sir George would know the right people. Just as he was about to drive to The Grange, his phone jangled. It was bad news from Bruce Murie, Sir George's Australian-born chauffeur.

The following day, the mystery of why construction vehicles were entering a barren field had been solved by the Bush-Cooks who, after a chat, convened a meeting in the local pub, drinks on them, to tell their fellow Woodfieldians what was happening. Charlie was showing distinct signs of wishing to speak.

"Hilary and I feel that you, our fellow residents and friends in this charming village, should know now, before you read about it in the papers, that the field, which we bought some time ago from Brian Parker, is to be used as a new television garden. I'm very proud to tell you that Hilary has been named as the main presenter of this new show, called *Gardens Now!* and we shall be creating a fine garden that we intend to open to residents exclusively, at least for one day a month, subject to filming requirements. It has been agreed with the producers of the new show that, from time to time, we can feature local gardens and gardeners and we hope that some of you will assist us on the programme. It's our intention that, apart from showing how to become successful gardeners, we want to grow fine vegetables and this leads on to something else we want to tell you."

The audience absorbed this news favourably and some even applauded before being hushed. What was coming next?

Now it was Hilary's turn.

"Thanks for that and we hope that you will all come into the garden, even if your name is not Maude." The joke raised as much laughter as a spade hitting an occupied gardening shoe and Hilary resumed at a pace usually only favoured by foreigners who wrongly think that they can speak English. "This will be a show for us all, not just the privileged professional gardeners and we want to have your ideas. But there's something else that we wanted to tell you. As you know, my wife, Charlie, is an excellent chef and we thought that, when the garden starts to yield fine local produce it would be a good idea for her to open her own restaurant. It is not our intention to make it an expensive eating place where only the foody snobs can eat. We want it to become your own restaurant and we shall be offering favourable rates to all those local residents who become members." This excellent public relations performance, unsurprisingly, not conjured up by a PR professional, was received with more applause. The Woodfieldians and the Bush-Cooks were happy.

Three who were not full of the joys of early summer were Rob Swagg, Sir George, who had not had a comfortable night in the pub, and his chauffeur, Murie, who still retained his Australian accent which resulted in some locals failing to

84

understand him. He had confessed that the scratch on the Rolls had happened when he had to pull into the side of the lane to avoid a tractor. Thus was Rob denied the opportunity to advance his career and the chance to ingratiate himself with someone who had connections. It was a hard world, but, sooner or later, one of the young louts, or YLs, as he called them, would surely succumb to temptation?

Chapter 7

The hapless Rob Swagg was becoming increasingly worried about his career. He had not made a successful arrest for some time and he had been set a target of not less than five a year. Worse still, despite living and working close to The Grange, the home of no less than 40 young criminals, he had failed to solve a case, as he was required to do according to the government-imposed targets. As he had not made any arrests, his paper work, unlike that of his colleagues in busier areas, was minimal and, that, somehow, emphasised his problem but that was a consequence of living in one of the most law-abiding communities.

The laptop, belonging to a senior civil servant had been mislaid, not stolen, the scratch on Sir George's car had been the result of his chauffeur's carelessness and he had failed to bring a successful prosecution of a man who had a penchant for hurling non-organic produce at politicians. All this was very bad. He, Swagg, not the veggie hurler, had to find a way of making successful arrests and bringing thugs to book, but the problem seemed to be that, quite simply, there was no crime. Would he be justified in arresting people for eating in the street, according to a very ancient law of which nobody else had any recollection? His research into other odd laws revealed nothing that was both practical and relevant. Somehow, he felt that he would have been ridiculed for even trying to bring charges against some of his friends, for example, for selling lemons without a licence or throwing paper out of upstairs windows on a Sunday. Just what could he do to save his rural career?

He had discussed this at length with his sister, Barbara, but she had no good ideas. As she said, so eloquently, and with an unanswerable logic that had elevated her to the position of partner in a group of solicitors in nearby Archester, "you can't solve crimes that haven't been committed". Rob, not as stupid as his sister had implied for many years, could not argue with this but he still had to do something.

The initial discussion in the Duck and Orange one evening had veered from what was going to happen, if anything, in the remaining 30 one-day cricket internationals in a very long season, to why technology was not used on a much wider scale to prevent such crass umpiring errors as had occurred in the earlier games. One drinker opined but quietly, "it's all very well, relying on the umpire but when they make such fundamental errors that cost one side the match and could possibly ruin a player's career, it's time that we moved on". The chat then moved on to what had happened to those characters who had been involved in the great Parker game nearly two years before. Stanley Stuart, who had been the WM umpire in that disastrous cricket match in the season before last, mainly because, as a former chemist's assistant, he owned a white coat, had been ridiculed in the local press for some eccentric decisions. Now he tried to change the subject, suggesting that all the English team, after nine consecutive defeats, had to fear was fear itself.

Mike Redding, president of WMCC responded.

"You can say that because you've never faced a bowler like Ray Miller whose stock delivery was at about 90 miles an hour and which was often aimed at your head. I've even seen you move almost too late when you've been umpiring at square leg, about 45 yards from the wicket." Somehow, Redding implied that he had faced Miller, a famous Australian in the late Forties, which was unlikely on grounds of age and inability to soar above village cricket club level.

Nat West, the opulent retired banker, pausing after buying everyone a drink, asked Mike about the club's performance so far this season.

"You've not been doing too badly, have you?"

"I'm pleased to say, yes, we're doing all right. As you know some of the team involved in that infamous match have gone. Will, our best batsman, as we all know, now lives and works in the States. Incidentally, I had an email from him the other day. He's enjoying his new life. He likes working for the American company and is obviously very happily married to Laura Two. It's odd, isn't it, that his first and second wives are both called Laura? I think that he may be coming over here before too long and it would certainly be good to see him again." All agreed.

Mike continued. "Malcolm, who came off the field in the big match, feigning injury, was banned by the local cricket authorities and has taken up tennis in Canada, where he went to work as a lumberjack. As I think some of you know, he said that it was something he had always wanted to do, having been inspired by the Monty Python show. That said, one reason for moving was that he couldn't look us in the face after being exposed as part of the Parker racket. He was seen as a cheat and members of our squad still feel that he was mainly responsible, after Parker, for denying them their lucrative reward for winning. Apparently, he was made redundant from his job soon after the match but I don't think that was because he was widely perceived as a cheat. It was probably because he insisted on turning up for work in the local council offices dressed as a lumberjack."

Someone else wanted to know about Hugh. "I haven't seen him in action this summer. Has he hung up his boots?"

"I'm sorry to say that he has. You remember that silly story in the local media about that game when he went berserk with the bat?

Not everyone did, so Mike reminded them of the headline:

88

Local cricketer damages church roof in savage daytime attack: vicar fears big bill

"As you may recall, he was very upset with this story as it portrayed him as an irreverent thug. As he said, he had attended church regularly for many years and was a great believer and refused to follow the leaders of the church down the road to agnosticism. The business about the church roof was the last straw.

"It was bad enough having a local vicar who didn't believe in God, sorry, vicar, I didn't see you behind that large tankard, but to be pilloried in the local paper in that way was, to use one of his favourite phrases, the last straw. In an effort to cheer himself up, he told the paper that he did not recognise himself from the story and the headline. He suggested that it must have been his altar ego."

Here, Mike paused but the pub congregation did not see the intended joke.

"In his letter of complaint to the paper, which, sadly, only served to give the story more oxygen, in the words of teenage media experts, he tried to be light-hearted but this approach only stirred up more antagonism. He wrote, frankly, very ill-advisedly, 'Pew, what a story. Aisle be pleased if you could kindly do me a service, as an organ of the press, and, if you still have a copy of the offensive edition in question, you could pulpit'.

"This did not go down well and merely provoked strong and sustained correspondence in the paper from the faithful who felt that his bizarre language betrayed his total lack of faith. The story, prodded by a further series of pontificating editorials, rumbled on until just before Christmas when news of the release into the wild of ten turkeys pushed Hugh off the front page.

"Poor old Hugh felt that the local cricket club should have had an insurance policy but they didn't. He also thought that the church authorities were rich enough to pay for a few tiles. It became a matter of principle to him, as he explained in various interviews, which, of course, kept the story running and running."

There was an interruption from the floor from a non-cricketer, who wanted to know if Hugh, whom he hadn't seen recently, had moved.

"Yes, he's gone to Archester, so that he is further away from his family, who always used to annoy him, especially after the court case and, as I just said, he's given up cricket. Anther reason, apparently, was that he was fed up with being asked if he was related to that cook girl who lives in the village and married Hilary, the gardener."

"Just as well he didn't live in a big city and was called Smith", observed one of the more sober members of the audience.

"What court case?" demanded some of the gathering.

"Eventually, he had to pay for the damage and that really annoyed him and, as he said at his second trial."

Here he was interrupted again. "What trial? A second trial? What on earth happened?"

"Well, as I just said, he really resented having to pay anything for repairs to the church roof, especially after one of the locals told him that it had been in a poor state of repair long before the cricket match. So he decided to refuse to pay the full amount as he felt that the church authorities were cheating. He offered to pay for a few tiles but that was all and he refused to consider anything more. That led to his first court appearance and it was ruled that he had to pay the full sum. Knowing that Hugh was a man of principle, you will guess that the decision did not leave him exactly dancing for joy.

"He had maintained throughout the trial that he was being asked to pay for the complete restoration of the roof which was absurd as he had only damaged a few tiles. He asked how a cricket ball could damage an entire roof but met with no sensible response. A local builder, who, coincidentally, had been asked to repair the roof, testified that by dislodging a few tiles, Hugh had effectively undermined the entire structure and that, in his opinion, based on two years' experience, in all weathers, a completely new roof was the only solution.

"Outside the court, the vicar was seen to be smiling broadly and giving a crude thumbs up gesture in the direction of his chums and telling his friends that God moves in mysterious ways. Hugh heard this and exploded, calling the man of cloth some names that are not usually heard inside churches or outside, at least in these villages. He also conveyed the impression that the identity of the vicar's parentage was in doubt. Hugh's comments can best be summarised as allegations that the vicar and his sanctimonious and hypercritical cronies were cheats and liars, and a disgrace to the church, who ought to be cast out. He maintained that, with so-called religious people like these running the church, it was no surprise that new sects were cropping up all over the country. I think that it was fair to say that these observations received a rather dusty reception from God's representative on earth.

"As Hugh advanced towards him, apparently to release a few more thoughts in a militant tone, the vicar, according to evidence submitted in the new trial, believed that he was about to be struck, so he raised his hand. Oddly, Hugh, too, thought he was about to be struck so pushed the unmarried vicar strongly, causing him to fall into the arms of one of the many spinsters who kept the church alive and who, doubtless, suddenly felt that her prayers had been answered. She was so surprised that she soon dropped the vicar, although not her faith, and the vicar suffered severe bruising.

"The magistrates did not accept Hugh's explanation of what had happened and noted that this was the second time that he had appeared before them in just a short time. He was told that "this is some kind of record. You are, clearly, a bully and a menace to society. It is our duty to protect our fellow

God-fearing citizens from atheists like you who have no respect for the church, its followers, or even for the law of the land."

"Hugh's efforts to inject a few facts, not least that he had been a member of the church for many years, until the cricketing incident, and that he was disgusted that the agnostics were now in control, and what did that say about society today, were totally ignored. He was to be jailed for 10 years, of which all but one week would be suspended. Hugh was released after three days as his behaviour was exemplary and now he has founded a new society campaigning for the restoration of religion in the Church of England."

There was much sympathy for Hugh and all agreed that it was a tale of our times. One drinker thought that it was remarkable that he had not been charged under anti-terrorist laws and, judging by the grunts, this was a popular view.

"What happened to Will after he accepted the job in the States?" wondered a non-drinker.

Jock was able to provide an answer.

"The last I heard was only a few days ago. As I mentioned to some of you earlier, I, too, had an email from him. Apparently he is very happy living with his new wife, Frisky, whose real name is Laura, just like his first wife, in a fine apartment near Houston and is really enjoying his work. The people he works with are very friendly and knowledgeable and some of his ideas have already saved the company a lot of money, which means that Will has benefited financially. He'll never come back to this country for good but I think that he's going to try to visit the UK before the summer is out, as Mike said. I'd really like to see him again. After all that happened, he really deserves to have a better life and I'm very pleased for him."

It will be apparent, even to readers not paying much attention, that Woodfieldians took little notice of events that happened outside their own lives and that of the village. So

Jock's question, on whether his audience had heard about what happened to Laura One inevitably prompted a shaking of heads. Jock always seemed well-informed on gossip and welcomed this opportunity of spreading some engaging tittle and a fair helping of tattle amongst his friends.

"Well, you know that after she had been exposed, if you will pardon the verb, as having hired two blonde models to follow Will around London, so he would begin to wonder if he was going mad, she went to work in the capital?"

Heads nodded. Their owners knew that much. Laura had been having an affair with Parker and thought that, if she could undermine Will's sanity or suggest he was having an affair himself, by having him pursued by two apparently identical blondes, a divorce would be easier and she could then turn to Parker, who had unknowingly financed the cruel jape. After that, Parker had rejected Laura and vanished.

"Later, after the messy divorce, generously covered by the tabloids in considerable detail, and on the back of selling her story to one of them, she tried to break into television. She failed and then tried her luck with a small local radio company broadcasting in the London area. Did any of you hear what happened after she had been working there for a month or two?"

Shaken heads indicated that the news, after some weeks, astonishingly, notwithstanding modern communications, still had not reached Woodfield Magna.

"Well, I was told by one of her friends, whom I've know for years, that she was involved in making coffee and other routine tasks that are performed in offices everywhere, nothing to do with radio. I gather that, allegedly, she was trying to seduce one of the bosses, not without some success, and she told her London friends that she was now in show business. In an effort to impress those who mattered, especially in television, she spent even more time taking full advantage of her natural good looks and figure. It would be fair to say that, whilst all the males lusted after her at the radio station, her increasing conceit and track record eventually deterred even the most frustrated senior manager from making the most modest of overtures. In a phrase, she became a spoiled and unpleasant but beautiful brat, still confined to routine office chores.

"She had been angling for a job reading traffic reports as a start to her new career, and, eventually, she succeeded in having a trial. This took place just a few days after she pretended she had been accidentally knocked down, not up, so remove those adolescent grins, by the executive who happened to be in charge of traffic reports. As he helped her up, she managed to let him, how shall I say this, inspect some of her assets. Unfortunately, her possible 'promotion' seemed to go to her head and she became even more objectionable. In her opinion, she was superior to virtually everyone else at the station and her sexy appearance surely, she thought, justified a job in television but she had to gain some broadcasting experience. In a word, despite her powers of attraction, that had seduced Parker and the head of traffic news, she was widely disliked by her colleagues. Now, when, she was being tested for the role of traffic reporter/reader, she had to read out a dummy report, which was, of course, recorded to hear how she sounded."

"So what?" demanded an impatient drinker, a former army man, keen to hear what happened to this sex bomb. Had she exploded or imploded?

"Just a minute and I'll tell you. I've the text of the test report here that a friend of mine sent me so let me read it out." Jock, with appropriate reverence, pulled out a piece of neatly-folded paper from his wallet. Judging by its appearance, this was not the first time that it had been extracted. Clearly, it was one of its owner's most interesting possessions, at least amongst those that could be stuffed into a wallet. He continued.

"It goes well beyond just traffic and was used to test Laura's ability to read out something very, very silly and totally implausible without laughing and without a prior run-through. It's a really ridiculous piece, one of the oddest stories I've ever heard and, of course, because she was so arrogant and unpleasant, the story, written by her colleagues who hated her, is much more absurd than those normally made to test potential broadcasters. Any normal person, of course, would have refused to read it after the first few sentences but Laura ploughed on, seemingly guessing that it was to ensure that she neither gagged nor giggled." Seeing that his audience did not know about gagging, Jock obligingly explained that it meant drying. His audience was still less than clear on all this gagging and giggling business but were too keen to find out what happened next to ask.

"I gather that these test recordings are always wiped clean so that they can't be used by elderly, smug, self-satisfied, so clever, presenters of 'out-take shows' to get their hands on them. But, on this occasion, for reasons, none of us could possibly guess, the recording was not only retained but copied by most of the males that she had offended. What's more, a printed version was produced and, as I said, I have a copy here."

The audience shuffled and, such had been their interest in the tales of Laura One, that most of them had not realised that not only were their glasses empty but they had been for some time. Stories of what happened to a conceited and arrogant sex bomb must wait. More important matters had to be rectified. Mike generously stumped up for another round and then Jock resumed.

"I'll read it out but be prepared for some lunatic writing".

His audience sat intently, keen to savour the moment, although few of them were unaware of the phrase and usually did very little savouring, unless drink was involved. Others, expectant and excited, were just very keen to hear the dirt and were sitting still, wearing anxious expressions like impatient bankers about to be told the size of their annual bonus.

Jock, keen to build up the tension, reminded his audience that what they were about to hear, which was completely absurd and illogical, was much, much worse than the audition for all other potential broadcasters. "I don't want to spoil it but I really can't understand why she didn't realise that the whole thing was a cruel hoax and stop after the first insane sentence. Any normal person would have refused to read this tosh but not our Laura. This is the most absurd piece that you've ever heard."

Sensing the increasing frustration of his audience he began.

We are getting reports of very severe traffic congestion building up in the West End of London and there have also been reports of major traffic jams in Truro in Cornwall, Dhahran in Saudi Arabia and on the outskirts of Lagos in Nigeria. Our security correspondent says that a totally unknown group, Paralyse all traffic, (PAT) has claimed responsibility for "taking out" all the traffic lights and has claimed that parts of the United States will soon "suffer the same fate".

Some sources are blaming a group of hackers from Hackney but other traffic control system specialists claim that a little-known group of angry anglers from Fishguard is responsible. A man from Chester told us that he was the brain behind the operation but his claim was rejected by a self-confessed rotter from Ottery.

This chaos occurs as hundreds of thousands of people are gathering in London to celebrate the recent resignation of the unpopular prime minister in a massive outpouring of joy not seen since England won the world tiddlywinks championship in 1923. They have come to express their relief at the political death of the worst prime minister in living memory, according to one visitor to the capital. The crowd outside the Palace of Westminster was so thick, like many MPs, that the latter were unable to leave the building, forcing them to spend time re-checking their expense claims.

Overseas visitors, too, are caught up in the crowds. Ten English patriots thought that some Chinese were showing insufficient respect for the UK as one of them was wearing

96

trousers, with the knees cut out, made from the Union Jack. Fighting broke out and 50 young men were stabbed, some seriously, but no arrests were made as, according to a senior policeman, that would have inflamed a dangerous situation. However, 95 photographers were arrested for filming the police as the latter watched the fighting. Another dozen press snappers were also arrested, for photographing their colleagues being taken into custody. It is understood they will be charged under anti-terrorist legislation. Mrs. Ethel Bodicombe, 82, of Penarth, will be appearing with them as she tried to take a photo of "such a handsome young bobby in action. He was just like my late husband". She told us that, apart from a driving offence in 1948, for speeding, she had never been in trouble before.

To make matters worse, very few people from the Home Counties have been able to travel to the capital by train as Paddington and Waterloo stations have been closed. The workers there are on strike, demanding an increase of lust, sorry, that should be just, 30 per cent in their wages and a two-hour lunch break. In a co-ordinated action, most of London's thousands of black cabs are blocking key routes into the centre of the city, to protest against the high tax imposed on diesel fuel.

Police say that it may take "many hours" before all those vehicles trapped around the West End of London are released and plans are being made to take the unfortunate drivers and passengers food and drink. This is being complicated by a major fire near the National Gallery in Trafalgar Square but Nelson is not thought to be in any danger. A spokesman for the London Regional Development and Preservation quango assured anxious enquirers that, "Nelson is above all this nonsense and piffle". Meanwhile, in Oxford Circus a burst water main has flooded the area and it is feared that several people may have been drowned on a single-decker bendy bus caught in the flood. Challenged on why the water supplies had not been turned off at the mains, the company said, 'we're in the business of supplying water, not curtailing it'.

The authority responsible for London's transport said that, naturally, it regretted any deaths but revenue would not be affected as most passengers now were so elderly that they travelled free of charge. The London Mayor, speaking from his country home in Buckinghamshire, has appealed for calm and described events as peanuts, compared to what happened in the war.

Now for sport. Torquay United have confirmed that they have appointed Andrea Pella as their new manager and that the club is 100 per cent pro Pella. Meanwhile, Britons may have failed to win the latest Grand Prix, Wimbledon and Football World Cup but England won the under 12 cheese-throwing championship at Mousehole, in Cornwall.

The weather is expected to be dry, except where it rains.

The audience in the pub was stunned, to a man, except the women, of course, and everyone agreed that they would not like to have read out that piece of total rubbish.

"So, did she get the job?"

"Yes, amazingly because she did not challenge the rubbish, but she became even more arrogant, prompting some colleagues to play the test report on the radio at midday, about a week later, and the clever operational boys, heaven knows how, ensured that it was played in full before the embarrassed executives could do anything about it. They also denied executives the opportunity to apologise immediately and to say that it was a juvenile prank, and, of course, totally untrue."

The pub audience showed surprise and some, clearly, very clearly, were gob-smacked, and, indeed, gutted and, in some cases, awe-struck as well, but, happily, recovered sufficiently quickly to ask what happened next.

Jock resumed his story to the gob-smacked, gutted and awe-struck audience who, astonishingly, had not heard the outcome of this odd event, even although it had made national newspapers. It just showed how isolated WM was from the real world.

"You can guess. Phone lines were jammed as anxious relatives tried to find out whether their friends and families were safe. The transport authorities, too, were besieged and, of course, the prime minister's press officer put out a strong statement condemning such cruel satire. The new PM would "continue to take tough decisions when tough decisions were required". Undoubtedly, the masochistic nation heaved a sigh of collective relief. They had become accustomed to tough decisions and would now miss them.

"The unions were up in arms for the suggestion that their colleagues were looking for such huge wage increases at a time when everyone, 'especially the rich and incompetent bankers who are responsible for this mess' should tighten their belts. In a word, it was chaos on a major scale."

But surely, asked the more perceptive drinkers, the broadcasting company apologised immediately and explained that it was all not true and that it was just a cruel joke?

"Well, as I said, they tried, but incredibly, there was a major power cut in the area which put the station and others off the air for a while just after the report had been read out live so the panic had set in before the station was active again. Apparently, the inaction was the result of some industrial action."

"Couldn't other media outlets, in other parts of London, not lacking power supplies, have denied the story immediately?"

"Yes, you would think that wouldn't you, but journalists decided that it was wise to visit the West End, to check the story, just in case, before refuting it. They felt that they couldn't run the risk of being made to look silly so had to check what was what. It might just have been true, at least parts of it, and all the editors were keen to run a new story instead of reporting more cases of swine flu and losses of computer discs containing confidential information. The tabloids were particularly keen to forget the illness as a story because they had exhausted their stock of alliterative headlines with *Swine Flu Season Swindle Stumps Surprised Specialists*. One paper carried a story of an elderly man who had swine flu, was cured and then claimed that he had gammon flu.

"As many other concerned citizens headed to the area, determined to gawp and take pics that they could then sell to other media outlets, the centre of London became too crowded as thousands of people had to see what was what for themselves. As a result, the journalists sent to rebut the story, seeing the crowds, thought that it was true and their reports, of course, initially at least, added to the panic and chaos.

"The broadcaster lost its licence, mainly because it did not stop the broadcast immediately and had not invested in back-up power facilities, and you won't be surprised to learn that Laura, who was fired, has been forced to take the only job available, as a waitress in one of the seedy parts of the capital. Now, like London itself, she always smells of onions, apparently. Serve her right as far as I'm concerned after what she tried to do to Will."

Grunts around the table indicated that these sentiments were widely shared but perhaps the most surprising aspect of the whole story was that the locals had not heard the story about London becoming so congested.

The intending drinkers recharged their glasses and made a note to discuss, on a later occasion what happened to some of the other local inhabitants who had been caught up in the great Woodfieldgate saga. The evening had certainly been more interesting than anything they had seen on television, which was not surprising as many of them hated television and did not own sets and who, therefore, had not bought licences. This explained why they were always being bombarded by letters from an organisation that could not comprehend that any citizen, in this century, could manage without a set.

Chapter 8

Naturally, PC Rob Swagg was pleased that there was no crime in Woodfield Magna but had remained very concerned that this fact, however, admirable, might be used against him. As he had told himself, repeatedly, his "superiors", always keen to cut costs, thus ingratiating themselves with not only their senior management but with the politicians, might move him to a larger area.

He had the use of a small but attractive cottage, on the edge of the village, and an elderly but effective police car that he could use to visit his very pretty redhead girl friend, Sandra Benson, who lived in nearby Morton Norton Major. It was really important to be seen to be active and, Rob, no fool, decided to try to take some of the credit himself for the lack of crime. Consequently, he gave lectures, to anyone who would listen, on crime prevention and other aspects of police work, including many of which he had absolutely no experience and which were unlikely to trouble the local villagers. He was a regular speaker at the local primary school and had even ventured to some villages near Archester. One problem was that he was running out of possible venues but he still had The Grange in his sights although he was not sure of the kind of welcome he would receive at the half-way house.

His range of topics was impressive. He had recently added one presentation, "21st Century Terrorism in a rural context". This had so alarmed some of the more elderly people in the area that he had decided to drop it. This was a pity because he had managed to acquire some graphic and blood-curdling footage from countries around the world. Woodfieldians did not curdle blood and were not in favour of seeing others involved in curdling. In short, there was no interest in curdling.

He toyed with the idea of adding new subjects such as *How To Survive Kidnapping* and *Are you being Blackmailed-An easy way out*. Sandra, sarcastically asking if it involved suicide or murder, nevertheless advised him that both topics were unsuitable and, anyway, he was unhappy about the latter as he did not know how to defeat blackmail but he liked the title. One presentation, on laundering money, had to be dropped after the elderly audience in one of the residential homes misunderstood the title and spent the rest of the day washing coins.

Sandra recommended him to concentrate on more relevant topics. Accepting her point he decided to develop a talk on *Dogs are not just for Easter*. If the first presentation went well, he could adjust the title, depending on the season. *Dogs are not just for Michelmas* and *Dogs are not just for Halloween* were planned but had to be cancelled because of a lack of demand.

Instead he researched a paper on *Drugs and How they can Damage your Health*. He had no feelings for the correct use of upper and lower cases but, nevertheless, he remained popular in the village. The first of the drug talks was to a group of elderly residents of one of the four residential homes in the area, at Tipton Poppleford Major. He was determined to make a powerful and memorable impression and it may be claimed, without false modesty on his part, that, in that objective, at least, he was totally successful.

His first and key point, which he repeated time and time again, partly for the benefit of those who, inexplicably, had dozed off and then rejoined the meeting, was that drugs can damage your life for ever. It was unfortunate that he carelessly added "however long that may be" after the word "life", but he thought that he had got away with it. He failed to notice that some of his audience, mainly those who were still awake, were looking frightened and those who had succumbed to slumber, looked well, lifeless. However, their friends ignored them so Rob decided that nobody had died during his chat which would have been embarrassing and unfortunate for his reputation. On further analysis, Rob realised that it would not have been too good an occurrence for the deceased.

He had just used the word "snorting" and this seemed to galvanise one member of the audience. Rob had noticed him earlier and thought that he looked rather more interested in what he was saying than some of his colleagues in confinement. His demeanour suggested that he was not afraid of public speaking and his opening salvo, delivered in a strong tone that belied his fragile appearance, confirmed this.

"Excuse me, young man, and I'm sorry to interrupt you" and here he raised his voice as some members of the audience were now snoring rather loudly, "but there's something that I must say. Your initial and continuing emphasis has been on the dangers of taking drugs. You've gone to great lengths to tell us about some of the pernicious effects that taking drugs can cause and I must say that some of what you said was really frightening. Now, you have warned us of the dangers of snoring. As you may have noticed", and here he had to increase his volume again, "many of my friends are snoring as we speak. I have two points to make which I trust you will allow?" Without waiting for Rob's approval, he continued.

"Every one of us, and you, one day, my young friend, rely on drugs to ward off pain or to make us less restricted in our movements, so that we retain some self-respect and are less of a burden to the nurses here who do such a fine job in looking after us. Indeed, it is one of the highlights of the day, when one of the gals brings in a trolley with our drugs on it.

"Whatever, you say, I for one, have absolutely no intention of giving up drugs I've been on them for many years and I'm still here and I don't think I would be if I'd had no drugs. Drugs have saved my life but you claim that they are dangerous. Not for me, they're not. I've only just one word for much of what you have said and it's jolly dangerous and silly poppycock. With all respect, you're just a village policeman and I'm sure that you mean well, but you're not   a doctor, and you've been talking nonsense."

A few grunts from those who were not asleep, or who had been woken by the resident's increasingly strident tone, indicated that he had voiced a popular view. Rob decided against commenting on his critic's apparent inability to count his number of words and wondered if there was such a thing as sensible poppycock.

The veteran wanted to resume so he did whilst Rob remained bemused.

"Now, and I'm sure that you are a kind and considerate man, friendly to animals and doubtless you respond favourably to market researchers on the phone and all that sort of thing but you have the effrontery, the impudence, to tell us that we should not snore. Look around you, at least half your audience is snoring now and, in some ways, it's a tribute to your eloquence that some of us are still awake even if we don't agree with what you've said. We all snore, even during the day, when we have a nap; nobody ever told us that it was dangerous and we don't know how we can stop it. Why has nobody ever told us about snoring and why should we believe you, a mere policeman, rather than the doctors who visit us frequently and have never warned us against snoring. What do you say to that, young feller?"

Rob, embarrassed and initially very worried, explained that he had said "snorting" not "snoring" and the audience looked marginally reassured, even if they did not understand the difference, before they returned to noisy slumber. Snorting, he explained, was a way of inhaling a powdered drug via the nostrils.

Another old boy, dressed in the uncoordinated style of several different decades, suggesting that he was using up his old clothes, was on his feet, or would have been if nature had allowed. "That's very interesting. I have the utmost difficulty taking my six pills a day and I don't mind telling you that swallowing some of them, they look like blasted small rugby balls, you know, is damned difficult. I've even tried eating them with toast and marmite but it doesn't work as I don't have too many teeth and, anyway, frankly, I don't like marmite. Strange stuff. Even the manufacturers admit in their ads that some people don't like it. I must admit that I like the idea of sniffing my drugs up my snout. I think that I must try it out. Many thanks for the idea."

Rob, wisely, decided that he could not participate in this discussion on this specific issue of the use of the snout and drugs and suggested that they should discuss this with the matron.

He resumed and began discussing drugs, *per se,* whatever kind they were. Nobody was using the *per se* drug apparently, judging by the blank expressions of those who were not snoring but one old lady wanted to know the properties of the *per se* drug and whether it might help her arthritis, which, she confided, was "something terrible that I wouldn't wish on my worst enemy". Regrettably, Rob's failure to define what he meant by "drugs" and the fact that he had not responded fully to the complaints from the floor, forced an intervention of the matron who, skilfully, explained what Rob had failed to explain and reason prevailed. She explained that the drugs that Rob was talking about were not the same "as we all have here in the home" and she explained the snorting business and even, boldly, sought to explain the *per se* drug issue.

"What our friend is talking about is those drugs that make you cheerful", as she put it so elegantly. Some of the inmates then announced that they had not been cheerful for decades and that they would be most appreciative for supplies of these drugs, as quickly as possible, "whilst there's time". One elderly lady said that she had paid her taxes and if there were some drugs that made you happy, she felt that she and her friends were entitled to a supply and, please could she have some. "I've a little money put by for a rainy day so I can pay if necessary." Her comments drew some appreciative comments from her friends all of whom would like some drugs to make them cheerful. One old lady said that the last time she had been cheerful was at her husband's funeral. Apparently, he was a "nasty bit of work". The matron, having plunged herself into the hole tried to extricate herself with some help from a bewildered Rob. If he addressed an audience like this again, he would have to write a new script.

Rob explained how to drive carefully, to the infants at the local school, now led by the admirable Julia Foxworthy. With hindsight, it was probably an error to show films of serious road accidents, but, at least, Rob told himself, the message had struck home, judging by the number of children who were crying at the end of his presentation and refused to cross the road, even with the active co-operation of the so-called lollipop lady, whose girth was such that she could have stopped a car travelling at 20 miles an hour just by standing still in its path.

He explained to many locals, some in their own homes, on how to safeguard their property. Prior appointments, (what other kinds were there?) were required at least one week in advance. He conjured up the slogan *Say goodbye to tradition, not to your possessions* but felt that it had as much impact as the punch line adopted by the erstwhile cabbage thrower. His point was that the old habit of leaving doors unlocked was, in effect, making life easier for the thief. His new slogan *Say no to thieves, yes to locking doors* suggested that he had been wise to eschew any career involving writing.

Although no burglaries had been carried out in the village for some time, he introduced *Past History (*what other kinds were there?) *is No Guide To the future.* Worried locals suddenly, in some cases, for the first time, decided that this "nice young man was right when he said we should lock our doors". Rob then noted, that, in the weeks following his lectures, he had many calls from distressed and elderly locals who had either locked themselves out of their homes or who had forgotten where they had hidden their keys.

Another of Rob's favourite themes was the need to fit locks to windows. This was an entirely new concept in the village, but such was PC Rob's reputation that virtually all the locals followed his advice. Unfortunately, Rob's emphasis on the possibilities of burglaries in the village had induced fear in some of the residents. According to local gossip, some were so concerned that they ensured that a stout stick was close to their beds so that intruders could be subjected to immediate justice. Indeed, such was the fear that now permeated the village that Rob had to give a number of presentations to reassure his fellow Woodfieldians that there was no need to be frightened. He spoilt his case by reminding them that, if they were to attack an intruder with "unreasonable force" whatever that was, they could go to jail. Eventually, the locals realised that all he was advocating was greater caution and the prospects of becoming a victim of crime was very low. Business in the hardware store in Archester boomed as the sale and fitting of window locks reached new heights, as it were, and the shop owner showed his gratitude to Rob by taking him out to an expensive lunch.

In addition, Rob had a column, once a month, in the local paper and he was forced to use his contributions for three months to reassure the locals that they had nothing to fear. Despite having frightened his fellow villagers, his stock did not fall. Yes, he reflected, it was a most agreeable existence and he felt that, for the first time in his life, he was really falling in love. Despite all his initiatives, he was more than ever convinced that his regional bosses, always keen to make economies, to redeploy human resources, change reporting structures, meet government-imposed targets and improve the collection of relevant statistics, which is what good policing is all about, would soon transfer him to another area and to a less agreeable job. Doubtless, this would be in the national interest but Rob was not particularly bothered about that and really wondered whether the nation was concerned.

So, when he had heard that 40 young criminals were to be housed locally, he had been more cheerful than he had been for some time, even without the drugs the use of which he condemned. His hopes, initially high, had been dashed, not only by the finding of the "stolen" laptop and the scratched Rolls affair but also by the immaculate behaviour of the inmates of The Grange. They had let him down. Everyone agreed that their behaviour had been impeccable and that all the worries that had preceded their arrival had proved totally unjustified. They were smartly dressed, always polite and, indeed, some had already made friendships in the village and had been entertained to tea by some of the locals, who now felt guilty for being so critical of the concept. By popular consent, the half-way house concept was a success.

Rob had wondered whether his early arrival at The Grange, on the very day that the minister performed the opening ceremony, to investigate the apparent theft of a laptop might have stirred some opposition. He had been quoted by the media, accurately, at the time, it pained him to admit, as saying, "these thugs are so thick, I expect we'll find one of them using it in his room, sorry, I should have said suite". In fact, one reason for this forthright comment, which was totally out of character, was to identify with the minister's senior civil servant. You never knew when such a contact could be helpful.

The inmates of The Grange had not, apparently, sought revenge but it was impossible to believe that, in some way, they had been deterred from committing new crimes by Rob's physical presence. He was only just tall enough to be allowed to join the force and he was slim and managed to convey an erroneous impression of physical frailty. That was one of the reasons that Sandra found him so attractive.

After frightening some of the more elderly locals, Rob's popularity had slumped very briefly but he was soon in favour again and his reputation had been shored up by the open garden plan in the village which had been his brainwave. So far, it had gone well and, mercifully, the days on which the gardens were open had coincided with the few good days in a summer that, according to the weather forecasters, was to be hot and sunny. However, there were at least ten more gardens that would open. The number was growing as it became apparent that it was such a popular idea.

All this was drifting through Rob's mind when his phone rang. He had an office in his cottage and his friends often used the police number, if only because that was the only line that he had. It was probably only an acquaintance seeking his company for a drink that evening at the Duck and Orange. Nevertheless, lest it was one of his superiors, of whom he had many, the inferior officer answered smartly. "Woodfield Magna police station. PC Swagg speaking. How can I help you?" What he heard next startled him and he asked for the information to be repeated. Could this be the call that would change his life?

Jane Parker was keen to help the village by finding a celebrity to open the fete. In a way, although nobody blamed her, she felt responsible for the damage that her ex-husband had done to the village and was eager to make amends. She had been very busy. Perhaps she had been premature in assuring her friends in the village that she would be happy to attend herself and she would be accompanied by a well-known famous face. Her first and only choice, Alice Heath, a journalist friend who lived in her street, was now unable to help her. She was required to visit the US and would be away for some months making a four-hour documentary on the impact that the Beckhams had made on US culture.

One of Alice's colleagues was an up and coming young television reporter who had already gained an enviable reputation after a fearless report on the UK's increasing disenchantment with traditional zoos and circuses. She had made history by being the first female television personality to interview a parrot which insisted that she was a pretty boy, but, apart from that, she was the very embodiment of all that young males and, for that matter, old males lusted after, if you will forgive nearly ending the sentence with a preposition, or, if you won't, after whom old males lusted. Concerned that she had let Jane down, Alice recommended Louise Lewis who said that she would be delighted to visit Woodfield Magna to open the fete. Apparently, she knew the Bush-Cooks "slightly" and would let them know she was coming.

109

Her name was passed to the fete organising committee who, once they had calmed down, duly inserted the appropriate moniker and an interesting photograph in all the publicity. The press release and pics, sent to no less than three local organs of the fourth estate, was duly and predictably devoured. The photograph of this charming young girl was to be seen on all the local lamp posts and telegraph poles. If any of the locals had visited totalitarian states it would have reminded them of pics of leaders plastered on state-controlled lamp posts just before a totally democratic election when the turnout exceeds 100 per cent of the electorate.

Chapter 9

Rob's phone call was not from one of his friends. Someone had been burgled. Rob said it out loud. "Burgled, burgled, in my patch". He assured the caller, Mr Roderick Farnworthy, that he would be with him shortly. Rob toyed with the idea of putting his siren on as he fell into his old-fashioned police car but decided to keep quiet, partly to avoid scaring the natives and partly because he could not recall where the appropriate switch was.

Farnworthy and his wife, Dorothy Evans Gibbs Knott-Taylor who had not wanted to be called Farnworthy, as she thought it was "such a dashed silly name", were not very happy but they were efficient. Rob asked them to prepare a list of what was missing and Farnworthy, swiftly inserting his hand inside a pocket in his tweed sports jacket which seemed to consist more of leather patches than the original material, gave the startled policeman the list.

Rob glanced at it and soon realised that, although some items were undoubtedly valuable, they were all small. Perhaps they were of a size that could be smuggled into The Grange without being detected and then hidden in one of the inmates' suites? DEGK-T said that much of what was missing was of sentimental as well as financial value. For example, the small cup that was missing had been won in her first swimming tournament at her school in Northumberland. "That's where I grew up" and she added helpfully, "it's in the north of

England, you know. Then there's that bracelet and we can let you have a photograph of that. Mr Farnworthy liked to take pictures of my jewellery in case it was stolen. I always told him that this was silly but he was right, wasn't he? I must admit that I never expected this to happen. That's all the thanks you get from the community after opening up your garden for local charity."

The lady of the house, who was literally and metaphorically wearing the trousers, continued.

"Do you think you'll find the culprit?"

Farnworthy shook his head and withdrew his unlit pipe, as if he were about to speak, but, in the apparent absence of permission from his domineering wife, changed his mind and remained silent. For no apparent reason he looked at his wrist, as if expecting to see a watch but then remembered that he no longer sported a timepiece as it reminded him that his remaining time on this planet was oozing away.

It was time for Rob to pay an official visit to The Grange.

The supervisor, Dick Goodfellow, was less than happy to see the uniformed Rob but soon offered his help.

"It gives the place a bad reputation and suggests to the locals that their hostility to the whole concept might have been right after all. I know that you're only doing your job, but please be as discreet as you can. The lads here have all had bad experiences with the police and I've spent many long hours trying to make them understand that the police are necessary in any society to preserve law and order."

Rob interrupted. "When you say that they've all had bad experiences with the police, you mean that they were all caught and subsequently sentenced for having broken the law?"

The warden repeated his offer to help. On hearing what had happened, he asked what evidence there was that one of his lads could have been involved. Rob had to admit that he had none but, at this stage, all he wanted to do was to talk to some of the inmates.

"When did this apparent burglary take place?"

Rob did not answer but assured him that he already had a list of what had been taken.

"So what?" hissed Goodfellow, who was beginning to belie the qualities suggested by his name. "How do you know that it's not just an insurance fraud? They may well have stuffed the stuff in their shed in the hope of stuffing us, and then given you a bell." Rob thought that there was rather too much stuff there and he was less than impressed by the slang expression for the telephone but he continued to listen. He was a good man: he could overlook matters that would have aroused ire, and possibly rather a lot of it, in his fellow men.

"Has it occurred to you that they led the campaign to prevent The Grange from being set up? Doesn't that suggest that they might do something like this to prove that they were right? Were they very upset?"

If this continued, Rob, who was having difficulty in barging in to the monologue, thought that he might have to charge this man, even someone called Goodfellow, with obstructing the police. The thought of actually accusing someone of an offence, so cheered Rob up that he omitted to say that if the inmates knew of the Farnworthy's objections, that could be a motive for one or more of them to seek revenge.

For the second time, Goodfellow asked on what day and at what time the "alleged burglary" took place.

Rob told him that it occurred last night between 7.00 when they went out to dinner and before 10.00 when the victims returned. They knew the times because Farnworthy had complained that he would miss the best news, on Channel Four, at seven, "Jon Snow's a fine interviewer" and that they had returned just before the BBC news at 10.00 although he did not rate the BBC any more under their feeble managers who paid the so-called stars too much and just "pandered to the ratings". The whole place, Farnworthy claimed, had lost direction and their failure to broadcast Test cricket was one of the worst decisions they'd ever made, he told Rob, before bemoaning their own losses and adding "damn fools", twice, for good measure. Rob was pleased to recount this as it showed that he had an ear for detail, even if it was totally irrelevant.

Goodfellow had a triumphant glint in his eye. "I can tell you that it definitely was not one of my boys." Rob, becoming both irritated and puzzled wanted to know why Goodfellow could be so sure.

"That's easy. We had dinner early last night so the lads could watch football on television. It was a good game and very close. Did you see it? England crushed Papua New Guinea one nil and all my boys were watching the game from the very beginning. I know because I was pleased that they were all here and not one of them left the lounge where we were showing it, in high definition, of course, on the new 50" widescreen set. The picture on such a big set is really good but we're looking forward to 3D television. We've already a set on order but it will be a few more months before it comes. Our current set is so good it even made the English team look less bad than they are. Do you have a big high-definition digital box and blue ray?"

Rob shook his head and felt uneasy, although it was not the size of his television set that had caused this new feeling. There was a simple innocence in Goodfellow's remarks but the police brain would not let him down.

"Wait a minute. The match kicked off at 7.30 and would have ended at about 9.15. That left over an hour, in total, unaccounted for." There's that preposition at the end of a sentence again but Rob felt that he had made a good point so excused himself. At least he had not used the word "stuff".

Goodfellow smiled triumphantly. "No, as you know broadcasters offer at least 40 minutes before the kick-off showing the teams and what they have done in recent matches, often in slow motion, before some so-called pundits discuss prospects. My lads were all here for the beginning of the coverage."

Rob was not defeated.

"But there was time between the end of the game and the time that the Farnworthys returned for one of you lads to nip out, walk into their lounge, and their home is only just down the road, help himself and come back to The Grange, undetected."

Goodfellow sighed.

"You're no football fan, are you? I said that it was an evenly balanced match. England only won in extra time and News at Ten was delayed accordingly and an edition of *17th Century Insects-where are they now?*, one of a series of 27 you know, had to be postponed, to the great regret of our matron who's got a thing about insects. She's got quite a collection and specialises in spiders. It was only then that my boys left the lounge and headed for their cocoa. I remember mentioning to the lady who serves the beverage that it was good to see them all together, showing an interest in something that they could all share. I must admit, 'though, that some of them did boo when England scored. I didn't realise that they had connections with PNG. Yes, sir, I can guarantee that all of them were in the lounge all the evening."

Rob was nearly defeated. "And you were with them the whole time?"

"Yes, the whole time and I was sitting close to the door so I would have seen anyone leave."

"Were any other staff members with you in the lounge?"

"No, I was the only one. Matron was busy reading a book about spiders in the staff lounge. I mean that the book was about spiders in general, not spiders in our lounge, of course, as that would hardly fill a book. The place is kept spotless by the 12 full-time cleaning personnel on the staff."

Rob thanked him for his time and retreated to ponder his next move. Who was the thief? It seemed that most of the village were watching the match or were chatting in the pub. It was unusual to see visitors in the village and, Rob's enquiries suggested that nobody in WM had seen any strangers that evening.

Chapter 10

The weather forecast for the day of the fete did not bode well and, although the conditions during the previous week had allowed those keen on advance planning to set up in what was called the North Field, rain had been predicted. Apparently, organised showers, although nobody knew who managed them, would give way to longer periods of sustained precipitation, followed by "bursts of rain as we head into the evening". There was a chance of thunder storms and a severe weather warning had been issued by the very same people who had promised that the summer would be long and hot.

Because of this prediction and the fact that the UK was in an economic recession, fewer families than usual had booked for overseas holidays, causing the package holiday companies to cancel many flights and hotel bookings. This significant extra capacity was greedily taken up by foreign operators. Then, as it became apparent that the gods who determine British weather were not prepared to grant sunshine to the depressed natives, there was a rush to seek the sun in overseas climes, notwithstanding the economic climate. Unfortunately, for the travel operators, it was too late to revive the flights and bookings, with the result that many thousands of families were disappointed or had to book with foreign companies who had a few vacancies left after selling holidays at the more favoured resorts.

This, in turn, led to a full-scale government enquiry after which those involved blandly confirmed that "lessons had been learned" and that all concerned would now go forward, having drawn the obligatory line in the sand, even if it was only on a damp British beach. Editorials and cartoons in the campaigning press pointed out that this was precisely what many frustrated families were not able to do.

Although weather forecasters had been the frequent target for jokes over the years, it was becoming evident that their accuracy in predicting short-term bad weather was sometimes uncannily correct. It seemed from an early forecast, backed by the fete committee's prejudices, that the organisers might have to contend with bad weather. Consequently, the 15 strong committee, now led for the 17th consecutive year by Alf Fox, had discussed whether some of the stalls should be accommodated in an expensively-hired new marquee. This provoked a prolonged debate. Some argued that a marquee was against the spirit of the event and others hinted darkly that it might even deter attendance. One advanced the proposition that he was in a marquee recently and it smelt but admitted that might have been caused by the presence of some 30 donkeys and what appeared to be discoloured and elderly straw.

Hiring such a large tent meant higher costs but it was agreed that charging an entry fee would be against the spirit of the event. Mrs Trumpington-Brewer, of the Surrey side of the Trumpington-Brewers and not from the Hertfordshire branch, as widely believed, had suggested that they might try to persuade the visiting celebrity, Louise Lewis, to pose, with local residents, for photographs for a modest fee, of, say, £5, so that costs could be recovered. She added that it was imperative that a reasonably large donation was given to the local hospice as she had heard that the nearby village of Nutley was predicting that, this year, it would be able to give a record sum to the charity. "We cannot be left behind, especially after Nutley won all that money for losing the cricket match and gave large sums to the elderly in the village. It's high time we did something for our own more mature residents." Since that meeting, John Gaitskell had generously

118

given the local hospice £10,000 from the sum he received from selling his painting so the financial situation was not yet totally dire.

One male member of the committee, was overheard whispering to a colleague of the same gender that he would pay considerably more than £5 for what he crudely described as "a 'decent' pic of that gorgeous bird". The purple-haired and pearl necklaces on the committee looked suitably offended and some even put their hands across their chests as if to protect themselves against an attack that would never have been launched in a thousand years.

Others, having lived all their lives in the UK, noted that bad weather was a very common occurrence in the summer and that, like Boy Scouts, "we should be prepared". That prompted one committee member, Colonel Arthur Whatarotter, retired, to reminisce on his time as a Boy Scout and he was able to assure his committee colleagues that tents did not smell, based on his life under canvas. His recollections were only halted by the chairman, to the obvious regret of the male committee members, just as Arthur was beginning a new anecdote which had commenced with "then, the following year, it was decided that we should organise a joint camp with the Girl Guides and I recall that year vividly because we..."

After a lengthy debate in the committee, it was decided that at least some of the attractions should be housed in the marquee, hired at some considerable expense from a firm in Archester. Unfortunately, other implications of bad weather did not receive the same detailed consideration. If it rained hard as it probably would, how would the visitors reach the marquee in the middle of the field, which was the only sensible place for it to be pitched? Some committee members spoke very critically about rain in general, which seemed unfair as it was not present to defend itself. It appeared that it was seldom wanted and it was high time that man, and for that matter, woman combined, across the nations, to ensure that it only happened when everyone wished it. Alf, finding himself drawn into this absurd debate merely pointed out that there would be no occasions when everyone agreed. That said, he pleaded for order and expressed a desire to make progress.

He was ignored. Rain was, as another former army man, Major Monty Nutter, averred, "a crafty fellow, it can sneak up un-noticed before tipping tons of unwanted stuff over its victims. It can rust steel and drown people and drinking too much of the stuff can cause problems". Alf, not entirely unfamiliar with water himself, being a plumber, pointed out that they were discussing rain, not all water and demanded that they return to the schedule. Monty, who was the sort of chap who when speaking in public would automatically grab his lapels, even if he were not wearing a jacket, had not finished. "The worst I've ever experienced was in Archester, last year, which was even more torrential than some of the monsoons I'd lived through in the Far East although they were pretty grim. I think I took shelter in the butcher's or was it the bookshop? Yes, that's right because I remember seeing all that glamorous gardening gal's books. Forget her name but damn good filly, or was it the baker's?" Alf assured him that it did not matter and that they were going to resume the business meeting.

"Fine, old chap, do carry on. Sorry I go on a bit myself now but it's because I live alone, know what I mean, always have done, well, for many years, don't you know, and have nobody to talk to, except that old dog of mine. He's 15 years old now but there I go again, I'll shut up now, not another word, quiet as a church mouse, not a peep from me. Absolute silence, lips buttoned up. Sorry to go on."

However, the good news, already conveyed to the committee, was that Louise, the visiting celebrity was keen to come and, although storm clouds were gathering over Europe, well, at least this part of the continent, she had, apparently, already prepared her opening speech. She had opted to speak from the modest 15 foot high platform, not from the marquee, as she had said that she did not want to be a pessimist and it might not rain, anyway.

The committee had organised local caterers to provide food and to the obvious satisfaction, the price for the franchise, as the chairman put it, had been agreed with the suppliers with no discussion on their part. This prompted some committee members to speculate whether the price for allowing the Archester company to sell food at the fete had been too low.

The committee meeting went well after this and it seemed that there was not much more to be resolved before the big day. Just to be on the safe side, the four men on the Fete Emergency Liaison Integrated Group, known affectionately to its members as FELIG, tried to exchange mobile phone numbers. This proved difficult: a quarter of its members did not have a mobile phone, 25 per cent had forgotten his number and a third member admitted that he did not know how to turn his on and when his grandson did it for him, all it did was to make funny noises. The chairman gave out his number.

Jack Scoop was in charge of publicity and had agreed that he would cover the story about the visiting celebrity for his brother, Ivor Scoop of *The Daily Clarion,* if anything newsworthy happened. Normally, such a parochial event as a village fete would not attract any country-wide attention but Woodfield Magna was still well-known nationally because of the cricket match scandal and the crime survey in which the village had come top and then bottom and then, of course, there was the enchanting Louise.

Jack's Archester-based company was now very successful and he had moved into one of the new executive houses that had been built on the edge of the village. With some help from his new parents-in-law, he had acquired the lease on the London building used by Ratty, Ratty & Fiddler, his old employers. Some time ago, they had been one of the most successful PR groups in London until the Parker affair, which was swiftly followed by a serious misunderstanding with one of the girls in the touring Patagonian Opera group. Jack let out the whole building apart from half of one floor, which he used as his London office and a flat. He had married his pregnant fiancée and was now the proud father of very young female twins, who, remarkably, resembled the cricketing Bedser twins in the Fifties. Jack had been reconciled with his parents-in-law who now saw him not as a failed PR man, and how they hated that profession and those who traded in it, but as a successful and shrewd business man who could really look after their precious daughter and their delightful grandchildren.

Previously, Jack, who was on the organising committee, had arranged for Louise, the visiting television star, to stay with Jane who still had a small flat in nearby Archester, but Jane was called away on the Friday afternoon, to meet an influential politician who wanted to sound her out about becoming an educational adviser to his party. Louise, too, would arrive late as she had to interview Cliff Steel, a pop star of the Sixties, who had lost his dog and was, according to his publicity agent, gobsmacked, shattered, and "in a word, totally and utterly gutted". At short notice, there being no hotel in the area, the only one had been converted to The Grange, and because Louise would arrive late on the Friday evening, the Bush-Cooks kindly offered to meet her at the nearest station, take her to their home and let her stay with them overnight.

Archester station had been in the news recently because a brief case found on the train had contained several government-owned computer discs helpfully marked "Highly confidential: only authorised personnel to use these secret discs". Apparently, they contained detailed information on all the higher-rate tax payers in the country, the names and addresses of tens of thousands of NHS patients and, bizarrely, the name of every Home Secretary since the post was founded. A few months before, such a discovery would have been at the top of all the national news bulletins, but now such finds were so common, that this discovery merited only the briefest of mentions in most of the national newspapers.. One tabloid almost welcomed the story as it was able to use a feeble heading that had been reserved for the next such find:

DISCovery embarrasses PM: More AWOL computer records found on train

Louise was pleased to see her hosts and she commented very favourably on their home. It was a large detached house, with a garden that suggested that one of the couple knew what was what, and what should not be what, in matters horticultural. A very green lawn sloped down elegantly to a small lake and, beyond that, there was a modest wood. Hilary B-C said that this was his favourite retreat and that he spent hours there, planning books and Charlie conjured up menus there. He expected that she would soon be entrusted with the dinner for the important meeting of G119 nations in London. He explained, in a patronising patter, that this was an event of major international importance, when the leaders of the world gathered together, seemingly to debate crucial issues affecting the whole of mankind. Although their subordinates had spent many months discussing and then agreeing major issues, H B-C explained, the leaders then failed to agree in public what they had agreed in private, forcing their underlings to produce bland statements designed to satisfy everyone. Helpfully, he added, "they satisfy no one. Assuming that Charlie gets the contract, and we've been tipped off that it's coming our way, please don't tell anyone, it's important that we offer the best possible food. The future of the world may depend on it."

Louise obliged. She would not tell anyone.

Bush-Cook, H, as befits all professional gardeners who can do anything in the world of culture, media and the arts, was planning to write what he called a definitive history of the world. After that, he planned to produce five novels, based in part on the work of the secret service. So far, in his writing, he had reached 55 BC, which he conceded, almost as if betraying a secret, was a very important year. "That, incidentally, is Before Christ, not Bush-Cook." Louise was, of course, most impressed that a simple gardener knew so much and said that that was most interesting. She decided against any further discussion with this jumped-up gardener who seemed to have become very big-headed since she first met him, albeit fleetingly, at the opening of a garden centre. She had also been involved with him on a television show. This man now was really pretentious and rude. She despised most television cooks as a bumptious, conceited, ignorant breed and could never bring herself to consider them as chefs, apart from Charlie, whom she liked very much, but this man could make her feel the same way about gardeners.

123

Louise and Hilary had worked together, just once, on a reality gardening show, *Find My Weeds* when they each led teams consisting of two parents and two children, who were charged with identifying what was a weed and which was a flower. The show had been planned to run for 12 episodes but only lasted for one edition. Hilary had undermined the programme's *raison d'être*, as all he said, during the entire programme, was that a weed was just a plant in the wrong place. This was welcomed by Friends Of The Dandelion, which was fast becoming an important pressure group in matters horticultural. It was unfortunate that he implied that this definition could also apply to, for example, good men who became politicians. However, this absurd comment had been forgotten and Hilary was now in charge of the new television garden in Woodfield Magna. It was only in its early stages but it was going well and, as Charlie told the local media, with a telling phrase that her husband used in relation to his researches on 55 BC, it was early days.

Louise looked out of her bedroom window and compared it to her view from her own home. She lived in a London flat and her view was over the roofs of houses and supermarkets. One day she must move to the country, or, now that she had moved out of the poverty zone, buy a second home for weekends.

Her career, like Hilary's history book, was in its early stages but she knew, already, and she was a modest person, that she was going to make it. Her looks would not last for ever, but television gave her an opportunity to be better known and she intended to take full advantage of everything she could. She was just 20 so she should have already begun work on volume one of her autobiography but a start would be made in the coming winter. She was believed to be dating a famous footballer, although some keen observers of show business maintained that that was just unfounded gossip that her PR man had conjured up, and she had already had an offer to give, no, sell her name to a new brand of perfume. Her agent, Bernard Graspitt, was also looking at potential modelling and other advertising contracts and Louise was keen to be associated with some of the nation's leading charities. Bernard claimed that it was all about publicity. Woodfield Magna District Hospice was but a small step on a long journey, she told herself. She knew what she meant but was not entirely satisfied with how she had expressed it.

After a brief rest before dinner, she changed from her seductive black trouser suit into a stunning knee-length red dress, which brought out the best from her shimmering blonde hair. She ambled attractively down the broad and "Gone with the wind" type staircase to join her friends.

Louise said that she had seen all the very favourable publicity about the Bush-Cook restaurant. Charlie said that it was doing very well and that they had been very pleased that, although it was some miles from Archester, many of the bookings were coming from people in the city. They were planning a more modest lunchtime menu for the locals who had given them unstinting support. Tactfully, Louise asked if they could dine there that evening as it had attracted so many good reviews. "My friends will be jealous when I tell them that I have eaten there and I expect then that they'll try to wangle a trip to this wonderful part of the world, know what I mean?"

The restaurant was only a short ride from the Bush-Cook residence and, because it was then about 8.30, there were few residents who saw Louise ooze with rather less care than was necessary from the B-C executive car, although it could be argued that she was not to know that that was precisely the moment that the wind decided to have a brief and rude blow. Jack was a real professional and his camera was fast becoming one of his best friends. Both were there to record the three celebs entering the restaurant.

The Bush-Cooks and their famous guest were shepherded to the best table by Figaro Jones, the head waiter, a cockney from Clapham who was failing, conspicuously, in his efforts to develop an authentic and sustained Italian accent. The B-Cs and Louise graciously said good evening to their surprised fellow diners. Few knew Louise's name but were sure that they had seen her on television, appearing in an ad for a car company but could not recall the make of car. Others had definitely seen her reading the news, but could not remember the station, whilst some insisted that she was a weather forecaster, although they could not name the channel on which she appeared. One man even said, "You can tell by that white jacket over her red dress she's wearing. If that isn't a forecaster's jacket I'm a Dutchman. In fact, I can remember seeing her once and she was actually wearing that jacket." "Shush, dear, calm down", was his wife's command as her next of kin was becoming over-heated.

A neutral observer might have thought it odd that, although almost everyone recognised Louise, not one could identify why she was well-known. Perhaps her looks had something to do with that or was it that she was well-known for being well-known? Such was the nature of contemporary fame.

Hilary took advice from his two female guests and then ordered the wine. He and his wife tucked into a chateaubriand and Louise chose beef Wellington which she devoured enthusiastically. She was looking forward to the fete the following day, especially as the forecasters were now predicting a fine, hot summer's day, but could not have anticipated events that were to have an impact on her career.

The following morning, Louise allowed herself a modest lie-in as her interview with the ageing pop star who had lost his dog had proved particularly emotional. Apparently, the canine, of unknown origin, had been his constant companion over the last ten years during which the celeb had gone though the traumas and "gut-wrenching heartbreaks" of six difficult divorces after what he described as five loveless marriages. Later he reversed the figures on being pressed, verbally of course, by Louise. He had broken down at this point and, outlined against his riverside mansion, wept openly, on camera, of course. It was only his fans, to whom he owed everything, absolutely everything, and whom he loved, every one of them, and Fido Three, that he had survived. He repeated, lest there was any doubt, that he loved them all and Fido Three received another commendation. If the wretched animal had been watching the performance, he might well have been sick. Some cynical viewers doubtless felt that the canine deserved to be congratulated for legging it: a life on the road would have been preferable to living with this so-called national treasure whose vanity seemed larger than his home.

Louise, trying but failing to choose her words carefully, had asked if, in the continued absence or even death, of the current dog, as she thoughtlessly described the celeb's friend, there would be a Fido Four. At this grim prospect, the National Treasure broke down again and Louise ended the interview as the camera closed in what could only be described as a truly gob-smacked and wet face as tears trickled down the lines on the tanned and well-creased visage in much the same way that rain drains down a vertically and recently ploughed field. When she was certain that the cameras were off, Louise immediately apologised to the famous pensioner for her "rather harsh and insensitive final question". "Not at all, my dear, it was fine, just fine, thank you." She was impressed that he had recovered so quickly, but, presumably, that was what makes a celebrity.

Because she had caught up on her sleep on the Saturday morning, Louise had not had time to read the very favourable tabloid coverage of the interview and the "genuine grief from an unhappy nation for a national and much-loved treasure in his hour of need." Indeed, the new prime minister, as ever, keen to appear as a man of the people, said that it was his "fondest wish that Fido Three returned home, but, meanwhile, he assured the National Treasure that the nation, "and we all love dogs, don't we" was praying for the safe return of dear Fido Three".

Now, after Louise had had a light brunch with her friends, she, Jane, the B-Cs, locals and many more from the surrounding villages, were eagerly awaiting the opening ceremony. Alf Fox, who always enjoyed being the centre of attention, and who generously chaired many of the local committees, knew that today, he would be in the spotlight for only a few minutes. He had to make an impressive short speech before introducing Louise. He was nervous and his best friend, if he had had one, for the use of the superlative implied that he had at least three, would have admitted that Alf's skills did not extend to either writing or making a speech. A sharp whistling and whining noise through the loudspeakers preceded by a rushing sound and fingers tapping the microphone, suggested that the chairman of the Woodfield Magna Village Fete was about to speak.

"My fellow villagers, unaccustomed as I am", Here he paused, waiting for the audience to expect him to saying "to speaking in public". There being no discernable grunts apart from a few of his drinking acquaintances, who had been living down to their reputation, he continued and removed his pompous hands from the lapels of his blazer, "to opening fetes" and here he paused again, "on this, the 17th and the last time I shall perform the function, as I am retiring, I welcome you all." Once again, there being no reaction, he finished his sentence, disappointed that his loyal service did not, apparently, merit even a mild ripple of applause. A professional to his very lapels, he continued, tugging enthusiastically on the part of his jacket that has already received too much publicity.

"I'm really pleased to see so many of you all here today and I extend a warm hand of friendship to our friends from Nutley and to our friends from other villages. You're all very welcome. In particular, I want to thank, on your behalf, our friends, Hilary and Charlie Bush-Cook, for their consistent support, ever since they joined our little community, and Jane Parker who has contributed massively to this year's event by managing to persuade no less a celebrity than lovely Louise Lewis to open this year's event."

This drew considerable applause and some males even cheered and there was enough whistling to engage the attention of any local football referees. Alf, upset that in all the times he had opened the show, he had never had such a welcome, had to wait a few moments and wave his hands in a motion designed to suggest that whilst clapping was a good thing, you could have too much of it, especially when a chairman wanted to resume. He continued.

Turning to Louise, he said that, "As I think you must realise, we're all delighted that you have been able to fit us into your busy schedule and we thank you so much for coming. It's a great pleasure for us all and whilst we know that your time is limited, we hope to see as much of you as possible whilst we can, if not here, then on television in the future." At this point some vigorous "hear hears" suggested that a few males in the audience had detected some salacious ambiguities in Alf's last sentence.

"Before I ask our charming friend to open the show, there are a few items of information I want to pass on. I'm sorry to tell you that Mrs Benita Welsh, who has offered horoscopes at the fete for many years, and who's acquired an enviable reputation for accuracy, has withdrawn because of unforeseen circumstances." Some of the more perceptive of the audience allowed themselves a slight smirk and one or two indulged themselves in a full-blown smirk. What Alf did not add was that her reputation for accuracy was based on her knowledge of local gossip. He continued. "Happily for us, Mrs. Georgina Harris has agreed to deputise and we thank her very much."

"However, as well as some of the attractions that you have enjoyed over the years, we have some new ones. For example, you can guess how many pebbles there are in a large glass jar. Whoever guesses closest to the correct figure will win a prize. We are also running a competition to determine who can name the most television cooks, I mean chefs, gardeners and weather forecasters who have appeared on national television in the last year. I must thank our own famous couple, the Bush-Cooks for kindly agreeing to be the judges in this competition which, I know, will immediately appeal to all you TV fans.

"Another innovation will be provided by the boys from The Grange, our new neighbours, who are attending their first fete in this village. We welcome you", but before Alf could finish the sentence, some boos could be heard. He resumed. "And they will be trying to pick the lock of a car in under a minute. Provide your own car and prepare to be amazed.

"Our local cricket team will be challenging all you bowlers to hit their stumps from just 15 yards, sorry, 13.846 metres. You can throw the ball and if you get past their bats and hit the stumps, there will be a prize. As you know, we had this competition last year and it was very successful in raising some much-needed funds for the local hospice and I'm sure you're pleased that Ross, who was defending the stumps until he was hit on the head, is brave enough to come back this year except that he is now going to wear a helmet. Perhaps I should add that you must aim at the stumps, not at the batsman as we don't want a repetition of what happened last year although, of course, I'm not suggesting that Ross was hit deliberately. After all, the ball that hit him was bowled by one of his friends.

"I'm pleased that, once again, we have a competition for the most unusual fancy dress worn by children under the age of 12 and we've also introduced a slightly different competition this year for you dog lovers. Enrol you and your pet and show the judges that your dog is the most obedient. You'll remember that, last year, the competition ended in one dog savaging another after the aggressor had been given a drink of beer. For that reason, every animal, sorry, pet, must be kept on a lead and, please, please do not allow your dog to drink any alcohol. We don't want any beery bulldogs or sloshed spaniels."

Alf was pleased with this alliterative sally but the audience, if impressed, failed to reveal their feelings. They were that kind of audience or perhaps they were just bored by the perennial Alf.

"We had hoped to have an exciting marching band, led by teenage cheer leaders from Kingsbury Underhill, but they wanted to be paid rather more than we could afford so, instead, the primary school village band will be entertaining us and I'm sure that we all would like to thank Julia Foxworthy, who is doing such a good job after replacing.." Here Alf's memory failed and he ended his sentence lamely, after a perceptible pause, by saying."her predecessor".

"Before I forget, our local MP has asked me to apologise for his absence this afternoon but he has an important meeting with the party leaders and some House of Commons officials on some financial matters, which I'm sure means his expenses. I'm sure we all wish him well." The silence, broken by a few rude comments to the effect that he was a cheat of dubious parentage, implied otherwise.

Alf resumed.

"Ladies and gentlemen, I must tell you that the display given by the falcons will not be taking place this year and I'm sure that we're all delighted that the children who were attacked by the birds last summer are now better and no worse for their experience. We can't say the same for the falcons which, you will recall, were deterred by members of the cricket club using some old stumps. Their trainer has asked me to apologise, once again, for the action of his birds. He says that it was the only time that they had behaved in this way but the HSE has ensured that such an incident will never happen again by insisting that all the birds were killed immediately after the fracas." This news produced what, in a greater number of children could have been called mass hysteria but the instant blubbing from the boys and their sobbing sisters suggested that the demise of the birds was not regarded as a triumph for the brave men and women of the HSE.

"I have some bad news that I must impart. As you all know, we have always, at our fetes, tried to keep our young guests amused. I know that the children have enjoyed the work of our specialist entertainers, except, of course, those falcons. Sadly, this year, each and every one of our friends has turned down our invitation, not, I hasten to add, because they didn't want to come, because they did. The reason that they are not here is that the government now requires children's entertainers to go through an expensive vetting process which is required to prove that they are not a danger to children. This idea may be dropped but, at present, that's how things stand."

Here he paused as the crowd, unaware of this latest official absurdity, looked amazed. He continued. "Understandably,

131

they are not prepared to acquiesce in the expensive nonsense to prove that they can be trusted with children. We all know that these friends of ours have been our children's friends and to even imply that, in this crowd any one of such evil intent could be successful is totally absurd. We're sorry that you all have been affected by this latest piece of government lunacy and I hope you'll lobby our MP, who should have been here today, to change this daft regulation. It's appalling that normal, decent child-loving people have to pay to prove that they're not paedophiles. Sometimes I think that we are going mad in this country."

At this point, Alf's comments attracted some sustained applause. Surprised but gratified that he had provoked such a reaction, he paused before continuing.

"I must thank all the parents who brought their children and their children's friends to the fete this year. In future, parents who give reciprocal lifts to friends' children may have to undergo official inspection by the government and I understand that many have decided not to do this. Let's hope that, by the time that the next fete takes place some of the lunatic regulations will have been cancelled and the signs are that sense is going to triumph."

At last, Alf had the audience on his side. The applause was warm, genuine and sustained.

"Your committee decided that this year, as the weather has been so bad, presumably because of global warming, although I think we'd like some warmer weather ourselves, we ought to go to the expense of hiring an marquee where you will find some of your favourite stalls and where we can continue to enjoy today's event even if it rains. However it has cost us rather a lot to hire this marquee and we're anxious to make a significant contribution, once again, to the local hospice.

"Now here comes some good news. I am delighted to say that Louise has promised to help."

Those who had previously uttered hear hears when Alf expressed the wish that the community should see more of Louise, immediately started speculating on the nature of the assistance. One yokel made a few lewd suggestions that caused his friends to giggle in adolescent fashion. Alf, in an effort to drown out their laughter moved closer to the microphone, causing a predictable whistle. Undeterred, and this is where those who have previously chaired 16 fetes come into their own, he continued.

"Louise has agreed to have her photograph taken with anyone who so wishes for £5 a picture, which she will sign later, and the proceeds will be given direct to the local hospice. I must also embarrass this charming young star who, we all hope, will grace our television screens for many years to come. She asked me not to say this but I think that I it's only right that I tell you that she has already donated £350 to our hospice fund."

Wild cheers greeted this announcement. Clearly, very clearly, she was a very good egg.

Alf had not finished. "We cannot control the weather but let's hope that the gods will be kind to us, although I don't like the look of that cloud that seems to be sitting over Jock's house." He glared at the hapless Jock with all the ferocity used by a departmental store's Father Christmas whose corn had just been crushed by a juvenile customer, and somehow implied that his friend was responsible for the cloud and its movement towards the fete.

"Finally, make the most of this fete. From next year on, the insurance that has to be taken out is crippling and I'm not sure how we can meet the cost. Please do what you can to ensure that these faceless bureaucrats do not take away some of our simple and   innocent pleasures that have been enjoyed in the countryside for many decades.

"That said, I thank you all for coming and hope that you have a most enjoyable afternoon. Before I finish, in the interests of public order, I should tell you that the queue for the photograph with our charming guest will be by the hoopla stall and she will be here until the last customer has been satisfied." Here, again, some young males detected some ambiguity in Alf's remarks. One remarked that he did not realise the extent to which Alf was obsessed with sex.

"Without further ado, and with no more words from me, as I must stop now, lest I outstay my welcome, it is my great pleasure and indeed, honour to introduce our charming and generous guest of honour, Louise Lewis."

The generous applause doubtless indicated some relief that Alf had finished and was to give way to someone who was probably more attractive than anyone whom the Woodfieldian lads had ever seen in the flesh. Louise was warmly applauded for several minutes. A natural blonde, she was wearing a pale yellow pleated skirt, a white frilly blouse and a navy jacket. Her appearance did not disappoint the males in the crowds. She rose to speak. Glancing upwards, nervously, at the clouds and then, confidently, down at the crowds, she began.

Jack opened his notebook at a new page and pulled out his camera from his pocket. He had listened carefully to the speech of welcome and would be covering the event for his brother. Experience told him that you just never knew on occasions like this when something might happen that can be used to commercial advantage. Besides, he had promised the local paper, whose editorial staff were away in Paris on a weekend bonding trip, that he would write 500 words and take a pic for the following Wednesday's paper. He already had one tabloid-worthy pic of the blonde as she was getting out of the B-C car last evening at the restaurant and any more photos now would just be a bonus.

"First of all, I must thank you all and especially Alice Heath for going to America which gives me the chance of visiting this beautiful village. I am really pleased to be here with so many happy people. I must admit that I felt depressed last night after my interview with Cliff Steel, one of our National Treasures, who's lost his dog. I know that we all feel deeply moved and hope that he is soon reunited with Fido

Three." The crowd, including those who despised the NT and who admired the dog for legging it, applauded the sentiment lustily. The truth was that almost any remark from the celebrity was going to be given a very warm response.

"I'd also like to thank Alf, the chairman of the organising committee and his colleagues and of course, my friends, the Bush-Cooks, who, despite their own busy schedules, allowed me to stay with them in their fine home and who treated me to an fantastic dinner in their new restaurant and I'm very glad that it seems to be doing well.

"Of course, I had heard about Woodfield Magna before, although I have been warned by your chairman that I should not talk about Brian Parker's attempt to organise the result of a cricket match and his offer to local councillors a large sum of money, for, apparently, doing very little work, presumably and allegedly in the hope of securing planning permission to build more houses. I must not comment on any of that because I gather that, although some new big houses have been built, the construction of the new affordable homes has not yet begun and it's a sensitive issue.

Alf seemed to pale on hearing these remarks.

"Let me turn to happier aspects. This is, undoubtedly, one of the most attractive villages I've ever seen and I can understand only too well, why, as one local told me, you're not keen on incomers. Well, I'm an incomer and, everywhere I've been in the short time I've been with you I've been treated very well. You are indeed, very fortunate to live in such a marvellous part of the country and, perhaps, one day, I might look for a second home here, when I've scraped a few more pennies together."

She added this last phrase as she looked around and realised that she probably earned, no, received, more in a week than most of her audience earned in a year. If she had been more perceptive, she might have noticed that this remark caused some more mature locals to bristle but there was a distinct lack of any bristling from the younger males in the audience, who were staring at her with glassy and vacuous expressions. If incomers looked like her, they could have as many second homes as they liked.

Louise continued.

"I don't want to sound patronising, but I think that it's so important to maintain old traditions in this fast-moving world and thank heaven that there are dedicated and hard-working people like you who remind us that there is an alternative to city life."

Such sentiments were warmly applauded.

"I've never opened a fete before so I'm not entirely sure that I know what to say. I've opened many things in the last year or two but not a fete. For example, I've launched a few ships but I don't think it would be appropriate to express good luck to all who sail in this fete and to smash a bottle of champagne against this dais. I've opened a new secondary school for boys and I must say that they were probably the most attentive and interested audience I've ever come across but I can hardly wish you well and express the hope that hard work will result in your having good careers, whatever you choose in your lives. Apart from anything else, that might sound like a spam advert."

Few of the audience had any real knowledge of computers and did not understand this apparent hostility to a luncheon meat that had sustained the nation in hard economic times.

"Before I finish, I would like to thank you all again for organising this event and for inviting me to open it. I hope that yawl, as our Texan friends say, have a good time and that you'll raise lots of money for that most deserving of causes, the local hospice. All that it remains for me to say, then is that I ...."

At this point, Louise suddenly looked pale, failed to finish her sentence and, with a significant and uncharacteristic absence of elegance, fell into the arms of the committee

136

chairman who had been following her speech with attention that could justly be called rapt. With admirable presence of mind and bearing in mind that, in his arms, he was cradling one of the sexiest girls in the country, he asked if there was a doctor in the crowd. It was unfortunate that, at that precise time, the storm broke and the rain pelted down with a rare venom, soaking Alf's precious parcel and doing nothing to enhance her dignity. Jock's cloud had moved on and had decided to attack the field in which the fete was beginning. The audience ploughed through the instant mud in the direction of the marquee.

Carrying Louise over the 30 yards to the huge tent was, as he admitted later, one of the most exciting events of Alf's life, which, he conceded to some male colleague committee members, had, thus far, been rather boring. Mrs Alf, incidentally, was at home, looking after their three children and four cats so did not see her husband's heroic efforts.

Puffing heavily, Alf reached the marquee and put down his precious cargo, very gently, on a long table. The noise of the rain and the mutterings of the astonished audience, now audibly worrying about their celebrity, mean that it was difficult for the chairman to be heard. He tried a second time. "Will someone ring for an ambulance, NOW?"

Immediately, five separate calls were made for assistance for Louise. The much maligned National Health Service rose to the occasion magnificently. Within 10 minutes, no less than five ambulances had arrived, all manned by males, keen to see Louise in the flesh. Some had been diverted from a serious fracas at a football ground, just over the county boundary, where the local club were playing an under 14 match against a touring team from Jersey in what was either a very late season fixture or an early one in the new season. Apparently, some of the children, unhappy with the referee's decision to award a penalty, when one member of the home team had punched an opponent in the face, attacked the unfortunate official, whilst other children filmed the event for YouTube and national television.

137

A tall man pushed through the crowds. Louise, ever the professional, was now awake again and had managed to re-organise her damp appearance to advantage and was busy trying to apologise to everyone. The tall man assured her that he was a doctor. The booming voice belonged to the recently retired Dr. Tiny Pye, he who favoured erotic topiary. His critics maintained, cruelly, that his medical knowledge came from the weekly supplements in a popular newspaper and a 20 year old American book that was displayed permanently and prominently, on his desk. That said, he knew what he had to do now. He was keen, if not downright enthusiastic, without infringing any medical codes, to assist in any way that he could, and, of course, he would have shown the same solicitude and professional care, to, for example, Alf if he had collapsed. Pye laid his giant hands at different places, on Louise, all totally legitimately of course, and, whilst he was doing this, he asked if the gentle pressure he was applying cause the young lady any pain. She was fine, she said and there were no pains. He asked a few questions and was about to come to a conclusion and dismissed the ambulance crews who legged it with obvious reluctance back to the football match, where two of the parents had been stabbed in the scuffles.

Jack, realising that he now had a good story for his brother's paper, had positioned himself strategically so that he could follow and then report on developments. He had taken some pics of Louise as she slumped before being caught by the chairman. One or even two of these could be sold to the local paper but he had some that would be reserved for *The Daily Clarion*. One of these was taken as Louise began her inelegant and downwards spiral and one was as she was being caught by the alert chairman. The third was as she was in his arms. Fortunately for the tabloid, two of the pics had been taken as her skirt rode up, revealing rather more than would be expected at any location except on a Brazilian beach or in an expensive club patronised by wealthy footballers.

Tiny had not finished his assessment.

"What have you eaten since you left London, my dear?"

138

Suppressing a smile, she told him that she had dined early last night at the Bush-Cook restaurant and that this morning, because she had so liked the place so much, she had returned there to have a fine brunch.

Pye asked if she had had a pie for dinner.

"No, it was beef Wellington, the best I think I've ever had."

"And what did you have for breakfast?"

" Fruit juice, coffee and toast."

"Anything cooked?"

"Yes, smoked haddock."

The doctor had heard all he needed to know.

"I'm please to say, my dear, that there is nothing seriously wrong. You've just had an attack of food poisoning."

Jack could hardly credit what his auricular appendages were conveying to him. He would sell all this for a large sum to his brother's paper. The editor did not like celebrity cooks and would give this story the prominence it merited, or, failing that, what he decided it deserved.

Louise was now recovering swiftly and was keen to thank the chairman who had caught her and saved her from falling badly to the floor of the raised platform. She was still sitting down in the marquee but she caught Alf by the hand and dragging him gently towards her, she stretched forwards and planted a big kiss on his lips. "That's my way of thanking you", she whispered seductively. After that, having restored her hitherto pristine appearance with the assistance of a towel and some makeup, she went to the section of the marquee that, because of rain, had been reserved for the photo-hungry males and helped to raise over £300 for the local hospice.

Jack, who had contrived to take yet another photograph, surreptitiously, wondered how he could do something for her which might be rewarded with what, in his adolescent days would have been described as…well, it didn't matter now but he seemed to think that it began with an s and had eight letters. He was going to make a packet out of this fete.

Alf, suitably embarrassed, had tried to assure Louise that it had been nothing, implying somehow, that catching distressed young blondes and being thanked in so physical a way was, frankly, part of his everyday life as a part time chairman and full-time plumber. A few moments later, as the fuss had died down, and the audience retraced their steps towards the outdoor stalls, as it had now stopped raining and the sun was out, the chairman confided to a fellow committee member. "It's just as well that there were no journalists present as poor Louise fell. Imagine what the tabloids would make of it. Thank heavens there were no photographs of the crucial moments. I saw her starting to fall and it was just instinct that made me lean forward and catch her. "Frankly", and here the chairman looked around to ensure that nobody else was able to hear, "I must confess that, catching her and then carrying her to the marquee gave me more of a thrill than I've had in my married life for years. Just think, how many millions of young men would have given to be in my shoes, muddy as they are, especially when she kissed me later to thank me. It made me remember my earlier life: do you know, I haven't had sex since my tortoise died."

Jack had indeed, captured the moment.

He took several more pics before the fete was closed for another year. Fortunately, the field had dried out very quickly, prompting some villagers to ask why a gamble on the marquee had been taken. Two acts had been scheduled to perform in the main arena. The first was a demonstration involving dogs who ran around, over and inside barrels and, generally did things that respectable dogs don't do every day of the week, unless their tucker was dependent on their performance. No doubt some in the audience were reminded of the disappearance of Fido Three. Polite applause greeted the end of the act.

Another act was staged by a young man, clad from top to toe in a silver fire-resistant suit. He drove his motor cycle amazingly fast over a short distance and performed all manner of tricks whilst retaining control of the bike. However, one of the dogs from the previous act, seeking more excitement or a new career, or perhaps just jealous of the greater applause accorded to the rider, broke loose from the canine collection and ran towards the bike. The fire-resistant suit, seeing the dog when he was but a few metres from it, attempted to slow up abruptly, which caused the bike to assume a vertical position. The dog, enjoying the show at very close quarters, tail wagging enthusiastically, jumped up so enthusiastically that he landed on the driver's shoulders, before sliding off and on to the ground.

The bike, effectively deprived of a human in control, decided, after minimal consideration, to conform to the law of gravity and returned to a more acceptable horizontal position but without its rider whose balance had been upset by the sudden addition of a dog where most people might wear a scarf. He fell to the ground and the dog, which had jumped clear at just the right moment, somersaulted as he landed, in what was patently a crude attempt to milk the audience's applause. The canine artist then ran over to the prostrate human, as the audience speculated that they might have just seen a fatal accident. The dog licked the man's helmet in gratitude or perhaps because he liked the taste. We just don't know. Dogs like to lick the most unlikely of objects. In fact, they're known for it. The rider still did not move and the audience feared the worst. As the bike had taken off, assuming one of the fundamental characteristics of a helicopter, it was clear to those who had done some advance thinking that it had to land somewhere. Mercifully, it landed between the dog and the rider who now struggled to his feet and, showing enormous professionalism, he picked up the dog and cuddled it. As the audience cheered, thinking that this was all deliberately staged, he muttered in the mutt's ear, "I think we got away with that, didn't I?"

The following day both Ivor and Jack were more prosperous. *The Sunday Clarion*, the sister paper, had used all the pics that Jack had sent his brother, including the "private" one when Louise had kissed her saviour. The captions showed the popular paper's purposeful punning propensity:

Louise falls for fete boss
It was just my fate says fete boss
The catch of the season in cricket-mad village
Feted village low jinks
A kiss for the catch in time
Married fete man's happiest-ever moment-with Louise

Jack's earlier pic, taken the evening before, as Louise went to the B-C restaurant was also used with the caption reading:

Louise ill with food-poisoning after visiting celebs' restaurant

What was much more troubling was the adverse publicity for the restaurant which, unsurprisingly, was to suffer a sudden decline in patronage.

The story was to upset not just the Bush-Cooks but the whole village as it was yet again given undesired publicity on the front page of a national paper. Alf's wife suddenly decided to visit her sister in the north of Scotland without giving an explanation although he thoughtfully reminded her that she disliked her sister and the remote area in which she lived, where there were more sheep than people. This had produced the rejoinder that sheep could be trusted. Apparently, you knew where you were with sheep. After some reflection, the fete chairman wondered, if, just possibly, it had been because of the tabloid story. How on earth had they got the pics and the story? The local paper was to stir up the story later, despite, or because of, the tabloid's massive coverage but Jack's story, "written" by his brother, was the one that did the damage.

Sexy Louise falls for village fete boss
Bush-Cook restaurant closed after food poisoning scare

The organisers of the annual village fete in Woodfield Magna, home of the television cook and gardener, Charlie Bush and Hilary Cook, were looking forward to their annual event. But, as they burned the midnight oil, planning what was one of the leading social occasions of the year, nobody could have guessed that it would be one fete that everybody present would always remember.

Bubbly Louise Lewis, widely regarded as the sexiest girl on television today, had agreed to open the fete. Although this stunning blonde upset some in the large audience by referring to the incident two years before, when a local businessman attempted to fix a cricket match and, allegedly, to bribe some local councillors into granting planning permission for big new homes in the village, she cheered up the males when she said that she might buy a second home in the village. However, as Louise reached the point when she would have declared the fete open, she fainted.

As she plunged to the floor, the quick-thinking balding fete chairman, Alf Fox, 56, father of three, and a local plumber, rushed forward and caught the falling star. At that point, the heavens opened and a panting Alf and his sexy bundle rushed through the downpour to the large marquee where Louise was laid carefully on a long table and Fox recovered his breath. "I must confess that, catching her and then carrying her to the marquee gave me more of a thrill than I've had in my married life for years. Just think, how many millions of young men would have given to be in my shoes, especially when she kissed me to thank me."

Later, retired local GP Tiny Pye, notorious loco'   'is erotic topiary, examined the star. He told her '
suffering from food poisoning. Louise had
overnight with the Bush-Cooks and had er
breakfast at their restaurant.

The Bush-Cooks immediately dec'
eaterie, The Cook and Gardener
Magna, as a precaution. Foo'
haunt of the famous will be c'

claims made for the well-known restaurant is that it uses some of the produce from the local television garden, run by Hilary Bush-Cook. Meanwhile, Alf Fox, the fete chairman, who was presiding over the event for the 17th and final time, was unavailable for comment. His wife, Cynthia, and children are thought to have gone to the north of Scotland for an unplanned break.

Louise was fit enough to travel back to London late last night and is expected to be able to fulfil her engagements, none the worse for her experiences in the seemingly ill-feted village of Woodfield Magna.

Chapter 11

Louise was distressed that the B-C restaurant had been closed and was determined to clear their name as rapidly as possible. Having returned to London, she visited a doctor friend in Harley Street and told him, after he had finished examining her, that she now remembered eating a dubious burger, the food favoured by Americans, not a suspect continental citizen, on the train. Could this have caused the food poisoning? His reply stunned her.

"It might well have done but I don't think that was the real problem. I think that it is much more likely that you fainted because of the hot weather and the pressure of opening the fete."

Louise smiled. "I can assure you that, in my television work, I face much greater pressure than I did when trying to open a village fete. Just a few days ago, for example, I was interviewing Cliff Steel about his lost dog." The specialist looked puzzled so Louise explained that he was a former pop star and had now lived long enough to have reached the level of National Treasure which just shows how fame has been devalued.

"Yes, but I think that what may have caused the problem, was not a horrid haddock, as implied in the press, or a bad burger but the fact that you are pregnant."

Louise was shocked and looked very faint. She had no idea that she was to add to the global population, which had not been her intention, and she asked for a glass of water.

"Congratulations my dear. I'm very pleased for you." Then seeing the blank and bewildered look on his friend's face, he added "I hope you are too." Louise assured him that she was but it was such a surprise, she was having some difficulty in absorbing the news.

Later, at a promptly-organised press conference, convened to avoid interminable gossip and to clear the Bush-Cook's good name, her partner, one of the few English footballers in the Premier League, was asked how he felt about the news. Sadly, his command of English was weaker than that of his foreign colleagues. "Gutted, just gutted", he responded, glowering at the assembled media but, prompted swiftly by his agent, added "with joy at this brilliant, fantastic, awesome and amazing news. In a word, I'm gob-smacked." Then, gaining in confidence, he confirmed that he was really "gob-smacked".

As a result of this revelation, the Bush-Cooks decided to sue Dr. Pye for his false diagnosis, which had damaged their reputation, but were dissuaded by Jack Scoop. He argued that this would look like some wealthy celebs challenging a simple local village doctor who had tried to do his best for their friend Louise. Instead, he drafted a statement which said that the B-Cs were delighted to learn that their good friend Louise was pregnant and that they wished her and her partner well. They were also delighted, there was a lot of it about, to have seen their friend in their Woodfield Magna restaurant which was proving very popular and which used local produce, which "reduced the food miles element" which benefited the global environment and helped local producers.

Rob Swagg was mystified, perplexed, puzzled, and, if only one word is allowed, baffled. He had not discovered who burgled the Farnworthy residence and was now under more pressure from regional headquarters to make some progress, not least as the owners of three other houses had suffered the same fate. His sister, Barbara, did not have any ideas but agreed that it must be more than a coincidence that the thefts only began after The Grange had been opened.

"I know, like you, I'm convinced that it must be one of those young louts but so far, I've absolutely nothing to go on. For example, after the Farnworthys had been burgled, I went to The Grange and it seemed that all the inmates are crazy on football and spent the evening watching the England game on television. According to Goodfellow, who was in the lounge for the whole match, nobody left the room. I'm not sure what to do but I may have to think of something unorthodox to solve this case."

Barbara wondered if watching England play football was part of their punishment, but then said that she could understand her brother's frustration. "But do remember that what you can and can't do these days is very complicated and weighted in my humble view, although I'm only a mere solicitor, in favour of the crook, although I presume we can't use that label now. I suppose that we have to refer to such people as legally-challenged. Instead, why don't you try to get to know Goodfellow better, he might be a good ally, although I imagine that he's very keen to defend his charges and the concept of providing a half-way house for the young criminals."

Rob thought that this was a good idea and on one of his days when he was not speaking to infants about dangerous driving or pensioners on the impact of dangerous drugs, he went to The Grange, mainly to develop a relationship with Goodfellow.

"I think that we got off on the wrong foot when that civil servant's laptop went missing. I'd like us to be friends now and I'm sorry for immediately thinking that it must have been one of your lads. You can't blame me for thinking that."

Goodfellow nodded, smiled and stretched out a hand which Rob took and shook enthusiastically.

"Tell me something about yourself, Dick." The warden stirred his coffee slowly, possibly to give himself time to decide where to begin but begin he did.

"Not much to tell really. I was brought up in the East End of London and it's fair to say that the family was far from wealthy. In those days, one of the main occupations in the area was theft. It was almost a way of life but I was determined not to succumb. As soon as I was old enough, I moved out into the suburbs, but it wasn't easy."

"How did you earn your living?"

"I was very lucky. I found work, a few miles from where I lived, in an old-fashioned ironmongers and it was fascinating learning something about all the products that the shop sold. It promoted an interest in DIY that I have sustained to this very day. I was keen to learn and the owner, whose name I've long since forgotten, so don't ask me, didn't have a son to pass on his skills so he was happy to teach me about tools and how to use them."   Rob, obediently, refrained from asking the employer's name.

"Then what happened? Did you stay with him?"

"No. A large DIY store opened up just down the road and the shop had to close. Just typical of what's happening all over the country. Economics first, the people last. All that was some years ago now but it seems like yesterday."

"Yes, the older we get, the faster time flies and incidents of years ago seem as you say, like they took place yesterday. For me, every few minutes it seems to be Tuesday afternoon."

Goodfellow resumed.

"That's odd. With me, it's Wednesday. I'd read about rising crime rates, even in the suburbs, and I recalled my own difficult start in the East End, so I managed to find enough money to go on to a government course which, apparently, might lead to a job. They wanted to put me on a course on fork

148

lift truck driving but I argued and eventually was given a place on a course on how to assist young crims when they came out of prison. I knew about crime, first hand, well, I mean second hand, and to some extent, all those years ago, about punishment as some of my friends were arrested and did spells inside. In a way, I felt sorry for them as in some cases, they were victims of circumstances.

"Then I got a job in Social Services, in North London, but eventually I became totally disillusioned with how they worked, pushing paper around and to hell with the people who needed help, and then I saw an ad for this job. I thought that it sounded different and that it might be a chance to put some of my own ideas into practice. So far so good. I think that the lads here are good at heart and I just pray that by giving them their freedom, or at least part of it, we're really preparing them for life in the outside world. What we can't tolerate is making these young people hardened thugs by allowing them to mix, for years at a time, with professional crooks. We don't want them to go straight back into prison when they're released. Some prisons I've visited, when some of my old friends were doing porridge, were more like universities of crime."

Rob nodded. A lot of what Dick had said made sense to him.

"How are you getting on with the local community? As you know, there was a lot of hostility towards The Grange but it seems to be less vigorous of late."

"Yes, I think that people are beginning to tolerate us but I know that local confidence could go up in a puff of instant smoke if any of my lads are found to have broken the law. I can't prove it but I wouldn't be surprised if someone tried to implicate us in even a minor breaking of the law, just to justify the closure of The Grange. We rely on you, Rob, can I call you that, to make sure that my boys are not accused of anything unless there's solid evidence. Incidentally, I must thank you for scotching the idea that any of my boys could have been involved in the Farnworthy theft. As you know, we were all

149

watching that England game on the box. Any progress on that case yet? "

"No, I must admit I'm baffled. As you know, some of the villagers are convinced that one of your lads did it but I don't accept that myself. One of my biggest problems is arguing that, just because this crime happened after The Grange was set up, it does not mean that the inmates are responsible."

"I'm happy to hear that Rob. Tell me something about yourself."

"Not much to tell about me, actually, Dick. I always wanted to be a copper. I managed to get in although, as you may have noticed, I'm not the tallest policeman in the country and went to the training college before working in London. It was all drugs and knifings and that was just at the college." Seeing Goodfellow wince, Rob assured him that he was joking. "I didn't enjoy working in the capital and when I saw that there was a vacancy here in Woodfield Magna, I applied and got the job and I've been here for about three years now."

"There must have been keen competition?"

"Strangely, not really. I think that most cops felt that it would be too quiet and they wouldn't be seen by the people who decide promotions. With the government's obsession with statistics, if there's no crime to solve, it suggests that my crime solution rate is nil and that won't help my career. Now, confronted by the burglary that I haven't solved, my crime solution rate, at zero, hasn't changed but, unless I make progress soon, I'll be back in the Met and I really don't want that. I enjoy being virtually leaderless. My boss tends to leave me alone, but he's getting distinctly ratty and he wasn't too pleased that my fellow local residents attacked the journalists earlier this year, although, privately, I know he hates the media."

"Do you have any time for hobbies, Dick?"

"No, not really, I read a lot and enjoy photography but that's about it."

"So you won't be going to the remaining open garden days?"

Dick smiled and broke into a hollow laugh although it would have been tricky for a passer by to determine whether it was hollow or solid. Convention decrees that a smile followed by a cynical laugh, must be a hollow laugh, so hollow it was.

"Me, gardening? Not likely, it's too much like hard work. I don't even enjoy walking around other peoples' gardens when they have done all the work. I can't tell a weed from a flower. No, it's not for me. I guess it's because I was brought up in the east end of London. Only the toffs had gardens".

Chapter 12

Steven Brown-Hassett, who had spent his early life in WM before he and his parents returned to Australia, was in the pub with Godfrey Murray, the guru of gossip, who had become Steven's personal adviser on Woodfield Magna affairs. The visitor wanted to know what happened to some of the other characters involved in the great WM crime, as he dubbed it.

"Well", said Godfrey, cuddling his now empty glass.

"Hold on, let me get you a refill."

Suitably refreshed, Godfrey resumed.

"You remember the farmer, who made a well-known television interviewer look silly when he put some questions to him?"

"Yes, I read a little about him. Is he still around?"

"That was the chap called Farmer who was also a farmer by profession. The television twit thought that Reg looked very ancient and asked him whether he minded if he asked him how old he was. Reg said that he didn't so the famous face had to ask the question specifically and Reg, who, I think, is now well over 60, claimed to be 45. Then Reg was asked if he was looking forward to the match. As he had taken the trouble not just to turn up but to pay someone to look after the farm, it seemed such a silly question that he gave a sarcastic reply. There were repercussions from all this. Within days, Reg was offered a lucrative contract to advertise some agricultural chemicals. The line was that he was so honest on television that you could buy products that he, himself, used on the farm, with confidence.

"Yes, but you said that he was over 60, so he lied."

"Sure, but the ad agency, I think that's the right term, they just took him at his word, filmed him endorsing the product and gave him a large cheque."

"Is he still in the village?"

"Yes. A local told the advertisers about his lie but they decided not to take any action. They would have looked silly, I suppose. As I say, Reg still lives in WM but about a year ago, he retired from farming, not that the agricultural chemicals company knows, and went to New Zealand for a long holiday with his daughter-in-law. Sadly, his son was crushed to death by some angry sheep and it was thought that they had become wild because of the food that they had been given which had been treated by some chemical or other. I don't know if it was supplied by the company he worked for. He's back in the village now and I think that he's deeply involved with opposition to this affordable homes project. We don't want them here. We can't afford them, we don't like incomers and we guess that the new homes will become second homes, as that Louise said at the fete."

"What about Will? I gather that he's coming back for a visit before too long?"

"Yes, that's right. I've kept in touch with him. He should be here within a week or two, now. The good news is that he'll be with his new wife. She's a Texan called Frisky and we can but guess why she acquired that name. Will's old company ran into trouble after he'd gone. Will had been working very hard to find a specific component for a potentially very successful safety-related product. He was the one person who really knew about it and he should have been promoted to General Manager because it was a very important breakthrough. Instead of that, the directors promoted someone called Hopkirk who soon demonstrated why he had been made redundant so often in the past. Apparently, he was related to one of the directors, but this close relationship, astonishingly, was to prove no substitute for engineering competence, which presumably, surprised the executives who had backed Hopkirk enthusiastically, after hearing a strong recommendation from his brother-in-law.

"Will had worked really hard trying to find the new part and the time he spent on work had something to do with his divorce. The American company, which had been able to make the crucial part, then offered Will a senior job in Houston and he took it. He also married a very attractive, intelligent and witty colleague. None of this would have happened if he'd been made a general manager and it might now have been even worse. He could have been facing redundancy, had he stayed, so there's been a happy ending. Within months of Will's departure to the States, there was a plaintive cry from the unbelievably stupid Hopkirk whose knowledge of business was approximately equal to former US president Bill Clinton's knowledge of Torquay United Football Club. He, that's Hopkirk, by the way, not Clinton, wanted to know if Will would consider returning to his former company to take charge of the project. Will told me in an email that this was one of the most amusing jokes he had heard since the performances of Tommy Cooper and Les Dawson, which reminds me, have you heard why a man imitating a chicken was arrested?

Stephen, who hated this kind of joke, lost no time in saying not.

"It was for using foul language."

"When the effort to encourage Will to return failed, the UK company suggested a joint venture which gave Will and his new colleagues something else at which to laugh, as pedants concerned with ending sentences with a preposition would have said.

154

"Incidentally, I should have mentioned that Will's new wife is the marketing boss for the American company and they met in London when they signed the contract for the   new part. He certainly wasn't going to turn the clock back by returning to his old employers. The company was really badly managed, even by British standards, and then was confronted by big problems in the sector. They moved from near London to Archester but the rumours suggest that they're still in real trouble."

"Godfrey, you're a mine of information. It's fascinating hearing about these people. I remember some from my early days, when I lived here as a young lad. You told me earlier about the infamous cricket match but I wondered about that young fast bowler that won the match for you before Nutley were awarded the match because he was ineligible?"

"He didn't know about the rule that said that only local residents could play. Statham was his name. The season after he played for us in that infamous match, he did well for the county second eleven and won a first team place earlier this season. He was very successful and was on the verge of the England team just a few days ago until an unfortunate incident in the practice nets."

"You mean with the English players?"

Godfrey confirmed that this was the case and that, yes, he had been very talented.

"What happened?"

"The papers said that he had been included in the squad by mistake. The selectors thought that they had invited another fast bowler, with the same name, but that they had made a mistake and invited young Statham from Ottershire. Odd, really because no other first class cricketer has the same name and some newspapers thought that they might have meant a promising young lad called Brian Trueman. In fact, I added up all the suggestions and no less than 12 other cricketers were suggested but we'll never know the truth.

"Well, young Statham caused a little bother when he played in the nets. The England captain had been hit by a bumper in the previous game and wanted to rebuild his confidence. Statham was asked to bowl some short stuff and he did as bidden but the problem was that he managed to hit the captain on the helmet so hard that he was unable to play in the match that was only two days away. Then, still in the nets, he clean bowled the player most likely to replace the skipper so easily that the man's confidence drained away too. His stumps were hit three times in 20 minutes and the selectors decided that he should not play in England's next match as he was so out of touch and seemed so weak against quality fast bowling."

"What about Statham? After that, surely he deserved a place in the England team but I don't recall hearing about him?"

"Yes, he was then selected but trod on a ball during pre-match practice and was out of cricket for two months and he's never been the same since."

"That was bad luck."

"Yes, he's a good honest lad and we all hope he comes back to his best form."

"I know what happened to Jane, Parker's wife and Laura, Will's first wife, but what about Jock?"

"We must be careful as nobody ever knew for certain that he was the source of the story about the potential for illegal activities on the planning committee but he gave up his council seat and his position on the cricket club committee soon after the crucial match. Now he just enjoys watching the club in what he calls action."

"I gather from what I've heard that the Scoop brothers have done well out of all this."
"Yes, Jack was the key figure in exposing the Parker scam and, eventually, he was able to set up his own company in

Archester. Of course, I don't know but I suspect that he was the one that wrote up the story about lovely Louise and the fete."

"Anyway, it's time that I was off so behave yourself young Steven and I expect I'll see you later in the week."

Chapter 13

Although Parker's great Woodfield Magna housing estates plan had collapsed, the authorities, encouraged by central government, had given prompt permission to a foreign-owned large group to build 12 executive style houses within the village boundaries. However, one condition was that they were to build 25 "affordable" homes on land to the north of the village, some distance from the mighty downtown area, the non-throbbing centre of the village, on a relatively flat spot high up on one of the hills. These new homes had to be built within three years of the beginning of the first project and a failure to meet this deadline would incur serious financial penalties.   Nearly two years had passed but little had happened. Seven of the executive homes had been built but no work had even started on the so-called "affordable homes".

Although the company took obfuscation to new heights or should it be depths, which would not have shamed the shameless politicians who effectively invented the approach, it was clear that it did not want to build these smaller units. The profit margin in the executive homes had been significantly less than expected and the overall condition of the national economy did not favour house-building. That said, in the truly unforgettable words of the local MP, who had foolishly campaigned apparently tirelessly in favour of the new homes, in the face of opposition from his electors, a contract was a contract. Privately, he had been rebuked by his party's Chief

Whip for such an unambiguous comment which "could so easily come back to haunt us in many other contexts".

As Godfrey had maintained in the pub, the locals had never been keen on what they regarded as a significant number of incomers flooding the area that they had been so anxious to preserve. Ironically, therefore, the builders and locals now shared a view on the new houses but there was nothing that could be done. Central government knew best and it wanted to provide new homes for up to 100 more people in this smug and self-important village. As the relevant minister admitted to a colleague, not long after the great stamps row, "we've go to show who rules this country. It's like the miners, all over again, but this time, it's these rural peasants."

Will had arrived at Heathrow with his new wife, Laura. This was not a mere chance: it was the planned destination so everyone was happy, not least the plane's pilot who had always intended to fly to Heathrow. Laura was not over-awed by the airport, as he had been on his first visit to Houston, and, of course, she had been to London before on business. She was in good form as the 757 touched down and its cargo, human and otherwise, was decanted. This was one of those rare, if not unique occasions when Will's luggage was almost first off the carousel. However, this advantage, predictably, was lost as the machine then failed, after two youths had jumped up and down on it before discovering the emergency button at the side which was more fun as it brought the unit to a complete halt. Eventually, the youths were persuaded to desist, not by an official, as most of the security staff were on strike, but by a rather large man whose frightening appearance suggested a short but unsuccessful career as a professional pugilist.

Laura's luggage appeared just before panic set in.

Will was determined to call her by her real name, even though it was also his first wife's name. "Frisky" might be fine when they were together and alone but it was not appropriate when in public. The couple had at least eight weeks in the UK, and probably much more, which was deemed to be long enough to allow Will to complete the work on a new project,

159

which he and his colleagues had been pursuing initially in Houston, as well as to have some holiday. He was looking forward to showing Laura off in Woodfield Magna and he wanted to visit some relatives in the north of England. His parents had died when he was in his early teens and he had been brought up by an aunt and uncle.

Before that, they would have some enjoyable days together in London. Laura was looking forward to being a tourist. Their stay happened to coincide with one of the few spells of good weather that the capital was to enjoy that summer. Inevitably, a sensibly pessimistic Will had warned his new spouse to pack warm clothes so one of the first jaunts was to some of the better clothing stores. Will was surprised, that in the short time he had been away, London seemed to have gone downmarket. Some of the smart stores had been replaced by emporia selling rubbish and Piccadilly Circus smelt of onions. Laura, brought up on the view that London was one of the world's great shopping cities was disappointed too, but still managed to spend more than a little on some "classically-cut bargains".

The South Bank of the Thames between the Festival Hall and Westminster Bridge had changed almost beyond recognition as far as Will was concerned. It had been some years since he had strolled along the riverside walk. Although he had used the line from nearby Waterloo to Archester, he had seldom had the time to amble with the masses along the side of the river. He and Laura strolled, hand in hand, absorbing the atmosphere and marvelling at some of the quaint ideas conjured up by the street entertainers, many of whom were painted all over in garish colours and only moved in robotic-like jerking motions. Others, more old-fashioned in their attempts to part visitors from their money, played various musical instruments. The scene, illuminated by rare sunshine, was one of innocence and gaiety, as Brits and foreigners alike strolled along the side of the river, just enjoying the spectacle.

One human was crouched in a box that resembled a kennel. He or could it have been she, no, surely not, was in a dog-like suit and his head was encased in what appeared to be the head of an Alsatian. All that could really be seen of him was his head, or, to be more accurate, the dog's head. Occasionally, if only to attract attention, he would growl and some passers-by lobbed coins into a bowl that its makers had intended to be used to store liquid refreshment for canines.

Will imagined a conversation between the dog-man and his father.

"Well my boy, what are you going to do now you're a grown-up graduate with a first in information technology?"

"Dad, don't laugh but I thought that I'd spend my summer months, wearing a dog suit and the head of an Alsatian, in a wooden box, built like a kennel, on the South Bank river walk. I'll leave a bowl outside the kennel so passers by, impressed by my initiative, will give me money."

The father, who had spent a small fortune on his son's education, but had given up trying to seek a sensible return, merely grunted at first and indulged himself with some senior sarcasm.

"Frankly, lad, that's extraordinary. When I was a boy, all I wanted to do was to dress up as a Cocker Spaniel and sit in a kennel by the Thames waiting for passers-by to put money in a bowl. As you know, it never happened and I had to be satisfied with life as a nuclear scientist. Still, having spent a fortune on your education, I feel you're doing the right thing. Just don't tell your mother or pick a bone with her. After all the scrimping and saving to pay for your education, I just feel that she wouldn't understand. She's never been that keen on dogs, especially Alsatians that's she thinks are dangerous and foreign."

Street entertainers were dressed as frogs, dragons and bears and all seemed to be doing well financially, judging by the squeals of delight, coming from the adults and the children seemed impressed too. The one failure was the dog in a kennel. The problem was that all the other entertainers were as tall as most of the adult pedestrians but the dog was below eye level. This prompted some more vigorous and realistic barking which caused some children to leap in the air, whilst their parents, ignorant that this was a human being in a box, muttered something to the effect that dogs should not be confined to kennels in this fine weather and that they should be given water.

Laura had a ride on the noisy merry-go–round although Will objected to the £5 fee for five minutes of whirling round seeing the same scene time and time again. Then she noticed that there was an exhibition of Salvador Dali's work in one of the buildings alongside the river. This was a show that she had wanted to see for years so Will, outraged by what he thought was the exorbitant entrance fee, was then irked by what he saw for the next hour. Laura seemed both excited and absorbed but to Will, the engineer, it was all rather pretentious and, to him, suggested a twisted mind. He was reminded of Dr. Pye's erotic topiary.

Then they spent some time deciding whether either or both of them wanted an ice cream and a snack. After some minutes, without having to call in an intermediary to arbitrate, it was decided that it would be wise and Will removed his vividly blue British cardigan. He did this, not as a pre-requisite to consumption but because of the heat. Earlier, having lived in England all his life, he had felt that the garment was essential at the height of what passed for summer. They walked past the London Eye which Laura said would make her feel a little queasy if she were to sit in one of those bubbles which moves, logically, in a gentle circle showing more of London than can be seen from anywhere, except possibly from a helicopter. They spent a few more idyllic days like this, behaving like tourists.

However, there was one odd incident that was to cause Will some embarrassment later. They had been dining at a famous and expensive London restaurant, in Soho, often patronised by actors from the world of film and theatre. Will knew that it was difficult to book a table so had done so some weeks before. After they had been seated for them long enough for them to have time to decide what to eat, a waiter emerged to

162

take their order. It was good that someone was keen to do the work for which he was paid. He was, of course, foreign.

Will was becoming accustomed to Laura's sense of humour but he was unprepared for what came next. Laura addressed the waiter. "Hi there, I'm Frisky Bennett. I'm a producer from Hollywood and we're here to select some possible venues for our next film, some of which will be shot right here, in London. My friend here, Rocky Halliday, is one of the stars in the film and he's here to improve his British accent.

"I think he's awfully good-looking, don't you?" Laura said, jokingly, temporarily forsaking her Texan accent for a highly improbable English aristocratic accent. Then, turning towards the waiter and ignoring Will's gaze only with some difficulty, she said what she "would take" in the way of food. Texans seldom order food but they helpfully indicate what they will take.

"Your turn, now honey, what do you fancy?", she said to her husband, staring at him provocatively. As she said this, Will was under even greater pressure not to laugh. The waiter, accustomed to empty English celebs, was most impressed. Laura was his first Hollywood producer and Will was his first American actor.

"Mr Halliday, what I can I get for you?"

Will, still struggling to avoid laughing, took some time before realising that he was being asked to order. Laura helped by saying loudly "you must forgive him, he's only just finished filming a major television drama series and he couldn't sleep on the plane, despite being really comfortable on your British Airways first class. I'm just so sorry that they seem to be having so many financial troubles but I guess that's true of all the world's great airlines." The waiter, being an alien, was not particularly interested in the fate of the British carrier. He always used the budget airlines.

"What do you want to eat, honey?" Laura asked.

Will decided on smoked salmon to start with and fillet steak to follow and conveyed this to the waiter, carelessly including the word "please" which to a discerning ear, would have immediately cast doubt on his tacit claim to be an American ordering food. The waiter, too flattered to be serving this illustrious pair, did not notice.

An astute Laura waved her hands around excitedly.

"Don't you think he's got the cutest English accent and did you notice that he said please, just like a real Brit? I think he's got it, he's really got it. Don't you, sugar?" The waiter, unsure if he was the intended recipient of the comment, played for safety and said that his accent was "cool, real cool" and expressed the view that he had "got it, really got it".

The waiter, too young to be familiar with the musical *My Fair Lady* repaired to the kitchen to place the order and to tell his colleagues, all of whom came from Eastern Europe, so that their command of English was enviable, that a famous Hollywood producer and actor were in the restaurant. One by one they took a peep and two of them confirmed that they had seen him in a dubbed film at home. Two rich old ladies, effectively intruders in the restaurant, in that they had nothing to do with the film or stage worlds, had overhead the conversation. As they left the restaurant, they joked with a freelance paparazzi photographer who was hanging around outside in the hope of taking a pic of someone famous. He had asked if the ladies would like their photographs taken. "Oh, no, we're not famous, but look inside. See that attractive girl and the man sitting opposite her? The cameraman nodded.

"Well, she's Frisky Bennett, a Hollywood producer and he's Rocky Halliday, a famous actor who's just finished filming a major series for American television. They're over here to find suitable locations for a new production to be filmed in London and he's here also to improve his English accent. We heard him order his meal and we both thought, didn't we, Dorothy, that his accent was perfect." Dorothy nodded dutifully.

164

"He sounded just like an Englishman although I thought that I heard just the faintest sound of New York in him, didn't you Dorothy?" Dorothy nodded again. "Yes, now that you mention it, there was a slight nasal twang."

"I'm sure that I saw him in that war film, what was it called?"

"Was it the Longest Day, Ethel?"

"No, not that, on second thoughts, I think that it was a musical, was it Detroit?"

Dorothy smiled. "I think you mean Chicago."

"Yes, that's it, didn't he play opposite that Welsh girl?"

"You mean Charlotte Church?"

"No, I remember now, it was someone called Jones. The one who married someone much older than she was and became stinking rich."

After a few more minutes, they both agreed that they had seen Will perform, although there was still some doubt on the roles that he had played.

The photographer waited until the American couple emerged and took several pics, totally unobserved. Within minutes the photographs and relevant captions were on the desk of he who decides what should appear in the capital's leading evening newspaper. This modest story and pics did not justify the space, especially on a day when it had been revealed that a London MP, a lifelong friend of the editor, had claimed £900 for a gold-plated fish tank in his office. It was at that point that the editor changed his mind on the Halliday story. The public were probably bored with the large scale fiddling by Members of Parliament. It was time to give them something more attractive. Where was that pic of the glamorous Hollywood producer and a famous actor? He would use one of those shots. By now, the deadline was too close to allow any checks to be made but, anyway, he thought that he had heard of the producer and the actor certainly looked familiar to him. The photograph was printed, together with the suggested caption and modest text, as relayed to the snapper by the two old ladies.

Passengers from Waterloo often left their newspapers on the train, to be picked up, read and sometimes taken home by those who lived, for example, in Archester. John Harvey, who happened to be the editor of *The Archester Chronicle* and who was a friend of Will's, had been in London and was turning over the pages of the paper he had picked up earlier on the journey. To his astonishment, there was a photograph of a man who could easily have been a double of his old friend, Will. He did not know what his new wife looked like so was not suspicious. He toyed with the idea of running a pic of Will, perhaps after the game with Nutley, alongside one of the American actor. First of all, however, the following morning, when he was in his office, he carried out a check and could find no reference anywhere, to an American actor called Rocky Halliday.

Instead, he decided to use a photograph of a successful student, celebrating having achieved two passes in the GCSE exams. The usual photograph was of a slim sensual short-skirted blonde girl, leaping attractively into the air in an appealing gesture of unconfined joy. This year, he decided to use a pic of a significantly less photogenic girl, whose weight prevented her leaving the ground without assistance. Her facial expression was not one of glee but one of modest satisfaction at having achieved ten passes. However, the editor's intention to give a fat and plain female some publicity backfired. Angry correspondents condemned the poor girl for her bulk, automatically assuming it was the result of greed. The majority of letters and emails said that this photograph showed, "beyond reasonable doubt, that the government's plan to tax fat people is justified". As one correspondent, who had often written to the paper in defence of smoking, wrote, "if nothing is done to deter these fat and greedy people, they will be using up all the money we pay into the National Health Service".

The following day, Will told Laura that it was time to go to Woodfield Magna. He had hired a plush car and was able to show Laura some of the English countryside. She had never been to the village and had formed a picture in her mind, aided by some of Will's photographs. They were to stay for a few days with Janet and Ray Fabian, Will's neighbours when he lived in the village with Laura One. Janet, who had been a friend of his first wife, had effectively disowned her when it was revealed how she had been unfaithful to Will and tried to undermine him with the two similar blondes campaign. They, Will and wife number two, not the two blondes, were made very welcome and his erstwhile neighbours immediately took to the new Laura. Will had a soft spot for Janet who, although she had been Laura One's best friend, always managed to suggest to Will that she knew what was going on and had great sympathy with him.

In the pub that evening an impromptu party began and as the drink flowed, Will was asked the obvious question. "Well, Will, is it just a holiday, or knowing you, will it also include some work?" The response was just a smile. Everyone would find out before too long.

John Harvey had a question.

"See this pic?" he said, brandishing the London paper in front of the locals.

"My god", shouted one old timer. "That's my Willy."

When the laughter had subsided Will took a closer look at the pic and said that he would leave Ms Bennett to explain. There was more laughter in the pub that evening than for many months. It was good that Will was back but what was it that he had been asked to do by his American bosses? Could it possibly affect Woodfield Magna?

Chapter 14

Constable Rob Swagg's determination to solve the crimes, which were now occurring more frequently in his patch, was not in doubt. What he needed was a clue. He was still convinced that the solution lay in The Grange but he had no proof that anyone there had perpetrated the crimes.

Early one Thursday morning, he answered the phone. He did this whenever the instrument made a noise, partly because it was his job and partly because he could not think during the noise and he had much about which, that's to please the pedants, to think. It was yet another angry and elderly local who wanted to know how long it would be before someone was murdered in his or her bed. It was good to know that a killer might not differentiate on grounds of gender. Rob was tempted to say that killing a villager was rather different to taking some of their possessions but decided that this intended reassurance might be misleading.

His phone seemed to ring more often now, since the thefts, than at any time since he had been in the village. They were not all calls reporting thefts: some were from the local newspaper but the majority were from concerned local citizens. Indeed, one of the regular letter writers, who always signed himself as "concerned citizen", and whose letters usually concentrated on the dangers posed by children riding on pavements, made the necessary mental adjustment and commented adversely on the "authority's basic failure to protect us".

It was clear that the paper was going to extract maximum coverage from the thefts. The circulation had increased significantly as the story gained momentum and the latest edition detailed those who had been burgled and their background. Apparently, the article, not the thefts, had been done with the total co-operation of the victims who were "angry at what had happened and determined to do all that they could to ensure that the crooks were caught and stuck inside for a long spell which they richly deserve". It was clear that all the correspondents felt that it was more than just a coincidence that the series of thefts had begun after The Grange was opened.

Within a few minutes, the phone jangled again. This was more bad news. It was Mrs Sylvia Prendergast and she wished to report a burglary. She had been away over the weekend, partly, apparently, to recover from the effort of preparing her garden for the great British public and the benefit of the local hospice.

"I'm sorry to hear this, Mrs Prendergast. I do hope that you have not lost too much."

"Anything is too much. I feel as if I've been violated."

"Yes, I quite understand and I'm sorry. If you could please draw up a list of what's missing and I'll be round as soon as I can."

Mrs Prendergast, a stalwart of the local church, who sat on most of its committees, was not in a very forgiving mood when a few minutes later she opened the door to the perplexed policeman. She was dressed for summer and was wearing black trousers and a white, sleeveless blouse. Rob thought, possibly illogically, that it was odd for a woman of the church to be sporting such an array of tattoos, which, to judge by their strength, had been etched some years ago. It just didn't seem right, no, consistent was the word Rob was seeking, for her to have so many anchors and a heart with what looked like the letter R in it but it was fading so might have been "engraved" there some years before. Her arms looked dirty and he looked away.

"It's all happened since that damned half-way house was opened." Her role in the church, apparently, did not prevent her from using the D word. "I knew it would cause trouble in the village, but, of course, we only live here so nobody took any notice of us. It's high time it was closed. How many thefts do we have to suffer before it's closed? Or, perhaps the weak-minded idiots who are supposed to govern us are waiting for a murder or two or would a rape or a fire do the trick?"

Rob winced. Being brutally frank and cocking a quiet snook at political correctness, there were very few females in the village that might interest a discerning rapist and Prendergast, who was probably much younger than she looked, would not have been in the top five but, immediately, he was deeply ashamed that such an appalling and politically incorrect thought could even creep into his head. This crime wave was having a bad impact on him.

He was inclined to agree about the politicians who had imposed The Grange on the village but could not say anything, partly because he did not know what to say. He sought to assure the Prendergast woman, as she was widely known in the village, that he would do all he could to recover her stolen items. She was regarded as so self-satisfied, sanctimonious and full of her own self-bestowed righteous importance that some in the village might even have been pleased that the thief or thieves had decided to relieve her of some of her possessions. She was not liked.

As he stood silently, accepting the verbal brickbats, she told him that she had compiled a list of what had been taken.

Rob studied it and noticed that, once again, small but potentially valuable items had been stolen. He wandered around the house but did not see any obvious forms of entry. Either the thief had gained access via an unlocked door or window, or he, and presumably it could not have been a she, had been allowed to enter. There was no sign of a struggle which was not surprising as Mrs Prendergast had been out, having dinner with friends. Mr Prendergast was in the Middle East, apparently looking for new supplies of crude oil, which was very decent of him as global supplies were running out. So far, Woodfield and the world did not know if he had been successful. The church stalwart confirmed that she had only noticed that someone had entered the house when she returned at about 10.30 pm. She denied stoutly, not a pretty sight, that she had left any windows or doors unlocked.

"Do you mind if I take a more detailed look?"

"Of course not."

Rob carried out the promised more detailed look and, this time, noticed some marks close to the lounge doors that led to the garden. The scratches were new and were too high for an excited and hungry squirrel, as had happened to his neighbour's door. The lock seemed flimsy. Rob made a mental note. For reasons that he did not understand, he did not mention his new find to Prendergast, S. He was also surprised that, having looked closely at all the houses where a burglary had taken place, this was the first time that he had seen any signs of an apparently forced entry. Was this significant?

"I haven't seen a burglar alarm, Mrs Prendergast. Do you have one?"

"No, I feel that they merely suggest to the lawless thugs that houses with alarms have something worth stealing. And a friend of mine, who had a new one fitted when she moved into Nutley, about a month ago, has hardly had a night's sleep since. It goes off if an emaciated mouse creeps past in the lane, after a good night out in the fields. It's a blasted nuisance." Her flippant response prompted the question of whether a fat mouse which had not enjoyed its time in the field could cause even more havoc, but this was not the time to discuss such matters.

So Rob ignored this as he did with much of the invective, or was it helpful advice, offered by his fellow Woodfieldians.

"I'll be frank with you Mrs Prendergast. At the moment we don't have any real leads on who is causing so much trouble in the village." He said "we" because that sounded more assuring but the reality was that the "we" was the royal "we". He, Rob Swagg, was both the most senior and most junior person on the case.

"A detailed inspection of all the houses where the thefts had taken place hasn't revealed anything significant although I still have some ideas which I, I mean we, shall be following up immediately. Whoever was responsible for this disruption certainly knew what he, or, for that matter, she, was doing and I think that we're dealing with a professional."

"You mean it could be a woman? I think that's highly unlikely. We don't do things like that. If women were in charge of this country, we wouldn't be in such a mess now. You ask that Harman woman, the politician."

"I, I mean we, are very keen to solve these crimes and I can assure you that no efforts will be spared to find your valuable possessions." As he gave that assurance, they both felt that it was more PR than crime detection. Mrs Prendergast hurled one more snide remark at the officer.

"You really haven't a clue have you, not a single idea not a clue?"

Rob ignored this sally and, if he had been staring at Prendergast, instead of a massive fuchsia bush in her front garden, he might have detected just the faintest trace of a smile at his failure to reply.

He left to have lunch with his sister Barbara, at her home in Tipton Poppleford Major. She was a hard working solicitor and she was at home today, using up her holiday allocation from the year before last. That's how hard working she was. Rob discussed the crime wave with her. He was feeling very upset because his bosses at headquarters were now putting him under even greater pressure to make an arrest and it was only a matter of time before others would be drafted in to help him after which he would be drafted out. In short, he was feeling the draught. Whereas previously, he had been worried that he might be moved because there was no crime, now he feared that he would be transferred because his crime solution rate was precisely the same as it had been when there was no crime. One small consolation was that the two young constables who had been sent to help him for a few days had proved useless and the finger-printing team had only found prints of the owners of the burgled premises. So, the culprit wore gloves, which suggested either a professional law-breaker or someone who watched crime on television or, indeed a criminal who enjoyed television.

He picked up the local paper on his sister's lounge table. He had started to read it at home when the Prendergast woman had phoned him at home and now he resumed his perusal. He wished he hadn't. The editorial was headed:

Man on the moon? Yes. Solve some local burglaries? No.

It was nonsense of course and opportunistic and harsh nonsense which was even worse. The shallow-minded "journalists" had doubtless been prompted by all the publicity surrounding the 40th anniversary of man's landing on the moon and wanted to show how clever they were.

The article commenced:

We can put a man on the moon, but we can't catch a tinpot thief who's stealing under our very noses. It's high time to bring in more experienced crime fighters if our local force cannot make any progress.

If the idea was sustained, and the crimes were not solved in the next few months, Rob anticipated another heading based on an anniversary:

173

Second World War victory? Yes. Solve some local burglaries? No.

Barbara, who was feeling very sorry for her beleaguered brother, asked him if the victims had anything in common. Rob shook his head.

"No, nothing, as far as I can see. They live in different parts of the village and know each other, in some cases, because they play bridge together, but that's not much to go on. Apart from the Prendergast woman, they've all been on holiday some time this year and used the same taxi company to take them to the airport. Still, that's not too surprising as there is only one company in the area. I've checked the drivers very carefully and I'm convinced that they've nothing to do with it. Some of the victims went on holiday earlier in the year and have only just been burgled. Why would a thief wait for months before helping himself, after the victim had returned from a holiday, when he or she could have helped themselves whilst the owner was away?"

Barbara speculated, but quietly, reflecting the quality of her upbringing.

"Perhaps it's someone in the village, who never wanted The Grange here in the first place and is carrying out these burglaries to throw suspicion on these young criminals."

Rob had thought about this.

"No" and to emphasise the negative, he shook his head. There've been six break-ins so far. Two of the victims were the sternest critics of the new scheme but two were great supporters of the plan and even spoke up for it at that public meeting we had in the church hall, you know, the meeting where some participants failed to keep cool."

Barbara grinned. "That's one way of describing what some would have called a riot."

"So?"

174

"If someone from The Grange has committed these thefts, which could lead to its closure, would they steal from those who had been in favour of the plan?"

Barbara had not finished. "It's possible. Let's remember, we're dealing with a criminal here. Anyway, how do you know that they have been burgled? It's only what they told you, isn't it? You haven't any proof that the burglaries were genuine."

Rob looked stunned which was not unreasonable as he was stunned. It had never occurred to him that any of the "burglaries" might have been staged for insurance purposes but there had been six and this would have been too much of a coincidence.

"And you told me that at each house, there has been no obvious forced entry?"

"Yes, but the last house, the Prendergast home, that I visited this morning, had scratch marks on a door which were compatible with an attempt to force the lock. I thought that was rather odd. Another thing, which I'm sure is not important, is that the Prendergast woman has tattoos on both arms. I know that such personal decoration does not debar her from being a great supporter of the church, but, somehow, it just seems inconsistent."

Barbara asked whether, at all the other houses, there were any signs of a forced entry.

"No."

"That's very odd, don't you think?"

Rob, who had just admitted that he had thought that was rather odd, nodded, implying that he had not changed his mind in the last two minutes.

"Are you suggesting that she staged the theft just to cash in from it?"

"I don't know, but it does seem curious that only one house has signs of a break-in. At all the others the thief either picked a lock or gained access through an unlocked door or window, unless it was an inside job, in which case the Prendergast case could be the only genuine one."

Rob was getting confused and said that all the victims had given him a list of the "missing items".

"And you believed them?"

"Well, I hardly had grounds for calling them liars."

"If I were you, my young brother, I'd check on their backgrounds, just to make sure. It would be interesting to find out if any of them, especially that ghastly pompous Prendergast woman with all her superior airs and graces, has any record for making a false insurance claim."

Rob listened to all this very patiently but with little hope that this would lead to a breakthrough. Then, saying that it was time to leave, rose but as he did so, he saw an ad in the local paper for the remaining open garden days. Suddenly, it struck him with the force of flying wheelie bin that two of the victims had said that they went away for a few days to recover from the impact of preparing and then opening their gardens for charity. Why on earth had he not realised this before? Could this be the clue he needed?

Back in his office, believing that now, at last, he might be on the right trail, he checked the other victims. All had opened their gardens during the season. He grabbed a leaflet and to his profound gratitude, he saw that at least two more would be open before the end of the summer. Happily, he knew the two owners very well and would ring them. He had a favour to ask.

Acting on a hunch, he decided to see what he could find about the tattooed Prendergast woman but his computer could not help. Regretfully, he reported back to his resourceful sister the following morning. Unfortunately, she could not give her brother any additional assistance and was about to leave the office to have an early lunch with an old friend.

At about three that afternoon, Rob had a call from his sister who was showing some unaccustomed excitement. Could her brother come round to dinner, in, say, three hours, as she had something to tell him? Rob was delighted to hear this but a tiny part of him recalled that in many crime dramas such a call often led to the murder of the informant. He rejected such nonsense but was, nevertheless, more than usually pleased to see a bubbling Barbara. After providing some drinks, she lost no time in opening the conversation.

"You know that Prendergast woman has always claimed that her husband was an oilman working in some God-forsaken country? I've discovered that she used to live in London, apparently, some years ago and moved to this part of the world about four years ago. In that time, I haven't seen the husband and, what's more, nobody in this office has ever seen the other half."

Rob wondered why such trivial information was even mildly significant and was about to express such thoughts when a slim but un-ringed finger was waved at him and its owner announced that there was more.

"I wonder if she's married and if her real name is Prendergast. It's nothing to do with me, of course, but if I were you, I think that I might try to find out if Sheila Pemberry has a record."

"Sheila Pemberry?"

"Yes, I had lunch today with my friend Belinda Morris and she asked about your crime wave. Belinda's a solicitor in this company, but in another office in this region, as you know." Rob didn't but apparently the remark did not require an answer.

Barbara resumed "after lunch we did a little shopping in Archester when she tugged my sleeve and asked me who the woman was who was waiting to cross the road at the traffic lights. I said it was Sylvia Prendergast. I'd never spoken to her but I knew her name because I read about her devotion to the church in the local paper and I'd seen all those pious and smug pieces she writes for the church newsletter.

"Belinda used to work in London and what she told me next was fascinating and I just hope that it's relevant to your case. If not, at least you'll have a free dinner and thanks for the wine, incidentally. She's got a reputation for remembering faces and people. If she wasn't a solicitor, I think that she could earn her money at it."

Rob was keen to hear the next part of the tale.

"Where does this Sheila Pemberry come into the story?

"My friend then told me that she was sure that Prendergast was really Sheila Pemberry. Belinda remembered her from some time ago. Apparently, Sheila, or whatever her name was, had been in court in London for some offence about six years ago, but Belinda couldn't remember what the alleged crime was or whether she had been found guilty."

Rob was really grateful for this information and, had his sister not prepared steak and kidney pudding, one of his favourites, he might have legged it back at speed to interrogate his police computer.

His machine, having let him down before on the matter on the Prendergast name, knew Sheila Pemberry and gave Rob some real encouragement. She used to live in East London and had a criminal record, having been found guilty of receiving stolen goods. Further research showed that the government had been encouraging judges to "clamp down" on such crimes at that time but she had escaped jail after the judge decided that "this fragrant young lady has been, to some extent the victim of circumstances beyond her control and the prevailing culture in which she was raised. I don't think that her offence justifies removing her from society and I shall therefore give her a second chance. She deserves it and from what I've seen in court, she exudes remorse".

The following morning, Rob phoned Belinda, introduced himself and the solicitor, when prompted, recalled the case vividly.

"Yes, it's all coming back to me now" she told Rob.

"Sheila, on hearing the judge, and not sure what remorse was, and not therefore clear on how to exude it, took a chance and gave the judge a beatific smile which knocked his wig sideways. He returned the compliment by fining her just £10 but my contacts told me that he had probably intended to fine her £100 but became dazzled by her smile, which, you may recall was beatific.

"From what I can remember, her friends and relatives outside the court cheered her as she left, according to her foreign-born solicitor, "without a stain on her character" which was a little difficult to reconcile with what had happened. He was later involved on the wrong side of the law and is still inside. That's one reason why all this has come back to me. Solicitors are known for being good people."

Rob thought he detected a smile in her voice, thanked her profusely and said that he would like to take her out to dinner "when this mess was over", to show his gratitude. She accepted immediately and Rob suddenly felt very cheerful although he was not sure how all this fascinating information was going to help him stop the Woodfield crime wave.

He continued looking at computer entries for Sheila Pemberry and was not disappointed. Some six months after the beatific smile, a blog claimed that she had subsequently expressed her gratitude to the judge in a physical way which resulted in her showing an overall profit of £240. The story, allegedly, had been given to a tabloid paper but the blogger claimed that it had been suppressed just before the editor of the paper was knighted.

Rob summed up what had happened. There was no one, apart from his long-suffering sister, to whom he could fully explain the recent events, as television detectives do, for the benefit of those who have exercised sound judgement or gone to sleep during the middle of the programme. He knew that "Mrs" Prendergast, who had claimed to have been robbed, was totally opposed to The Grange and all it stood for. She had a criminal record for receiving stolen goods. She had probably lied about having a husband, as Rob could find no evidence of her having played the leading, or, in these days of equality, even a supporting role in any nuptials. But, of course, none of this meant that she was now guilty. It was still, just, for the authorities to prove guilt, rather than for the defendant to prove innocence. One little detail bothered him. Well, no, many large details bothered him. Why was the Prendergast door the only one that bore scratch marks and why would someone who was, apparently, so dedicated to the church have an armful of tattoos that would have been the pride of a seasoned sailor?

Nevertheless, Rob now had his first, albeit slender, hope that the crime would be solved before more police were drafted in for an indefinite period and he was taken off the case. At present, despite the anger and local criticism, regional management had decided that it was not worth injecting more much-needed manpower into the village whilst there was much crucial paper work to be done and statistics to be compiled, apart from solving crimes in more important places, such as cities and constituencies represented by government ministers. From now on, Rob would keep a close eye on Mrs Prendergast. Another positive lead was that most of the victims had generously opened their gardens for charity just a few days before they were burgled. He kicked himself, again, for not noticing this before and, of course, it might prove to be totally irrelevant but it might just be the clue that he wanted.

Like his fellow Woodfieldians, he remained convinced that one or more of the WM inmates were responsible but he would have to tread very carefully. He must not make bland allegations in the pub. It was all too sensitive. The government had invested much money and hope in the project and if he, a mere village copper, even implied that an inmate were responsible, his future would be distinctly less promising and his victim would probably sue the force under the human rights legislation. He must move very carefully. It was time that he became better acquainted with The Grange and its inhabitants.

A few days later, Rob was in the Duck and Orange. He was there mainly because he was thirsty but his professional side wanted to find out the reaction to the thefts. He need not have worried. It seemed that most of the drinkers did not blame him. It was the politicians' fault for planting the young crims, as they were now called, in their midst. Rob began chatting to one young man. After a few sentences, or it might have been one over the eight that "few" implies, their chat became a conversation. Rob recalled that he had met him before, at The Grange. He had been very polite and helpful and it was hard to believe that Charles Bell had ever committed a crime. He was well-spoken, clean and well-dressed, at least by the standard of modern youth. Rob bought him a pint and the two resumed their conversation.

Mrs Prendergast was sitting, with several friends who, judging by their loud comments, shared her views, fulminating furiously about the crime wave and the fact that the police didn't seem to have any ideas. Her chums agreed. "It must be one of those young hooligans in The Grange". She turned round and pointed rudely at Rob and Charles. "Look at him now. Our policeman, doing nothing to find the crooks, spends time in the pub with one of the inmates from The Grange." Her friends did not ask how she knew that Charles was one of the young crims.

"I shouldn't wonder if he's not buying him a drink." Even before her fellow cronies could work out the double negative, breaking news confirmed that another drink was about to be purchased. "Yes, look, there he goes", she thundered as Rob headed for the bar. She went on in similar fashion and, judging by the grunts and nods, she was speaking to her own people.

Charles was keen to chat. He was articulate and defended his fellow inmates vigorously. "Admittedly, some of my 'friends' will always be at odds with society and I see no hope that even half-way houses like The Grange will change things. It's in their very DNA and I really cannot see how anything will overcome the colossal burdens imposed on them by their background and culture. But, for the moment, they are enjoying the freedom, even if they know that many villagers hate them."

Rob asked, tentatively and carefully, why Charles had been "put inside" as he put it.

"My father was always fighting with my mother."

Rob interrupted.

"You mean arguing?"

"No, I mean hitting her. One night, when I was just 18, he came home, violently drunk and knocked my mother over. She had always been a frail lady and completely incapable of retaliating. I decided it was time that I defended her. A voice inside me asked whether I was a man or a mouse." Charles continued without throwing any immediate light on the outcome of the question but Rob assumed that he had decided that the answer was a humanoid not a rodent.

"I pushed my father back and he stumbled, hitting his head on the corner of our stone fireplace. He looked really awful and I was afraid that I had killed him. We called an ambulance but he died on his way to hospital. I was charged with manslaughter and, although my mother, many people in the local community and my school teachers spoke up for me, I was sentence to seven years inside. Eventually, after about two years, our local MP, who had also defended me and denounced the decision to incarcerate me, managed to persuade the Home Secretary, you know, the man whose wife rents porno movies and charges it to the taxpayers, to review the case. I was freed subject to my good behaviour and my agreeing to spend a year at The Grange." Charles failed to mention that, earlier in his young life he had been convicted of arson but it did not seem to boost his portrait of an innocent so he wisely omitted it.

Rob sympathised but apparently, Charles was lucky.

"One inmate had failed to pay his road fund licence and he was there for life."

"An incredulous Rob gasped. "Really?"

"No, I'm joking."

As the two men laughed, it seemed to irritate the Prendergast camp.

"What's it like at The Grange?"

"Obviously, it's better than jail and, of course, it's very comfortable. That said, if I wanted to become a professional criminal, the other inmates would make very good teachers. Frankly, I'd be surprised if many of them go straight as the newspapers would put it. They think that this just proves that society is a soft touch and that they can take advantage of it."

"What do you do all day?"

"I'm studying for a degree in economics and I play a lot of cricket, although the village team won't let me play for them, presumably in case I nick their boots. At The Grange, the big 50" television is always on and 'my', and here he stumbled for the precise phrase before settling on 'colleagues in crime', "enjoy the reality shows and, of course the soaps but their favourite programmes are the crime ones which means most of the output for most of the time. They like sneering at the police and, in particular, the more senior cops who always seem even thicker than those whom they supposedly lead. Still, I suppose that's necessary sometimes for the story line. At least it allows the cop to explain to his dumb boss what's happening. Their comments on why the crooks were caught are most illuminating and I think that we've all learned something."

Rob smiled. That was one of his own favourite hobby horses.

"What about sport?"

· "As I said earlier, I like cricket but most of the lads like football so we all had to sit through that most boring of football matches when England humbled Papua New Guinea one nil, after extra time."

"So you're not keen on football then?" the ever-astute Rob noted.

"No, I'm not but the odd thing is that Goodfellow, you know the so-called warden, hates football himself but he said that watching the game was compulsory, for everyone. We even had to sit in a very dark room, with the heavy curtains closed so we could see the game as nature, whatever that had to do with it, and the BBC intended. It was so dark, you could hardly see other guys in the audience and I'm sure that many of them went to sleep. Judging by the way they played, I think that some of the lads in the England strip also succumbed to slumber. Of course, they might have been worried on how to make ends meet on just £100,000 a week or less. I must be fair."

Charles had to leave to meet the curfew of 9.00 and Rob shook him by the hand as the two parted. The gesture was noted by some of the drinkers.

Out of the corner of his eye, he saw Mrs Prendergast talking animatedly to Dick Goodfellow, who, surprisingly, had joined her group whilst Rob was listening to Charles. Presumably she was laying down the law and telling Goodfellow what she thought of The Grange and its inmates. Now that Rob knew that the voluble lady had a criminal record, he decided that he must watch her and it might be a good idea to listen too. Very carefully, he moved quietly to an empty table and cocked an ear in the right direction. As he had expected, Sheila Pemberry/Prendergast was generously conveying her thoughts to Goodfellow.

"All these thefts started only when you and your young criminals were planted on us by this spineless and dictatorial government. It's quite plain that these thefts must have been carried out by these young thugs. We've never had any trouble before like this in the village and you and the police seem to be totally impotent."

Goodfellow did not appreciate this adjective and protested that, like the police, he did not know who had carried out these thefts but "I'm definitely not impotent. I'm doing the best I can in very difficult circumstances. Anyway, the policeman, what's his name, Rob, is just as impotent." It was unfortunate that this word was suddenly released twice more into the atmosphere as those who had missed it the first time then heard it again and in the most-gossip-worthy and misleading context.

An embarrassed Rob, now impotent in the ears of those who had not heard the whole conversation, slid out from his new seat and sought fresh air.

Two days later, he visited Barbara. He told her that he had discovered that Sheila Pemberry, alias Prendergast, had lived in East London. Interestingly, he had seen her denouncing Goodfellow, the warden at The Grange fiercely, in public, but it seemed just a little contrived, as if it were being staged for the audience.

"Why do you say that?"

"Well, it was odd. Goodfellow didn't make much of an attempt to defend the idea of The Grange or his lads. It was almost as if he had forgotten his lines. I also wondered why he moved over to join Prendergast and her cronies. He must have known her views on The Grange as she has been so outspoken and so loud about the project for so long.

"There's something else. I was talking to Charles, one of the inmates, and he told me that Goodfellow had insisted that all the boys watch that boring England football match, you remember, that it was on the same night as the first burglary. What was strange was that he insisted that they watched it in a really dark room, which must have meant that one or more of the inmates could have left the room, carried out the theft and returned before the end of the match. What's even odder is that Goodfellow hates football. It doesn't add up. Both Goodfellow and Prendergast had lived in East London and although I know it's a big area, it's just possible, isn't it, that they knew each other before meeting again here in Woodfield Magna?

"And...",

"My word, there's more? My little brother has been busy."

"Yes, I've discovered that most of the people who have been burgled had previously allowed members of the public to have a nose around their gardens, in return for cash for a charity. What's really disturbing is that I dreamt up the scheme and I should have picked this up weeks ago."

"So you think that the thief has a good look at the homes, whilst pretending to take an interest in matters horticultural?"

"Precisely, Melvin. Many of the owners have taken photographs of their gardens on the open days but when I spoke to the garden owners, they all told me that, oddly, because we sold many season tickets, they thought that not many visitors had been to more than one garden. They know that because all those who open their gardens always visit all the others but, of course, the gardens are open for some hours so that doesn't necessarily mean much."

Barbara looked puzzled but waited for her brother to resume.

"There are two more gardens that are due to open before the end of the season and, fortunately both belong to good friends of mine."

The following day, he called on these two friends but, before that, he phoned the newly-appointed crime correspondent of the local paper. Having previously been charged with covering the local flower show, road accidents and new births, mainly to the vicar's wife, he was very happy to carry an interview with Rob, who had phoned his boss and, having explained his plan, was authorised to proceed as he wanted but he was warned to be careful, very careful.

Rob was intentionally helpful and very generous on the provision of quotable quotes in his chat with the new crime correspondent. "No, sadly, despite all our efforts, we are no further forward in solving these crimes than we were at the beginning of the summer. Frankly, we're baffled and just haven't a clue. We just don't know which way to turn at the moment, but we're hoping to have a lead before the winter. We owe it to the patient and good people of Woodfield Magna." Then, just to ensure that his words had penetrated, he repeated "we just don't have a clue".

Rob's words were duly reproduced in a scoop for the local paper and the headline, predictably, was

Baffled police admit "we haven't a clue"

From the point of view of the overall police in the whole country, this confession created not a ripple. City police were being severely criticised for their control of the crowds in London who were protesting against the possibility of a ban on Premier League clubs signing more foreign footballers and their colleagues elsewhere were busy removing strikers who were occupying factories which were about to be closed. Leader writers on the national papers did not see the article and so did not feel any more opposed to the police than they did before.

Rob's two friends, whose gardens were to be exposed to the critical gaze of the fellow Woodfieldians, readily agreed to his plans. Next, he had to ensure that what he was organising was legal. Apparently, it required official permission and much form-filling. It was unlikely that approval would be granted until long after the open garden system had finished for the year. Rob thought about this for a little while and then called

Philip Marston, who was the photographer on the local paper. He and Rob had been friends since Rob moved into the village. Marston, sworn to secrecy, lost no time in saying that he would be delighted to assist if his paper could have the exclusive story if anything emerged. That had already been agreed with the new crime correspondent, who sensed a second world exclusive if the plan succeeded.

Now, at last, Rob thought that he was making some progress.

His friends were to open their gardens on the Saturday and Sunday, respectively. Philip was in position, in an upstairs bedroom and was just checking his equipment. He had brought two cameras in case one failed. It was his task to photograph all the visitors and this performance was to be repeated on the following day. It was unfortunate that the gardens, in the same road, were to be opened on successive days as the organisers thought that this would probably reduce the overall attendance.

Happily, in a predominantly damp summer, the weekend was dry, hot and sunny. Philip tried to photograph as many visitors as he could but Rob decided to take no chances. It would not be a good idea for his press photographer friend to be seen "snapping away" in the garden, so Rob used a small and simple camera and went into the garden, pretending to be a keen gardener who was eager to take as many photographs as he could. The operation was repeated the following day, when for the second day in succession, the weather gods relented. Rob analysed the photos. Contrary to what he had been led to believe, many Woodfieldians visited both gardens but several of the photographs, taken at both houses, intrigued him. One visitor, who had gone to both gardens, was snapped in each, pointing his camera at the house, not at the garden. What was even more helpful was that Rob recognised him and knew that he didn't like gardens or even like looking at other people's gardens.

The next part of the plan was for the local paper to reproduce some shots of the two gardens that had been opened, alongside a short article, which mentioned in passing, that both hosts were due to be taking a short break after having brought their gardens up to the required standard. Rob and several colleagues from Archester mounted a discreet vigil around the two houses. The Woodfield man was confident that, following his confession that the police did not have a clue, the thief would not want to miss this last opportunity of the season.

As darkness fell, a person approached the first house of the two in the road. It was difficult to see his, or her, features as the visitor was wearing a hood, as well as some other essential clothes, the absence of which might otherwise have offered a clue or two to the identity and, indeed, gender, of the intruder. The face was daubed black. The visitor moved to the back garden, where some more of Rob's colleagues were stationed, and, then, looking around and seeing nothing untoward, he, or she, pointed what looked like a screwdriver at an elderly lock on the lounge door. Within a few minutes, he, and let's leave out the she to avoid slowing the tale, but, of course, that's not a clue, had gathered up some valuables, ostentatiously and deliberately placed on a side table and left, not knowing that he had just played a leading role in a new crime film. Rob and one of his colleagues followed the thief as he strolled down the deserted road, whilst one of the other officers radioed ahead to more colleagues at the house where the second garden had been on display.

The procedure was similar. Again, the thief entered the house from the room at the back, which, in this case, was the dining room. Within minutes, he left, having stuffed his new acquisitions into an expanding but sturdy bag. In line with Rob's instructions, the man, for it was surely a man, judging by the person's height and shape, was not apprehended but followed. He went to the village car park. There he was greeted very warmly and lovingly by a woman Robb immediately recognised. The two friends together put the bag into the boot of a car but, before they drove off, the gates to the park had been closed and Rob had arrested Sheila Pemberry and Dick Goodfellow.

The two were charged and pleaded guilty which was inevitable as the whole escapade had been filmed at both houses and the bag contained all the items that the trusting owners had left out so deliberately. They also admitted having undertaken the other thefts and many of the stolen goods were restored to their proper owners. The local paper was full of praise for Rob and he managed a smile when he saw the headline over a very flattering piece:

'Clueless' brainy cop ends local crimewave
Warden at The Grange and local churchwoman charged

Rob was congratulated and offered immediate promotion to sergeant to be based in a small station on the outskirts of London. He had feared a transfer if he had failed and now that he had succeeded, he was still to be moved. However, strong local support persuaded the authorities to switch him not to London but to Archester, where the sergeant would soon be retiring.

Chapter 15

It was a strange experience for Will as he drove up to the main reception area of his old company, even if it was in a new location. As his hired silver-grey S type Jaguar glided smoothly down the long drive, the sheep in the adjacent fields paused briefly and decided, after studying the visitor and his transport, that a prolonged interruption to their munching was not justified. Given their views on the posh car and its driver, very reasonably, they immediately implemented their decision. That's the way with sheep, no committees of enquiry, royal commissions or even *ad hoc* standing committees.

The drive led to an impressive-looking new two-storey office block which was surrounded by tall trees which had not been subjected to an Haitch SE visit, and an immaculate lawn in the foreground. Will, accustomed to tall and densely-populated urban office blocks, thought that the space per head must be generous.

Today was one of the days when the long-term weather forecast of "long hot periods of sustained sunshine and high temperatures" was justified. As the most recent forecast for the whole of the UK on the car radio had only been of five minutes duration, there had been no time for Donald "Mac" McDonald to comment on the weather expected in England, Wales and Northern Ireland. Unfortunately, for parts of the UK, the summer had been one of the dampest and coldest on record and, to Will's annoyance, like millions of his fellow countrymen, he had not been able to watch much cricket as the first three Test matches had been severely disrupted by rain. It was unfortunate, too, that the weather had not been good enough to allow him to take Laura to some of his favourite places around the UK. Until he had done that, their shared memories were based mainly on Texas. He would grant himself some days off if, and here he corrected himself, when, the weather perked up. He recalled the question apparently posed to Rudyard Kipling. "Will it stop raining?" His response was that it always had in the past. Perceptive chap, Kipling and now the versatile fellow makes cakes that apparently are rather good.

The news followed the forecast. A short item about an outbreak of fighting in the Middle East which could threaten supplies of oil to the west and jeopardise the slow pace of economic progress, was followed by a longer piece on the disappearance of the dog belonging to the ageing pop singer and National Treasure. The animal was still missing, many weeks on, and the new PM, again showing himself to be a man of the people, had appealed for anyone who had information that could return the dog to its grieving owner to contact the police immediately. He repeated the rubbish he had offered some time before. "I know that, as a nation, we all come together at times like this and I want to say, on behalf of the nation, our nation, our dog-loving nation, that it our most fervent hope that Fido Three returns home soon. Cliff, you and Fido are still in our prayers and we just hope that you don't have to acquire Fido Four."

The next item was about some UK companies which had been fined for not displaying the EU flag whilst another had incurred a penalty of £400,000 for displaying the Union Jack. One reason for the latter fine was that it might upset "those from a different background, whom, of course we welcome, who had chosen the UK as their new home". Will wondered about those long-established Brits who might just want to fly the country's flag and who might be irked by the decision. The managing director of the illegal flag-flying group said this financial penalty would drive his organisation out of business with the loss of 100 jobs so he might have to set up the company in Belgium.

A local charity, which had received a modest grant from the EU but which had failed to publicise the source of some of its income, was forced to repay the money to Brussels. These penalties were imposed after undercover activities by community enforcement officers attached to the Flag related activities team which were known as the F rats.

Now, in a further effort to gain popular support, the PM had announced that the failure to forecast the weather accurately, which had "cost the country dear and worried my colleagues and me" would be investigated by a new and higher-powered special enquiry. Those charged with this task, the PM assured an understandably nervous nation, all had had "direct experience of weather over a long period of time". The creation of this study group puzzled the manufacturers of barbecue equipment, who had done well in anticipation of a hot and dry summer, and the makers of umbrellas and rainwear who, against all expectations, had been able to sell substantial volumes when the weather deteriorated.

A think tank had been investigating the rising costs of the National Health Service. Their interim report, published only two years after the committee was set up, unexpectedly contained some firm conclusions. Apparently, there was a correlation between the total costs of the service and the state of the nation's health. This ground-breaking knowledge prompted the creation of a sub-committee that had discovered, for example, university graduates enjoyed better health than pensioners. It was recommended, therefore, that all pensioners should immediately be awarded a degree. A sub-committee, charged with deciding what degree should be granted, had opted for a first degree in living, which would be known as DIL.

Pensioners, delighted, or DILighted, as one of the tabloids was to claim, that they could put letters after their names and, even more pleased that they would now also enjoy better health, later told pollsters that they would be voting for the PM and his party at the next election. The slump in the polls for the main Opposition party would subsequently cause the downfall of two successive leaders although one had to go because he had been photographed wearing a silly hat. The prime minister was able to claim, at international gatherings in the future, that the UK had a higher percentage of graduates than any other country in the world.

Earlier today, satellite navigation failures had caused an unthinking driver to steer into a river and a leading Paraguayan footballer, yet to play for his country, had been signed by a Ukranian-owned club in Duxvill, in the north of England, for £52 million and 58 pence. His weekly pay was to be "just £175,000". His new manager, "over the moon" at the signing of "such a bargain", said that his would ensure that the club had "more results" this coming season but, and this must have been good news for their opponents, would "only play one game at a time". All this was greeted with what passed as rapture by the local community: some just grunted positively whilst others admitted, predictably, that they were gob-smacked at this fantastic and truly awesome brilliant news.

Yes, Will thought, it's good to be back in the UK. He was not a vengeful man but he did allow himself a modest smile. Now it was all to be so different. He was bitter that he had been overlooked for the position of general manager, after such hard work which had played a part in the breakdown of his marriage. He was also profoundly disappointed with the lack of support from management when he was seeking out the crucial component. On the credit side, he now had a very interesting and much better and well-paid job and, above, all he had found a new wife. If he had been stuck in his old job, he might now just be a sour bitter divorcé. However, Will felt sorry for many of his former colleagues who were suffering the difficulties caused by inept management "Keep an eye on them and give them a few more months to flounder and then we'll decide what to do, said the president of Will's new employers, Berkford Engineering International.

The months had come and gone and Will's friends, still struggling financially, had told him that the company was selling its office and laboratory near London and moving to a new industrial estate near Kingsville Parva, the other side of Archester. Apparently a few redundancies, voluntary and compulsory, had failed to stem the tide and the company, already dragged down by its own incompetence, lack of new products and management failure, now had to confront the impact of the recession. It was simple: the company had no new products and cuts in the research and development budget, to bolster share prices and thus bonuses, had been bravely imposed by a former chief executive, who knew that he would be retired, on a guaranteed and fixed pension, when the impact of the reductions was felt. He had almost undermined the company fatally.

Apparently, many of the better staff had seen the looming crisis and had left, keen to take any work, even outside engineering, that suggested greater permanence than might be offered by remaining on this sinking ship. Others had left because they wanted to stay near London but, although some good people remained, many of them were unlikely to be able to guide the company through the current crisis. The company was in dire need of new investment, new products and improved management.

The move to the country had been virtually compulsory but one good feature was that their previous office block and laboratory had been bought by a newly-formed quango. It was to investigate why so many companies in the private sector were leaving London and other large cities to move to more rural locations. The government, concerned that this could have a serious impact on urban economies, was worried that rural communities, which tended to favour the main opposition party, although, of course, that was irrelevant, would gain an unfair advantage.

The quango, staffed by personnel who, having little experience of business, were, therefore, not prejudiced, had a massive budget like all official and semi-official bodies, although the chairman of this quango had claimed that there were "frightening rumours that we are to be asked to cut our budgets by 0.05 per cent" which he described as "horrendous".

Being free from market forces, the quango had paid a very high price for the buildings.

Their preliminary report had been published although the final thinking on this "highly complex subject" was to be released only after five years, by which time, as critics pointed out, the data would be out of date, so the quango would have to start all over again. Some senior personnel working for quangos are not as stupid as they are portrayed. This first study had recommended that rural office locations should be subjected to a substantial tax to stop the drift to the country and to revive the flagging town centre economies. This report heralded a significant improvement in the government's fortunes, according to polls on voting intentions. It was, of course, a coincidence that the government drew most of its support from urban constituencies.

As he parked his car in the massive car park, which was four fifths empty, or it might have been about 17 per cent occupied, causing an uncharacteristically indeterminate Will to wonder which space he should occupy, he conceded that he did feel a little smug. Having thought about it for a moment, he came to the same conclusion. Instead of clinging on in a failing company, he had been very lucky.

Some things had not changed. Presumably, to save a little money, some of the old-fashioned signs had been brought from the previous location and they looked incongruous against the outline of the new building. Will wondered how long his old company could survive on its own, if it had to, especially when saw the crude hand-written notice next to the front door which indicated that they occupied the whole building.

Will's new employers and the founding family and owners of his previous company, had agreed that the US group would take over the British firm. They were glad to sell and terms had been agreed, but, because of the need for secrecy, news of the deal had been kept from the British employees. Will had been volunteered to break the news to the staff and it had now been agreed that he and Laura, who was in charge of marketing for the US group, would spend about six months in the UK. Will was to be the new chairman and chief executive, although the latter role would be given to a new British executive after a vigorous search carried out by a headhunter.

Will knew that the immediate future would be painful for some of his old friends. He had ensured that their redundancy payments were as generous as possible but there was no alternative in this harsh, money-dominated world. He had to let some go, make them redundant, fire them, dispense with their services, give them their P45s and, in two words, dismiss them.

There was some duplication of operations and even marketing and, where that occurred, most of it would be transferred to the US. Laura would be very active in helping her husband. That said, Will, who regarded himself as a decent man, was, nevertheless, almost looking forward to breaking the news to some of his old management level colleagues who had shown him such little support and faith.

He was particularly looking forward to seeing the miserable Goldfish who had effectively scuppered his chance of promotion by failing to back him at a crucial stage in the development of the project. Goldfish had sat on the fence, as he always did, until he saw, and was convinced that he saw, senior management's stance. At that time, he would slide off his normal position, with apparently minimal damage to his fins, trousers and reputation, and ensure that he was identified with senior management's views. This slimy tactic had served him well and, like scum, he had risen to near the top. The ghastly Goldfish was the man who had told Will that a decision on the appointment of the new general manager had been taken whilst he was in the US. That really riled Will.

Will picked up his briefcase, pressed a button which locked the car and strode confidently to the front door of the office block, which, presumably aware of Will's new status, sensed his arrival and generously and respectfully swung back. The entrance hall was impressive and about as big as many of the reception areas he had had seen when he visited some of the biggest engineering companies in the UK. It seemed pretentious for a company with less than 150 staff. The floor was marble and long maroon velvet curtains, surely dust traps and a fire hazard, bordered the impressively high windows. Some 20 brown leather chairs and sofas were minimal in style and therefore expensive, but Will wondered if the company had ever had so many visitors simultaneously. The glass table had copies of the obligatory newspapers and business magazines, designed to impress the gullible, although the local rag was, to judge by its condition, more popular than "management reading". One book, *Your Problem, Our Story, a management guide to handling emergencies and the media*, rested on one of the chairs. The walls were covered by the type of paintings that could be seen in economy hotels but there were some photographs of senior management, looking amazingly pompous and full of their own importance.

He was pleased to see Susanna, the receptionist, and even more pleased when she advanced from behind her secure fortress and embraced him warmly. She plied him with questions about his new job, home and wife, although, as she said, not necessarily in that order. Obviously, she did not know why he had come to the new headquarters. She assumed that he was looking in whilst on holiday as one of her friends had told her that Will and his new wife were back in Woodfield Magna for a holiday. Susanna, a natural and bubbly red-haired girl would not have claimed that she was beautiful, and most males would have agreed, but her outgoing and attractive personality, and, indeed, much else, was hidden deep inside a black trouser suit. Why was it that companies seemed to want to make their female employees look like men? Susanna wore a white blouse and a company tie under her double-breasted jacket. Perhaps, when the revolution comes, men will feel obliged to dress like women, assuming, of course, that they, the women, don't feel obliged to look like men. Will curtailed this confusing internal debate.

Susanna was obviously genuinely pleased to see him and the instant affection and her effusive welcome made the conservative and very British executive almost embarrassed. He tried to answer all her questions about life in the US and she said that, one day, she hoped to go there but her boy friend was reluctant to visit any country which had "elected" George Bush not once but twice. Will smiled. He had often heard similar sentiments. Laura One had declined to go to the US for a holiday a few years ago, although Will later realised that this was not the consequence of a political opinion but a desire not to be away from Brian Parker, her secret and now totally discredited lover.

"I know I shouldn't say this but we all felt very sorry for you when Harry Hopkirk was made general manager. We thought that you deserved it. I hope that you didn't mind my saying that." She blushed and Will assured her that what she had said meant a lot to him and he tried to repay the compliment by saying, rather meekly, in what was supposed to be a Texan accent, "I sure have missed yawl, well, most of yawl".

Susanna offered to ring whoever he was going to see first to let him know that Will was on his way. Will smiled and said "thanks but no thanks, let's make it a surprise but first I just want to think a few things through". He sat down on the modern yet surprisingly comfortable chair and picked up the local paper. As he flicked up and down the columns, he noticed an advertisement under situations vacant.

We want a powerfully motivated, dynamic well-rounded strong person who wants to make a real difference to society and the local community. You will enjoy the challenging issues and exacting work in an ongoing team-led context, occupying a highly visible role which exposes you to the community and its environmental aspirations, going forward. Significant communications skills are required as you and your colleagues prioritise and resolve problems and issues. You will need resilience and tenacity to ensure that everyone involved in the project remains focused on collecting and then delivering results. You will also have a role in driving the team, at least once a week, towards its predicated goal and you will enjoy limited travel. We can promise you that each day will bring a fresh and sometimes not so fresh challenge.

Applications should be sent to the Managing Co-ordinator UDMCRS, (Unwanted Domestic Material Community Removal Service) at the local council. Candidates should explain why they want to be associated with the reclamation scheme, RUBBISH (The Removal of Unwanted Bins and Bags Into Selected Holes.) Envelopes must be marked "Serving YOU: Working for the Community: RUBBISH.

Will smiled and wondered what had happened to normal English. He turned the page and saw a "case study". A man of 25, earning £25,000 a year, wanted to buy a house and retire at the age of 55, with a pension of £45,000 and he was seeking financial advice. The twit spent about £150 a month on a television subscription and on his mobile phone. Just below this piece was a survey which revealed that 55 per cent of all teenagers wanted to be famous when they grew up. There was no indication of what job was to assist them in this objective. Fame alone was the spur.

Will picked up one of the business magazines. As he opened it, the page fell open at a glossary of business terms.

Average: A standard that few people reach so it's odd that the level is so high

Basket of currencies: How unused foreign coins used to be taken to the bank to be exchanged for sterling. This was before airport shops selling junk were established to separate coins from travellers.

Bear: The opposite of a bull

Budget: A sum of money allocated to a specific project, frequently increased as costs rise, so that executives can claim that the budget has not been exceeded

Bull: The opposite of a bear

Business Cycle: An environmentally friendly mode of transport favoured by managers as photo opportunities and by politicians followed by chauffeur-driven cars with their change of clothes and business papers

Capital intensive: A company based in London

Cash flow: Money spent on a wet holiday

Credit squeeze: Too many plastic cards in a thin wallet

Demand: A perceived need, often prompted by advertising, usually backed by credit

Deflation: A longer-term reaction to a smaller pay rise than expected

Disinvestment: The process of selling assets usually because of a management blunder whilst implying that the sale is part of a deliberate and carefully-planned policy

Diversification: The policy of companies to move into sectors in which they have little or no experience. They do this either because they have failed in their main line of business or they have been so successful that they think they can do anything.

Durable goods: Those expensive household items, such as televisions or fridges, that go wrong just after their guarantees expire

Exchange rate: The mechanism by which the value of sterling falls just before a foreign trip and up again before you convert foreign currency back into pounds

Forecast: An estimate that will be altered immediately there is any change in the circumstances in which it was made

Glossary: A subjective selection of terms with equally subjective definitions, designed to fill editorial space when holidays and business trips preclude journalists from writing anything more sensible

Hot money: Cash used on a continental holiday

Imperfect market: A shop that does not have what you want

Inflation: The phenomenon that makes individuals believe that their income is always falling, irrespective of any rises in salary or wages

Interest rate determination: The mechanism that ensures that the cost of borrowing falls within weeks of your agreeing a 40 year mortgage on a fixed and higher rate.

Inventories: The application of imagination to stock levels

Investment: A phrase frequently used by partners in relation to a desired but totally unnecessary domestic object which will yield nothing and which will be put in a cupboard within two days of purchase before being given to an unpopular relative three years later

Mean: A retort from those whose plans for investment have been rejected

Merger: The name applied to a new alliance of companies after a takeover when both companies wish to disguise the fact that a takeover has occurred

Moving average: An emotional reaction to news that your salary is below the national average

Present value: The sum realised by selling unwanted Christmas presents

Random sample: A sample of views, from people like you, taken in the office, to save costs

Seasonal or statistical adjustment: A modification to ensure that the figure always fits the prejudice

Soft currency: Laundered money that has not fully dried out

Think outside the box: Ignoring the impact of television

Yield: What happens to an investment when the owner gives way to a bull or bear

Will enjoyed reading this and made a note of the author's name. He was the sort of irreverent chap who might help make some dull ads more appealing. Mr Carter, who had deliberately tarried to determine the level of activity, realised that, since his arrival, there had not been a single phone call or visitor. No member of staff had ventured into the marble hall which resembled an ornate airport lounge on a day characterised by industrial action.

He rose and told Susanna that he was now ready to see his former colleagues.

"As you haven't been here before, I should tell you that senior management is on the second floor, the engineering boys are on the first and we workers are here on the ground floor." She grinned and joked. "Sorry that we haven't got a mezzanine floor but times have been pretty tough here and we've had to economise, you know." Will said that yes, he did know. Susanna blushed and Will immediately assured her that he had not meant that as a rebuke. He tried to make amends. "Ah well, you never know, things may improve just when you don't expect it."

She smiled and Will thought that her smile could melt ice flows, providing that they were of a male disposition. Then he thought about global warming and how melting ice could cause even more trouble to a troubled world. He cut off his own ridiculous thoughts promptly not least as he was aware that his odd daydream had been curtailed, probably for the best, by another comment from Susanna.

She had resumed a more formal and official pose. "I should have signed you in, but I guess that it doesn't matter although

Stan Wilson, the head of our new six-man security team would have a heart attack if he knew. Will made another mental note. Susanna smiled again and said that the lifts were just round the corner, on the right and offered again to ring Will's erstwhile chums, although she did not use this phrase, but he said that he would prefer to surprise them. Reluctantly, Susanna acquiesced.

Will had a clear mandate from his new employers on how to deal with his former colleagues. He tried to ignore his prejudices and told himself, yet again, that, but for his efforts to find a nano-size widget, he might not, no, he would never have met Frisky. He wondered what the reaction would be when senior management, and in particular that useless twerp, Barry Goldfish had heard what he had crossed the Atlantic to say. Will was feeling confident and almost benevolent as he headed for the second floor. He was now in total control and it felt good.

The family had not wanted to tell the staff that the company was to be sold to Will's new employers. They had decided that the news should only be conveyed when some more details had been resolved and when Will was in the UK. It seemed appropriate that Goldfish should be one of the first to hear but before that Will was to see the managing director. He was another bloated, bureaucratic wimp whose laziness and obsessive attention to irrelevant details had contributed to the decline of the company. The MD's secretary was missing, and Colin Payne responded to Will's knock with a curt and imperious "come".

Payne greeted his former colleague as if the two had been friends. After some routine and boring pleasantries, in which the MD lied that it was good to see his visitor, a sentiment that Will demonstrably did not reciprocate, the eminent visitor said that Colin Payne was right in thinking that he and his new wife Laura were in the UK on holiday but he was also here on business. Payne asked if this was a belated desire to form a joint venture to market the new product, which, he had always believed, had enormous potential in the right hands. Will agreed, stressing "the right hands" and, alarmingly for Payne, called him Colin, which he had never done before. Someone blessed by a faster brain than that housed in Payne's bald head might, by now, have been a little suspicious but Payne was not a quick thinker.

"You know, I've thought a lot about this and Will, I believe that it could work. Between us I think that we could do well on both sides of the pond."

Will nodded and, encouragingly, said "Yes, Payne, I think, that in the right hands, and given proper backup, you could be right." The MD, a few seconds ago called by his first name, for the first time, had been relegated abruptly to his surname, also for the first time, and this irritated him more than a little. That had been Will's intention.

The visitor resumed. "I'd be grateful if, in five minutes time, you would kindly tell all senior managers to meet in the board room in 30 minutes."

Payne begged Will's pardon. "Did you just say what I think you said?"

"I really couldn't say, Mr Payne. I don't know what you think, and, frankly, never have. Indeed, given your track record, it seems to me that you never think. Thanks for drawing this to my attention. I shall remember it. As it seems necessary, I'll repeat what I said. "I'd be grateful if, in five minutes time, you would kindly tell all senior managers to meet in the board room in 30 minutes."

This was more than Payne could tolerate and he launched into his longest and most animated speech since joining the board seven years before. "You push off into the yonder, to the colonies, leaving us to pick up the pieces on that project of yours and then come here, on holiday and request, no, order, me to convene a meeting of my senior colleagues, just so you can say hello to them. It's a massive impertinence and if you want to see them, I suggest you organise a session in the pub, in their own time. Meanwhile, Carter, you can leave my office immediately and get out of the building before I call security."

Will just smiled, in a passable imitation of the Mona Lisa, as Payne's initial smouldering developed into a fire. It seemed that Will's facial expression incensed the managing director even further and Will wondered if Payne's pain might lead to a heart attack. Somehow, his bald pate had changed colour in sympathy with his reddening visage. It was an impressive sight but Will had more to say.

"You were right when you said that I had ordered you to convene an immediate meeting. You see, I'm your boss now and I can't help thinking that, in the circumstances, you might consider it prudent to do what I have asked, and frankly, to show a little respect. Here, you might like to see this letter, signed by all the members of the family which owned this company until recently."

Payne grabbed the letter, glanced at it, turned pale immediately, which, considering his recent red countenance was quite a colourful feat. It was as if a few moments ago, he had been in a particularly enjoyable dream, telling Carter to leave his office and now he was in a nightmare. He screwed up the letter and lobbed it into the waste paper basket. His timing, particularly for someone who did not understand what was collected on what day by the SROs, salvage reclamation officers, was excellent: waste paper was to be collected the following day.

Will had anticipated this and produced another copy of the document.

"In case you can't control yourself again, or your ability to read remains impaired, let me read it to you." Payne was beginning to look very unwell and he wanted to pinch himself, in the sense of applying pressure to a part of his anatomy, rather than to effect a theft, to gain confirmation that he was in the middle, or indeed, at any stage, of a vicious nightmare.

"It's headed TO ALL SENIOR STAFF. At the moment, that includes you."

Payne was beginning t
although he tried to banish
him that today was not going t
kind of acute perception that had
top.

Will read on.

Senior members of staff will know, from
with the controlling family, that the latter ha
disappointed by performance over the last few year
company's activities are being challenged not jus
inadequacies we have created for ourselves, which we
as a serious failure of senior management, but also by
economic downturn. Credit is difficult, staff morale is low an
our markets are shrinking in the face of the economic gale that
is sweeping through the world. Something must be done, and,
in the absence of meaningful initiatives from senior
management, despite repeated requests over a long period, we
have taken what we regard as the right steps in the right
direction.

We, the family, have stressed repeatedly, the need for new
investment, new product development, improved marketing
and the need to keep the best staff whilst encouraging those
who have not contributed, at whatever level, to seek other
employment. None of this has happened. When credit was
relatively cheap, our attempts to persuade senior management
to invest always were rejected and we decided, wrongly, with
hindsight, to follow the management line. We did not want to
second guess our own most experienced employees. How
wrong we were but we have learned from our errors whilst,
sadly, there is no such recognition from management. That,
too, has convinced us of the correctness of our decision.

Clearly, the failure to back Will Carter with a product
which had global potential was a major mistake and, by
failing to promote him to General Manager and, instead
opting to appoint a relative of one of the directors was an
unforgivable and very expensive mistake. Such a decision
should never have been ratified and management's decision to

ipany would
courtesy of
givable and
this in the
` be needed,
was worth
nething so
f late have
comments

have a most painful thought and,
t from his mind, something told
be one of his best. It was this
allowed him to rise to the

egular meetings
e been very
Now, our
by the
egard
the

1 without
t Berkford
npany for
the legal
effect the

..... .ow owned by our American friends who, of course, are free to take whatever action they feel is appropriate.

During the negotiations, we have stressed our desire that as many non-senior management staff as possible should be retained and we are pleased to say that this has been agreed. We feel that it is not their fault that the company has gone backwards and that they should not bear the main responsibility. That said, we recognise that BEI will have to let some of our colleagues go as some functions will be moved to the US. It has also been agreed that those who have to be made redundant, as opposed to being dismissed for sustained incompetence, and we hope that the numbers will not be large, should receive maximum redundancy pay.

However, we have made no such agreement in relation to senior management and their future rests entirely with our American friends. What we can tell you, and this we think will please the majority of the staff, is that Will Carter has been named as Chairman and Chief Executive of the new company and will remain in the UK for at least six months during which

*time he and his wife, who has been a senior vice president with
BEI for some years, will be re-organising the company. They
will also be dealing with all staff matters, including
redundancies and recruitment of replacement senior staff
where it is considered necessary.*

*We would ask all staff to co-operate and regret that it has
become essential to become part of a larger organisation but
we feel that this was the only alternative to going out of
business. We wish the new company every success.*

Payne looked as if his head had just thwarted a brick intent
on breaking the sound barrier. His face, usually a beery red
just after a very early lunch, was now pale and it was clear that
he knew his future with the company could be counted in
minutes. Indeed, Will told him that he had to leave the
building within 67 minutes of the end of the meeting that he,
Payne, was about to convene. There was no reason to select
67: it just seemed funny to Will. Security, hired for the day by
Will, not those on the pay roll, would be checking all those
leaving the building for the last time, to ensure that they had
not carelessly contrived to take with them any documents,
mobile phones or armchairs belonging to the company. These
human resources would never be allowed into the building
again.

There was one other former colleague that Will wanted to
see before he addressed the senior management meeting. Barry
Goldfish, who was the occupant of a palatial office down the
corridor, was an insult to a much-loved domestic pet. Will
hurried because he didn't want Payne to impart the news
before he could do so himself and rushed past a bewildered
secretary into BG's office. The stupid Goldfish, who had heard
from a relative in Woodfield Magna that Will was back in the
village, greeted him in fulsome fashion. Here, as in Payne's
office, there was polite patter before Will delivered the
bombshell.

"You know, Goldfish" and the use of the surname threw the
recipient but wisely, the latter kept quiet and waited until he
could be equally rude to his former and junior colleague. Will

continued. "You know that I worked my socks off, trying to find the necessary widget for our project, yes, Goldfish, our project, and you never gave me any support. You sat on the fence before implying to your fellow spineless cronies that the project would fail and that I was not suitable for the vacancy in general management. By your rules, I admit I was ineligible in that I was not related to anyone on the board of this damned awful company."

Goldfish tried to speak but Will's gaze and an imperious hand gesture silenced him.

"And then you and your fellow weasels, when I was in the States, after I had found the necessary part, acted in a cowardly fashion and appointed the useless and inexperienced Hopkirk. You told me that I had been passed over without the slightest trace of sympathy or sensitivity, then, when the project failed as the rest of the company knew it would because hopeless Harry was clueless, you had the nerve to ask me to come back. You're a big fool, Goldfish."

Goldfish managed to mutter a few words whilst Will, who was having the best time he had had with his clothes on for many years, took a breath.

"I really don't know who the hell you think you are, waltzing into my office, abusing me. Your rudeness proves that we were right and now you can get out before I call security."

Will smiled.

"You ask who I think I am. Let me enlighten you. I have no doubts whatever on not just who I think I am, but who I know I am. I'm your new boss and my first decision is" and here, as on gormless television programmes, hosted by gormless and noisy "celebrities", he paused, to allow the unimaginative Goldfish to wonder and worry about what was coming, "to fire you with immediate effect". Will had wanted to say this to Goldfish for some time and now as the words floated slowly, sinuously and satisfyingly from his mouth he could not recall ever having had so much pleasure in business from uttering so few words.

A spluttering Goldfish, now closer to the colour of the fish whose name he had appropriated, asked, and here the question loses something in the translation, what authority Will had to assume such powers. Thoughtfully, and this was so untypical of the man, seemingly thinking of others, even when his own future seemed uncertain, he asked Will if he had gone mad. The implication was that he was prepared to overlook this hostile approach in return for summoning medical aid. This was wasted as his tormentor produced another copy of the family's letter and handed it to Goldfish whose hands were shaking.

"I want you out of the building 67 minutes after the meeting that we are both about to attend in the board room. Incidentally, don't even think about taking any documents or machinery. I have hired some extra external security guards, who, oddly, are not related to anyone in this company, and they have strict instructions to ensure that nothing belonging to the company leaves with the dismissed staff. We shall be working out any payments due to you and will be in touch with you in due course. Incidentally, the reason I'm getting rid of you is for sustained incompetence. Now let's go to the meeting, shall we?

The ranks of senior management had gathered in the board room and it was clear from the remarks as Will entered that it was now common knowledge that the company had been sold, that Will was to be the new chairman and chief executive, at least in the short term, and that many of them would be dismissed. He had only told Payne and Goldfish but Will speculated that the secretaries, whose imagination had been stimulated by the raised voices, had heard their bosses being fired.

Will read out the family's letter and told them that Payne and Goldfish were leaving the company immediately. He was going to conduct a review of all levels of senior management and he warned them that many of them were likely to be

211

sacked, not to allow American executives to take their places, but because so many of them were sub-standard and should have been dismissed ages ago in any decently-run company. It was his intention to replace those whose jobs were still required with more-competent UK personnel. However, he said there was some good news and the stunned senior executives pricked up their managerial ears, like eager spaniels expecting more than a gentle pat on the cranium. Was there to be any good news for them? Will announced that many of the jobs below senior management would probably be retained. Somehow, that did not seem to cheer them up.

Next, Will returned to see Susanna who was oblivious of the explosions that had occurred over her head. Would she please organise a meeting of all the junior staff, in the main conference room, as he had something that he wanted to say to them.

Susanna looked embarrassed. "I don't think, I can do that without Mr Payne's permission. I'm sorry but it's worth more than my job's worth."

"I realise that, Susanna, but Mr Payne is leaving the company within the hour as is Barry Goldfish and others will be following later."

Seeing that Susanna looked more than a little puzzled, Will confided in her. "Don't tell anyone yet, but my American employers have bought this company, and by the way, I'm the new chairman and chief executive. One of my first decisions, incidentally, is to ask you to think about what uniform you would like to wear. It's wrong that you're made to look like a chap and, anyway, especially, however hard you're made to try, you never will."

Not for the first time that day, Susanna left her shelter and came round to the front and put out her hand in congratulation. Will, who had known her for many years, spurned it. "I think we can do better than that" and then hugged his old young friend. The new regime had begun. The meeting with the junior staff was very encouraging. When Will asked for any questions, it was clear that many of them had some excellent ideas that could help the company and Will explained that his wife, whom he had met in the US and who was a senior vice president of marketing, would be working with him for the next six months in the UK and would be delighted to hear their ideas on anything connected with the company and, of course, their own careers.

Over the next few months, Will and Laura re-organised the company and managed not only to save most of the junior jobs but found excellent replacements for those who had been "let go". Jock Carruthers, who had been instrumental in exposing Parker and had some years before had been dismissed after blowing the whistle on a crooked banker, was coaxed out of his premature retirement and became chief finance officer for the UK.

The new, streamlined company was linked in to the administrative and marketing functions in the US and, encouraged by a powerful advertising campaign, headed by the author of the business glossary that Will had seen in the reception area, sales soon improved. Will was able to appoint an experienced deputy chief executive, whom he had encountered in his search for the nano widget.

When the weather had improved, Will took Laura to parts of the UK she had not seen before. He wanted to see his aged uncle and aunt in their home in the north of England and they made the couple very welcome. Will played two games of cricket for the village, without apparent success, prompting Mike Redding to observe, "perhaps you've been watching too much baseball".

Chapter 16

Senior managers in the company contracted to build houses in Woodfield Magna, KEEPQT International, were feeling neither confident nor benevolent. The group had built only seven of the 12 executive style homes on the edge of the village and it had secured approval from all the authorities only after the intervention and support of the government and its success in an unorthodox auction. It was, of course, unusual for a minister to become involved in such a small development but the administration thought that it had to be seen to be involved in providing homes in the rural community, even if the rural community in question did not want any new homes which would be too expensive for the locals. Central government must rule, not pathetic little whingeing NIMBY protest groups opposed to any developments. This, after all, is a democracy, which means that a political party that was endorsed by about a third of the total electorate can do what it likes, providing Brussels approves.

The rumpus caused by Parker's apparent attempt to influence the local authority had prompted numerous pious editorials on the role of local authorities and the system of granting planning permission. They also discussed the influence of large building groups who were able to offer inducements, legal but possibly immoral, to councils, especially those keen to have a "free" new office block in which the bureaucrats could deliberate on their challenges in fully-merited comfort, with minimal regard for public opinion.

Another issue raised by the Parker affair was the "Not in my backyard" principle. Many urban dwellers, faced by city sprawl, could not understand why country folk should be allowed to preserve their fine views and quiet life at the expense of those who wanted new homes. It was impossible, according to the government, to build enough new homes in so-called brown areas to meet the ever-growing demand. The administration, which secured most of its support from the cities, clearly, disliked the countryside.

One MP, formerly a minor trade union official from the North of England, now supposedly the Minister for Rural Life and Community Affairs, whatever that meant, had complained about noisy and smelly animals when he made a publicity two day tour to the country. Candidly, he admitted that he could not understand what the villagers were saying to him. Later, challenged by a determined young local television reporter, he said that he did not mean the opinions they expressed but their "funny accents". The journalist had similar difficulties in understanding the minister and bravely emphasised this by asking him to repeat his long answer as she did not fully comprehend what he had said.

After the Parker affair, the government had decided that this village must be taught a lesson. The Woodfieldians, backed by large parts of the media, had ensured that no new affordable homes had been built for years in their lush green village. The NIMBY principle had to be defeated and opposition to a compulsory purchase of two areas around the village was organised. The combined efforts of the Bush-Cooks, the actress Jackie Lovely and a well-known weather forecaster, as well as many ordinary people, proved inadequate which showed the strength of the government's determination.

After much internal debate, the KEEPQT International group had bid for the right to build some new, desirable, executive-style homes in Woodfield. The company had been surprised that the government, effectively, organised an auction for the right to build in the village, especially after the rumpus caused by the compulsory purchase of the land. The national media were outraged: this was but "another stealthy move which runs counter to the traditions of the market place which should not be lightly jettisoned". This new snook was being cocked at the countryside, already well stocked with urban-produced snooks. Although only a small sum of money was raised by the auction, a careless junior finance minister, attempting to defend the indefensible, noted that the government had, at least, secured more funds to help provide some of the generous "severance pay" given to MPs who had decided to retire before the new and lower levels were introduced, following the great expenses scandal.

After the initial anger provoked by Parker had subsided, the residents of Woodfield Magna had been delighted to learn about the government's interference and greed. Surely, this meant that few companies would bid for the right to build as the basic "entry" level price was surely excessive. They were wrong. KEEPQT's bid proved to be the best of the three which, apparently, were submitted to the government. Trying to show that the bid was open and had attracted sufficient competition, a retired government minister had agreed with his erstwhile colleagues and with KEEPQT to set up two new building companies. They would all bid for the right to construct 12 new houses. When the media pressed for information on the other two groups and for details of their bid, the information was withheld as it was commercially confidential. Details of KEEPQT's winning bid were not publicised for the same reason. In fact, it was minimal but the whole affair was a closely-guarded secret.

From the time that the Group had decided to become involved, on the advice of the minister for housing, an old friend of the managing director, concern on the project had been growing.

KEEPQT had built, free of charge, a new but small office block in nearby Archester. However, it was not for the local authority, offered in return for their support, as had been intended: this fine new building, on the "advice" of the government, was to be the home of a newly-created regional government administration where unelected "representatives" of the local communities were to discuss matters of great importance to the local people in four one-week sessions annually. The local authority was not amused, especially as the new quango took over some of its work. This deception, and the imposition of yet another new and expensive group of bureaucrats, to be paid for by the taxpayers, had galvanised opposition to another condition of the contract granted to KEEPQT. The company was also and belatedly, required to build 25 new "affordable" homes to the north of the village.

It was not just the local villagers who were causing problems for the construction company. The value of their extensive land bank was plunging and they were committed to other developments around the country. They had been forced to abandon two large sites in the north of England and the manner in which they had left the unfinished estates had caused so much bad publicity that the company was obliged to spend many thousands of pounds tidying the site so that the residents could no longer, justly, complain that they were condemned to living on a building site.

The demand for new homes was plunging. This was because those charged with ensuring a stable economy had been stupid, ignorant, careless, arrogant or greedy. Some of the bigger villains were guilty of all of these characteristics. The economy had been allowed to boom, based on a tidal wave of credit that the recipients could never repay. House prices had soared, convincing the gullible owners that they were rich, then there was nemesis. As the economy moved from artificial boom to merited bust, the demand for homes slumped and thousands of home "owners" were plunged into negative equity. The market in "affordable homes" vanished as potential buyers worried about their jobs and potential builders could not afford to build at the new and lower price levels. The demand for executive homes faded dramatically, as so many executives lost their jobs, and prices tumbled.

Originally, it had been intended that some of the profits on the 12 executive homes would assist in paying for the affordable homes but with both sectors fading fast, the company was in a financial mess. The problem was that only

217

four of the seven executive homes finished so far had been sold and the company was required, as part of its contract, to begin the construction of the affordable homes before the end of the calendar year.

The KEEPQT board was meeting in the opulent board room in its London office in Mayfair. It had been suggested that the session might be staged in Morton Norton Manor, the country retreat owned by the chairman and chief executive, Sir Simon Pugh, because of the security aspects of what was to be discussed. However, an astute general manager had pointed out that it might look suspicious to the staff if all the directors were out of the office on the same day. He helpfully mentioned that this only happened during Henley, Ascot, Wimbledon, Cowes Week, the Lords Test and during Buckingham Palace Garden parties but, as far as he knew, there was no major sporting event taking place at the time of the proposed board meeting and the Queen was abroad. The two non-executive directors, MPs who represented northern constituencies, favoured meeting in London to allow them to claim generous overnight expenses.

The members of the board were not an inspiring group. One of the MPs, Jonathan Sterling, was known as "rent a mouth" because he popped up to spout up on any topics on the day's agenda. The broadcasters liked him because he was always available and his ignorance, on almost everything, made him look foolish, so he was good entertainment. He provided good practice, too, for young interviewers.

Some of the directors were close friends of the chairman. He had recommended their appointment and these men, for there were no women on the board, had done the decent thing and invited the chairman on to their boards. What nobody really understood was how most of these people had climbed the executive ladder in the first place. In some instances, family connections had played a part and friendships made during the wasted days of a university course accounted for other appointments. Some board members were genuinely experienced and intelligent and it was this group which had warned against impending and potential disaster. They were, of course, ignored by those who just knew "what was what", presumably because of their culture, upbringing or by some strange form of intellectual osmosis of dubious value.

Sir Simon outlined the problems. He implied that all the difficulties facing the company, "your company", thus passing some of the blame on to his colleagues, had crept up, undetected, almost overnight, and that nobody could have anticipated the developments that had posed serious problems for the company. "Indeed, we must and I repeat must, find some short-term solutions to the problems that confront us, gentlemen, as otherwise the group may well go to the wall and I don't have to spell out the consequences for us all" and he added belatedly "and to our colleagues" and then he added hurriedly, "and our shareholders". The group of knowledgeable executives, who had predicted disaster for some months, started to protest. David Askey was the first to comment, and, as it happened, he was the last as well.

"Mr Chairman, can I remind you that, at our meeting as long ago as last November, some of us predicted precisely that we were heading for disaster. You will find it under section 6, paragraph A of the minutes. Our suggestions on the action that we should have taken then, and now it's too late, were rejected with minimal discussion and I would like that to be minuted."

Sir Simon was in no mood to become involved in recriminations.

"Never mind that now, David, be that as it may, we need ideas on how to get out of our current difficulties, not how we might have avoided other, lesser challenges in the past. Let's try, shall we, to focus on what is important, not dwell on who did not do what which is not helpful." He was on the point of recommending that a line be drawn in the sand but, disliking clichés, decided instead to discuss "the ongoing situation, going forward".

"You all know that we have two, intertwined, interlinked, interconnected, associated and interrelated problems. One, of course, is the ghastly slump in the national economy, created

219

solely by our incompetent government and the repercussions that are having and will continue to have, on our sector and company, your company. We also have a much more specific problem in Woodfield Magna. Our difficulties here are compounded by the PR aspects. I think that there is widespread anger that we built there at all, after the way that government used us to bulldoze through their wish to be seen to be undermining NIMBY.

"Not only have we sold just four of the executive houses but we are very unpopular and we still have the major problem of how we can afford to build the "affordable homes" as we have to under the terms of our contract. The plain truth is that we cannot afford to build the affordable homes. If we fail, we shall incur a massive fine and let's remember that we must also face the wrath, yes, the wrath of the locals who don't want any new houses anyway. Right, gentlemen, I have spoken for long enough. Now it's your turn. Ideas, please."

There was silence. David Askey thought of speaking again, but he really could not be bothered. He had had enough of this company and was already talking to a larger and better-organised competitor who had sensibly diversified before the crash came. No, someone else could stick his wretched head above the parapet.

"Gentlemen, this is just not good enough."

Sir Simon was visibly annoyed with his colleagues as, to a man, they maintained silence. Complete silence. Bafflement on how to solve the problems facing KEEPQT International was truly rampant. It would have been difficult to find a group of senior executives who were more baffled or a scene where silence was more rampant.

It was time for some sarcasm.

"Can I remind you all that we are not talking about whether biscuits should be served with tea or whether you should all be given an allowance for new trousers as you spend so much time sitting on the fence, waiting for a colleague to speak and then assessing whether the majority agree with him before offering your own comments. What we are talking about here is the future of the company and, let me spell this out, as you're all deep in thought, your jobs are at stake. You've all seen the last quarter's figures and unless we make some progress soon, there's a possibility that the company will be driven into the arms of a competitor, in a fire sale. That will mean not only the loss of your jobs but a severe reduction in the value of your shares. Now, please could somebody begin this essential debate?"

Robin Brownlands, a keen and relatively young member of the board, responsible for building on inner urban sites, decided that this was an opportunity to make his name. If his contribution was rejected outright, at least he had tried and that might count in his favour. He wagged a small finger at the chairman, albeit very gently, implying not dissension but that he would like to break the silence.

Sir Simon nodded, smiled and confirmed that he and his colleagues were definitely all ears and looked forward to hearing him.

Nervously, he began. "Well, chairman, thank you. I think that we all realise that the wider picture is one that we cannot influence at present, at least not significantly." He was unhappy at the way in which he had started and realised that it was not easy to influence a wider picture, or indeed one of smaller dimensions, but he hoped that his colleagues knew what he meant. The good news was that he had actually started. Suitably encouraged by encouraging nods around the table, he gathered in pace and confidence.

"I would like to address the problem of the houses at Woodfield Magna. I checked just before this meeting and it appears that, as we all know, we've sold only four of the units we've completed. I was also told that there's little interest in the others and that bodes ill for the other five we are committed to build. Even ignoring the deteriorating economy, which is bad enough, we are disliked intensely by the local residents who are genuinely angry at the way in which we and

221

the authorities have railroaded, to use one word I heard lately, the creation of this estate." He was not sure whether the verb to railroad, assuming it existed, as he thought it did, was transitive or intransitive but he sensed that this was not particularly important at that moment.

"Now that we have been forced to abandon the site, at least for the present, the situation is even worse as those who have moved in complain, fairly, in my opinion, that they're living on a building site. Indeed, it is such a mess that television crews frequently film there to illustrate the stagnant economy and the decline of house-building. This does not endear us to the residents and I don't think that we can challenge their judgement as anyone who has visited the site will agree."

None of his colleagues had been to Woodfield, but some nodded agreement, so he continued.

"I understand from our on-site rep that those individuals who show any interest in buying have several complaints. One, predictably, is that there is no idea when the site will be tidied up and the estate will look like a group of up-market executive homes. The second most common grouse is that the houses that are empty look just that. They don't appeal because intending purchasers cannot imagine what the properties would look like when properly furnished. Thirdly, let's face it, gentlemen, we are very unpopular in the village and I'm sure that the locals' well-known resentment towards us has an impact on those who might otherwise consider buying these homes. It's a close-knit community, and, as things are at present, potential purchasers will not be keen to move in, especially as house prices are falling. Finally, if we are to build the so-called affordable homes, surely it's clear that we must make some money on the exec newbuilds as otherwise we shall be in real trouble."

Sir Simon was appreciative.

"Thank you that was an excellent summary of the problems, as I see them and I suspect we all see them." Hear hears around the table confirmed that the other directors were awake and hearing the boss's endorsement of young Browlands' analysis, indicated their assent.

The chairman wanted to know what solutions Brownlands had.

"Mr Chairman, I have some suggestions, some of which are simple and, in the overall context of things, are inexpensive to implement." The finance director, an astute fellow, suddenly recalling that he was responsible for financial matters, beamed. This man was speaking his language.

"We know that we shall not be resuming work on the site for what, some months, so why don't we clear the site and buy some plants and shrubs from local garden centres and employ local landscape specialists, not our own, and make sure that the local community benefits? We could even run a competition to determine the best concept for developing the triangle of land at the beginning of the estate on which nothing will be built, whatever happens?

"My second idea is that we spend some money buying, again locally, wherever possible, some furniture for the houses that we can't sell. People want to buy homes, not empty houses which, at the moment, is what we are offering. We need a more sophisticated approach. We should be able to negotiate with one or two of the stores in nearby Archester and they might welcome the publicity."

Approving nods around the table, implied that the rest of the board were just about to make precisely the same suggestions when young Brownlands had spoken up.

"My final idea may not go down so well. It's clear to me that we are regarded as the enemy in the village, as I said, and, possibly worse still, with the local media which sees a long-running battle between David and Goliath."

David Webb, the marketing general manager, firmly convinced that this meeting would be a waste of time, had fallen asleep. Hearing his name, and thinking that it had been suggested that he was in dispute with a man called Gol Liath, presumably from somewhere in Eastern Europe, or, just possibly from Wales, they always sounded similar, immediately rejected any absurd and ill-informed views. "I'm not in an ongoing one-to-one conflict situation on any issue with anyone in the area". Laughter from his colleagues who called him RV2W, RipVan Winkle-Webb, laughed at his denial. Realising that he must have succumbed to slumber, and on hearing his colleagues' laughter, Webb swiftly tried, in vain, to pretend that he had been joking.

Brownlands continued.

"We need to have a better reputation in the village and we need to occupy and sell the houses. This is what I propose."

His fellow directors, still silent, were amazed that one of their own number had thought through some of the problems and was prepared to submit suggestions before even knowing if Sir Simon approved of them. Still, Brownlands was young. Usually, the chairman was the only one whose ideas were presented and, by definition, any concepts suggested by others were wrong or impractical in some way. After years of being rebutted, they just did not bother any more and this was one of many reasons why the group was now in difficulties. On this occasion, Sir Simon had chosen to be silent and had out-smarted all his colleagues except Brownlands.

"We must be our own ambassadors. We need to be identified as individuals not as a large company, in league with the authorities, determined to impose our will and building on a reluctant village. I propose, Mr Chairman, that we ensure that the three completed but unsold houses are fully furnished and then occupied by KEEPQT employees. We can devise the details in due course. It may be that some of our staff can rent the homes and, possibly others may want to buy, at a reasonable price. There is no need to tell the media what we are doing but I recommend that we prepare all our answers for the time when, inevitably, the press and the rest find out what we're doing. Assuming that our own people are installed in some of the houses, they must then become active and agreeable members of the local community, without being pushy or perceived as PR lackeys from a large company."

"Thank you, Robin. That was very interesting and not a million miles from what I had been thinking myself. Does anyone else wish to speak?"

Now that it was clear that the ideas had the backing of the chairman, the hitherto silent, unthinking but well-paid wimps wished to speak. They took it in turns to assure the chairman that this was an excellent set of ideas and that they recommended immediate action. Brownlands smiled.

Sir Simon congratulated Robin and said that "if we all agree gentlemen, we must implement stages one and two with immediate effect. David, will you ensure that the site is cleared as rapidly as possible and that suitable furniture is bought locally as Robin here recommended, for the completed but unsold properties."

It was just as well that the chairman mentioned Brownlands as Webb had dozed off again, waking up just in time. Now he had a clue on who he could ask to find out what he had to do without waiting for the minutes. "Of course, chairman".

The chairman resumed. "I'm very keen to implement Robin's other excellent suggestion, but we must proceed carefully lest the idea backfires on us."

Ray Kelsey saw this as an opportunity to impress the boss. "I think, chairman, it might not be a good idea for any of us to move in or, indeed, any of our colleagues from this group company". At this point, he stopped.

"Why not?"

"Because it would look odd to the outside world and although the media, sooner or later will twig, what we are doing…" Here he was stopped by the chairman.

"Twig?"

225

"Sorry, sir, I mean rumble".

"Rumble?"

"Find out".

That linguistic mystery solved, the speaker was encouraged to continue.

"I have an idea."

This was such a novel feature of board meetings that his colleagues sat up bolt upright, pinched themselves to ensure that they had not, like RV2W, fallen asleep, checked that the view through the windows did not reveal any airborne pigs and awaited what the former prime minister Ted Heath, called "un moment historique" . Of course, it may well have been a favourite phrase of the band leader, or, indeed, any other Ted Heath, but history does not help us here and that's the problem. Historians tend to overlook wise words from band leaders, or, just possibly, they seldom say anything worth recalling.

"Yes?"

"You know that one of our distant sister companies in the group is a pipe-laying company?" All nodded because the chairman did but no other director knew of any such subsidiary company. "Well," said the speaker, "as you all know", which was not, of course, true, "they recently secured a large contract to lay pipelines from some distance the other side of Archester to Woodfield Magna. Some of our senior managers will be looking for accommodation. Why don't we rent or sell some of the executive homes to them, as they might be working in the area for at least a year?"

The chairman, enthused that someone had actually had a bright idea, nodded so enthusiastically that the clip on his bow tie came close to parting company from his shirt collar.

"I certainly favour that idea. Are we all agreed, gentlemen?" It was clear that they were, indeed, in favour.

One said that having pipeline people there meant that they were not immediately identified with the building company. He, for one, did not know that there was such a company in the group. Others, equally ignorant, looked shocked at this confession and gave the impression that they seldom thought about anything else apart from building houses.

Within the next three months, the executive homes site was cleared, landscapes had been landscaped and plants planted. Local business had benefited and even the local paper had run a friendly story or two, accompanied by some very favourable pictures. National television no longer used the site as a metaphor for the ailing national economy. Was the tide turning? Three of the pipeline company managers took advantage of the generous offer to buy or rent the executive and well-furnished houses. Nobody realised that the incomers worked for the odious housing group.

Jack Scoop, whose wealth was advancing at a very agreeable pace, had bought one of the new executive houses before prices had plunged, which did not please him. He had become friendly with the pipeline company employees and they and their wives had recently enjoyed a fine dinner at Jack's house. All that Jack had discovered during predominantly small talk was that they worked for an engineering company and, somehow, it never emerged that they worked for a KEEPQT group company. Days later, when drinking at the pub, Jack had asked if the trio if they were involved with the pipeline company that was tearing up some of the fields around the village. They had been instructed, by their patently inadequate PR person, just to say that they worked for the pipeline company. Jack decided to see whether his own organisation might be able to acquire a new client, so had done some research into the pipeline group and discovered all he wanted to know.

When he and his wife went round to one of the pipeline manager's houses for lunch one Sunday, his gentle questions about their employers met with only a bland response and there was no reference to the link with KEEPQT. Meanwhile, the houses were being looked after and the pipeliners were playing an active part in the life of the village, joining local societies. The wives played tennis and had helped to set up a ladies circle and were busy raising money for charity.

All that seemed reasonable to Jack, although as someone who could smell a big story a mile away, he sensed that this could be interesting. After another dinner at one of his neighbour's, he asked to use the loo and as he walked through the hall, he noticed a large crack between the window and the lounge door. Later he thanked his host for an excellent meal which he and Jasmine had really enjoyed. Just as he was about to fumble for the key for his own home, he recalled that he had deliberately forgotten his jacket. He returned and apologetically fetched the missing garment from the lounge.

Back in their own home, he asked Jasmine what she had thought of the house next door. She had not noticed anything in particular. "What do you mean?"

"You didn't notice any cracks?"

"Yes, they are like ours but I assumed that they were just settlement."

"I'm not so sure. I thought that too, about this house, but their cracks are much bigger. Tomorrow, when they're all out, laying pipelines and doing good work for the nation, I'm going to have a look at the outside of all these houses. I just have a hunch."

He was not the only one who had a hunch. The three pipeline engineers, having noticed the cracks, initially thought to be just the consequences of settlement, were worried and had discussed the problem amongst themselves. One crack, in an infant's bedroom, was widening at a frightening pace and it was now possible to put a coin in the gap. Not being members of Parliament, they did not claim the money lost on expenses. The trio decided that it was sufficiently important to pass on the potentially serious news to the head office of the building company.

The managing director, who was effectively the personal assistant of the chairman, had to take some decisions himself, as his master was on holiday and had given very strict instructions that, under no circumstances, was he to be contacted. Arthur Scott told his colleagues to ensure that, whatever happened, word must not leak out into the local community. Meanwhile the necessary professionals would be visiting the houses, under the guise of relatives, to carry out extensive but discreet investigations.

Jack had not lost his feel for a story as a piece in *The Daily Clarion* demonstrated. Together, Jack and his brother had researched and conjured up an article. Jack told his brother that this was merely the hors-d'oeuvre for something that was much tastier. All being well, he would be giving him another, bigger story on the following day.

Woodfield Magna angry at latest insult from building group

New "residents" are employees of KEEPQT subsidiary company in charm offensive

Why do so many people in high positions apparently think that the residents of the picturesque village of Woodfield Magna are fools? The disgraced building executive Brian Parker and some members of the local council, who also sat on the board of Parker's building company, thought so when they conspired, but failed, to defeat local opposition to new housing in the village. According to legal sources, they were fortunate to escape prosecution.

Then the government, determined to defeat an outbreak of NIMBYism, not in my backyard, used compulsory purchasing to acquire land around this beautiful village in Ottershire. They also conjured up new and instant legislation and even created an auction to determine which company would be allowed to build 12 executive homes and 25 affordable homes

229

in the village, still against the wishes of the local people. *Apparently, only three companies participated in the auction and the government has refused to name the other two organisations, on grounds of commercial confidentiality. Some commentators even believe that the other two companies are just paper creations belonging to KEEPQT International which won the contract.*

So far, KEEPQT have erected seven homes, three of which remain empty whilst equipment was left on site. Recently, following local pressure, the company has hired local labour and spent thousands at local garden centres trying to improve the appearance of the local estate but the villagers remain unimpressed. "If they think that by tarting up their building site and spending some cash in the region they can win us over, they're completely wrong, Sid Fish, 62, a local, who did not want to be identified, told The Daily Clarion.

Now KEEPQT have further tried to deceive the locals, and the market, by installing some of their own senior management in the executive houses. These men and their families have been told to become deeply involved in village life to improve KEEPQT's reputation. Reg Farmer, the chairman of the NO TO NEW HOMES campaign, who described this as a crafty move, was not impressed, and said that this latest twist in the story was a disgraceful insult. It appears that the newcomers are not employed directly by KEEPQT but by a sister pipelines company which is installing new gas lines in and around the village over the next two years.

The group described this as a sensible move as it brought in revenue for the company, provided much-needed accommodation for their colleagues who would be working in the area for some time and spending money locally whilst ensuring that the standards of the houses were sustained. This did not impress the villagers who told The Daily Clarion that they were fed up with organisations trying to deceive them.

Jack had shown photographs of the neighbouring houses to a group of key engineering and surveying specialists who visited the site during the day, when the pipeline engineers were out at work. They also examined the cracks around Jack's house, retreated to consider their verdict and met later that day to confirm and convey their recommendations.

Sir Simon Pugh, refreshed by his holiday at his villa in the West Indies, had convened an emergency meeting of all the senior managers. He was not in a very happy mood and he glowered menacingly at his colleagues.

"We have some bad news, very bad news. The executive homes that we have built at Woodfield Magna are subsiding at an alarming rate. We have carried out an extensive investigation and come to but one clear and very difficult decision. To begin under-pinning is not recommended by our PR advisors who say that we would have bad publicity over a long period whilst we carry out remedial work and then, given the sustained publicity, nobody would want to buy the houses. Our engineers agree with the PR specialists and they recommend that, despite the costs, we demolish the houses, with appropriate compensation to the owners. I don't think that we have any choice and, subject to any ideas that emerge from this meeting, we shall seek official approval to demolish the entire estate. This will impose a huge financial cost which may well send us into either liquidation or the arms of a competitor but I can't think of any alternative.

"This problem creates even more difficulties for us. Originally, we had planned that some of the profits from sales of the executive homes would help pay for the so-called affordable homes. Now we have lost that opportunity. As far as our lawyers can determine, we are required to build these cheap homes whatever happens to any of our other projects. Every way we look, we face trouble. The government has invested political reputation in this and will not let us renege on the contract for the executive homes. They have suffered reverses on, for example, the Post Office stamps issue and many more and will not want to be defeated on the politically sensitive issue of affordable homes, especially in Woodfield Magna. A member of the Cabinet, whom I happen to know from university days, told me the other day that they want to teach the village a lesson.

231

"That said, I must confess, here and in private, that we were so pleased to be awarded the contract that our own investigations may not have been as rigorous as they might have been. Speed was required by the government, as it was when it was trying to re-organise the banking sector. All this will be carried out under the critical gaze of a very hostile village. I suppose that one irony is that the locals don't want the executive houses, and, now, neither do we.

"Finally, and I must stress this, nobody, but nobody, outside this room, must breathe a word of what I have said. It is crucially important that we have some time to consider how this work can be carried out with minimal damage to our reputation and yes, to the environment. If anyone leaks this story, they can expect instant dismissal."

Jack had received the report on his own property and on the pics of his neighbours' houses and was busy writing. This is what appeared the following day, under Ivor's byline.

New blow for KEEPQT: Woodfield Magna homes condemned by structural engineers

Woodfield Magna, the ill-fated Ottershire village at the centre of a continuing storm of protest over the construction of new executive and "affordable homes" by KEEPQT International, will soon be thrust back into the spotlight. A secret report produced by top structural engineers hired by The Daily Clarion suggests that the seven executive houses built so far, some of which are occupied by group employees, are sinking. The specialists were unanimous in claiming that the subsidence is too serious to allow under-pinning and that in their opinion, the only possible solution is for the houses to be pulled down and the area grassed over.

This sensational news will be welcomed by campaigners anxious to preserve the village but is bad news for the government, which, according to critics, employed "dubious tactics" to ensure that the estates were built. The government acquired the land compulsorily and told the company precisely where they had to build the executive homes. The legal position is not clear but the builders were required to carry out their own surveys.

It's certainly very bad news also for the struggling KEEPQT empire, whose shares have halved in value this year. The company is also committed to building 25 affordable homes in the area. According to analysts, it is "just unfortunate" that the executive homes, which had been expected to help finance the cost of building the affordable houses, will now be demolished. The company will still be required to construct the other homes on other land compulsorily acquired by Whitehall and sold on to KEEPQT.

Reg Farmer, on behalf of the protesting villagers, welcomed the news. "It means the end of the executive houses, at least on that plot, and, with an election coming up, I doubt if the government has the time or inclination to compel any company to build executive homes elsewhere in the village. Now we must ensure that the so-called affordable homes, which are too expensive for us to buy and too costly for the company to build, and which will be bought by the wealthy as second homes, are not constructed."

Sir Simon had been pondering the latest disaster to hit his group. He sensed that the shareholders, having seen a major slump in the value of their shares, would not be keen to reappoint him and if they fired his useless board, well, that served them right. His own compensation, if he were removed from office, was satisfactory, or even generous but, irritatingly, well below the level attained by failed Scottish bankers. Now, his main objective must be to prevent the early construction of the affordable homes, and, ideally to ensure that they were never put up. He allowed himself a small smile. What on earth was an affordable home? The executive houses that had been demolished recently had been affordable to the rich. Now, it seemed that the locals would not be able to afford the lower-priced affordable homes. It was a truly mad world.

If the company was compelled to build the affordable homes, and how he had come to hate that label, the organisation could be driven out of business. The restoration of the site where the executive homes stood would prove extremely costly and probably even more than suggested by an experienced female television pundit whose views, according to Sir Simon, might have been affected by the fact that she was pregnant. What was even more painful was that the compensation due to the few outsiders who had bought the homes had taken into account the original purchase price and a generous addition for the inconvenience and the cost of the move. House prices had slumped since the lucky residents, including Jack Scoop, moved in, so they were able to acquire mansions, elsewhere, almost as big as Sir Simon's, for very little.

Now there was the problem of the affordable homes. It sat on Sir Simon's mind with all the weight of a careless elephant resting leisurely on a mouse. The hopes for an acceptable solution to his problems matched the prospect of the mouse emerging safely and in a condition that did not prejudice his chances of being recognised as a rodent. Sir Simon reviewed the options and came to a preliminary conclusion. There were none. The government, renowned for saying that it never shied away from tough decisions, had recently not only reversed its stance on banning post offices from selling stamps but had decided that the introduction of identity cards was no longer justified. This was odd as the administration had previously argued that, without them, terrorism would flourish, the flow of immigrants would be uncontrollable and crime would reach hitherto unknown heights. It had also reversed its stance on the need for every citizen to submit a DNA sample to a new EU centrally-controlled unit, the DNA Federal Trust. (DAFT).

It was clear that the administration could not tolerate another change of direction on the affordable homes. Admittedly, the government had bought the land and sold it on, but, unlike the site for the executive homes, when KEEPQT was pressed to move very speedily, and faster than it would have done in other circumstances, the company had carried out a major survey and found no reason not to build. Sir Simon continued to ponder this, even allowing his third coffee of the morning to go cold. That was a measure of his deep-seated concern. Suddenly, he realised that there was just one, very slender hope. It was not quite a "eureka" moment, but, if he had been a forehead-smacking man, a smack would have been administered but he was not, so no blow was applied.

If he was successful, the affordable homes would not be built, at least before the election in a few months time, and, if the Opposition won, as was expected, they would side with the locals, and prevent any building of either the executive or affordable homes. Suddenly, he realised that it was not necessary to stop the building, only to defer it before his friends, many of whom he knew from public school and university days, would be in power and would put an end to this expensive farce. Suddenly, a crucial truth dawned on him. The locals and the company now had a joint ambition.

He thought for a few more moments and then stretched across the desk to call his PA. "Miss Watson", he addressed her thus, not unreasonably, as this was her name. "I want you to find out the Woodfield Magna number for", and here he lowered his voice as it was essential that nobody should overhear, "and let me know it as soon as you can". She did as she was bid and later that morning an important call took place.

Chapter 17

A restaurant in the centre of Birmingham, many miles from the Head Office of KEEPQT and the home of a semi-retired farm worker from Woodfield Magna, was an unlikely setting for an important business meeting. So, too, was the timing. It was a busy Monday morning, just before the lunch crowds gathered. The venue was modern in that the lighting was modest, either to create an atmosphere or because the manager was using energy-saving bulbs, and the efforts of the sun to penetrate the inner recesses were thwarted by heavy and dusty curtains. It was an ideal place for secret meetings that never took place.

Sir Simon was in the restaurant first, and seeing his guest approach, accompanied by his chauffeur, Sir Simon's not one employed by his guest, rose and stretched out his hand in greeting. The chauffeur, whose headgear, still worn indoors, hid a particularly silly looking round face, although that was not relevant, as was the fact that he was aged 46, made the introduction and left, having established that his boss had his mobile number so could call him when he was required to take his guest home.

The knight beckoned his guest to sit down and a waitress approached.

"What would you like to drink?"

"A cider would be very pleasant", the bemused man said.

"I'm sorry, sir, we don't have any cider but we do have a vast range of beers."

She ended the sentence on a high note, as if questioning her own assertion that, in the matter of beers, the hostelry was well-stocked.

The waitress then reeled off about a dozen names and the Woodfieldian opted for the last-named for the very good reason he could not recall even one of the others. The country man looked puzzled and bemused because he was. The astute knight, who had not got to wherever he was by not failing to spot puzzlement and bemusement, took the initiative.

"I imagine that you are both puzzled and bemused."

The man's insight was amazing. That really summed up the guest's state of mind. It was truly incredible but presumably, that's how these chaps, they call themselves executives, isn't it, reach the top, mused the rustic gentleman.

"First of all, let me thank you very much indeed for agreeing to see me and for giving up so much of your time. I hope that Chadwick found you in the Archester bus terminal all right, as agreed, and that you had a comfortable journey here."

The still bewildered Woodfieldian nodded. This was a very odd day. He had never been this far north before and he had only understood the waitress's strange accent by concentrating hard. Fortunately, he had seen crime series on television, based on this area, so was not completely lost.

"I really must apologise for all the dagger and cloak stuff. Incidentally, I hope that this will compensate you for your time and trouble. I know that you have had to hire some staff to look after things whilst you were here." This was not entirely true but as Sir Simon fished inside his jacket pocket and produced an envelope which he handed over to a grateful Woodfieldian who placed it in his inside pocket, Reg Farmer saw no reason to challenge the wrong sequence of dagger and cloak and thought that this might be an example of executive humour.

It seemed that that handing over cash was the thing to do in when involved with important people. Reg was reminded of Members of Parliament being given envelopes containing money to ask questions in the House. Sir Simon's efforts to be discreet would have seemed furtive and suspicious to anyone watching but nobody was.

The Woodfieldian thanked the KEEPQT boss.

"Yes, it was a very comfortable ride, thank you, and thanks again for this." He patted what was now safely inside his inside pocket.

The knight continued. "Before I say anything more, I must also thank you for wearing a dark suit and white shirt and no tie. The reason was…" Here the Woodfieldian interrupted.

"That's all right. It comes out just for weddings, not that there's many of them, and for funerals and there's plenty of them. Wearing it for a meeting, that's really a posh thing to do."

The knight also wanted to thank his guest for not wearing his trade mark hat.

"After you gave that television interview, at the cricket match that Parker tried to fix, and you put that TV chappie in his place, you became well-known. Then, of course, you became really famous in all those ads, saying, 'You can trust me'. I didn't want anyone to recognise you, chatting to me and that's why I chose a midlands city, not well-known for its rural activities, to have a chat. I thought that if you wore a dark suit, white shirt and no tie, you would look just like a modern businessman."

The theory did not apply to bosses, however. Apart from a regulation but very expensive dark suit and white shirt, Sir Simon was also sporting a club tie and was wearing a waistcoat which matched his suit and one lapel was adorned by a large red rose.

Reg Farmer, famous farmer and a key member of the newly labelled and clumsily-titled "No to the Affordable Homes in Woodfield Magna in our lifetime campaign, (NTTAHIWMIOLC) nodded. "Very wise", he intoned, still uncertain why he was involved in this apparent subterfuge and added for good measure and to show that he knew some clichés, "no problem".

"Another drink?"

"Yes, thanks, same again, if I may."

A knightly hand immediately attracted attention and, as if by magic, a waiter appeared. Reg did not have that kind of influence even in the Duck and Orange that he had patronised for decades.

"You know, of course, that we are going to have to demolish our executive homes and that, according to our agreement with the government, we had to go ahead, whatever happened, with the so-called affordable homes?"

"Yes and I must tell you we are still totally opposed."

"Yes, precisely. A few days ago, wondering what on earth we could do, it suddenly dawned on me that we and you are on the same side and that, if we co-operated, we might be successful in what we both want."

Reg, who had realised this weeks ago, deemed it wise to express restrained surprise at this example of senior management thinking. He whistled quietly, feigned astonishment although he did not know he was feigning, and agreed.

"Dead right, squire", he said forgetting himself briefly. He apologised and his host expressed the wish, Reg, if that's all right with you, that, in turn, you call me Eustace."

Reg stuttered "sure but I thought that your name was Simon".

"Yes, it is but I like the gentle soothing sound of Eustace."

Eustace continued.

"Well, can we keep this meeting and what is said totally, and I mean totally, secret. You must promise me, Reg, that you will only tell key members of your campaign. Nobody else must know as even entirely unwittingly or accidentally, they might undermine what I'm proposing to do."

Reg had no experience of this kind of thing, but sensed that, as his host had just said that they were both opposed to the building project, something interesting was to be offered for discussion as a result of which the houses would not be built. Reg, "the farmer you can trust", according to all the advertisements, nodded enthusiastically.

"Well, my lawyers have been pouring over the agreements we had with government, who, as you know acquired the land from you villagers, through compulsory purchase orders, before selling it on to us, doubtless at a profit to the Treasury."

"We received a miserly £3,000 per acre" said Reg.

"We paid £400,000 per acre" said Eustace.

Eustace resumed. "We think that we may just, I repeat, just, have found a possible escape clause, or rather an omission of something important. We don't think that it will necessarily mean that the development will never take place but it may delay development until after the election. As it happens, the likely PM was at school and university with me and I know quite a few of his friends. I am firmly of the view that they will cancel the project, on the grounds that the site was not really suitable for development and that is the view I'm going to try to get across over the next few months."

Reg sat up, or rather, tried to in the comfortable chairs that were like chairs in fashionable London clubs, although he did not know that. Steeling himself, he asked "Well, Eustace, what's this magical solution? Are you planning some more subsidence?"

Eustace was not amused but his sharp response worried Reg.

"I'm not going to tell you."

Reg looked offended so Eustace continued immediately.

"When they torture you, I don't want you to blurt out what you know." Reg looked alarmed until he realised that this was executive humour.

"But, what I do want from you is an undertaking that you will reveal nothing to anyone except those whom you judge ought to know so they don't mess it up for all of us, including them."

Reg gave his word.

"As you know, not least from the tabloids, we have one of our subsidiary companies working in your area, digging ditches before laying pipelines so you good people can enjoy natural gas central heating. Well, where they're working is not far from the proposed site for the so-called affordable homes."

"Yes, I certainly do know, although they are working some distance from any homes, they woke me up with their noise the other Sunday, the only day I can have a lie in, at 8.30."

Eustace apologised and said that, in future, any noisy work would only begin at 9.30.

"Thanks".

"There's a large lake at the top of the hill, isn't there, if I remember rightly?"

"Yes, we call it Murdoch's Folly, but nobody knows why. Perhaps it's because it seldom sees the sun."

Eustace smiled and Reg continued.

"The water level can get quite high in the winter and then the Beckett, the little stream, floods when it can no longer can absorb the extra volume. But for the last ten years, we haven't even come close to a minor flood in the village, especially since all those new hedges were planted."

Eustace, showing no visible signs of boredom, listened politely.

"What I wanted to say was that if you or your friends see our pipeline team working during the night in that area, and I give you my word that they will be quiet, please, please ignore it. Anyway, it's some distance from any existing houses and of course, the lake area is much higher up the hill than the proposed new building site. Above all, don't report it to any authorities. I hope that I have made myself clear?"

Reg asserted that he had, and, imitating politicians, he said "yes clear, very clear" but refrained from any comment about tough challenges. The problem was that he did not have the remotest idea of what Eustace was going to do but it seemed good news that NTTAHIWMIOLC now had such a powerful ally. "You can rely on us. Whatever you have in mind, we shall support you wholeheartedly by seeing nothing, hearing nothing and saying nothing."

"Excellent, let's hope for the best and now what about a spot of lunch?"

A young waitress appeared in the restaurant and started to reveal what was available in the matter of food. Reg, not understanding the younger generations' new habit of ending a sentence on a high note, misunderstood when he heard the girl say "and we have curried chicken today". To him it sounded to him like "and we have curried chicken today?" Given this, he found himself saying, "I have no idea. I haven't seen a menu and I think that you are in a better position to know than me. I'm only a customer."

Later that day, Reg was dropped in Archester, which was part of the plan, and he found a taxi which took him home. Eustace had been generous. A friend, seeing a dark-suited Reg, asked "A wedding or a funeral?" "Sadly, a funeral". Reg, "the farmer you can trust", was alarmed at just how easily he had lied, but it was, he was sure, in a good cause.

Chapter 18

In the garden of the Duck and Orange, Steven Brown-Hassett was telling his young nephew, George, about some of the wildlife at home in Australia. The stories were going down well and Steven found himself offering to take his rellie, as they called them in Oz, to the Natural History Museum in London. Steven had heard all about the fixed cricket match, the fight to save the village from the new housing developments and the problems at the fete. He felt that a day away from all this excitement would be a good idea.

They joined the queue at the museum in the middle of the morning. Steven was surprised that there was a line to get in. George, an amusing, engaging and intellectually inquisitive little boy of eight, was able to explain. It was the school holidays and, at least for the present, admittance was free, "even for colonials". It was also his opinion that, when the next government looked at the economic state of the country it would, as he put it, "stare into a huge black hole of debt and decide to make visitors to museums, despite or even because of the view accorded to culture, stump up for entrance." He was nothing if not precocious but, somehow, he contrived to deliver these and other adult-type remarks quite naturally, without sounding like a well-educated young prig although the child in him emerged when he asked if five tow paths constituted a foot path. He also wanted to know whether a really bald man, these days, needed a three pee, rather than a toupee, to allow for inflation. He noticed the sign "Visitor's car park" and asked if that was because the car park was very small or was it because the management only managed to attract one visitor?

He also showed that he was normal by expressing a desire to have an ice cream and the two sat down and discussed the future of the world for ten minutes. Like everyone else in the village George was curious about the houses. Steven could only tell him what he had heard but he, was confident that, somehow, the houses would not be built. The topic then changed as young George wanted to know where Summer Bay, the location for his favourite Australian soap, was based. Fortunately, Steven knew the answer to this so his reputation did not suffer. "It's filmed near Sydney."

George was puzzled by some aspects of the soap. How did the schoolboys and girls afford all their new clothes and restaurant meals? "How do they get around as ' they're too young to drive? Come to that, even the adults don't seem to work every often and I wonder how they get their money. Then, there's that old chap, Alf, who must be about 90 but is always involved in rescues when someone has fallen over a cliff." Warming to his theme, he asked how some of the adults could afford to have so many children, not their own, and other adults staying in their houses, especially as they only had one bathroom. He concluded that if they attended properly to their hygiene, some of them could only emerge at about lunch time.

Steven's ignorance was about to be exposed so he suggested that they ventured forth to look for insects. These were a particular interest of young George who advanced swiftly in the right direction. Steven himself had always felt slightly guilty about insects. Apart from killing spiders who invaded his home, after all it was they who had crossed the boundary, wasn't it, he had slaughtered many butterflies when he was living as a young boy in Woodfield Magna. His technique had been to catch the butterfly in a net and then transfer it to a large jar. This contained chopped laurel leaves and there was a soft bed of cotton wool on top. The poor victims would soon be gassed and would die, without

245

damaging their wings. Then Steven, and he felt really guilty when recalling this, would push a pin through the middle of their bodies so that they were fastened in the valley of a white board. Their wings were then spread out on both sides of the narrow channel and then he and his friends could stare at them. Still, he thought, we all did it then and it wasn't thought to be wrong. That said, he always felt guilty whenever the absence of butterflies was discussed but, he reasoned, his actions could hardly have influenced the global butterfly population decades later.

George was staring, transfixed, at a glass display unit. He recommended his uncle to lose no time in gawping at the contents. Steven did as bid. "Look at that, uncle, it says that that beetle, the Ibnic, that red and yellow one, is very rare and lives in the Amazon jungle. Is that near where we buy books from?"

Steven smiled.

"It says that one was found in Ottershire, about 25 years ago. Did you see it? I'd like to see one. How did it get here then?"

Steven, reading the rest of the insect's rather indifferent cv, said that it would be very difficult to find because it turned green and hid under a leaf whenever it heard any noise. The yellowing notice claimed that it could detect humans at a range of 100 yards which, using his mobile phone-toothbrush-camera-calculator, the Aussie told his young friend was 92.31 metres. Steven noted that he could detect some nationalities at a range of 200 yards when he was on holiday on the continent. Apparently, the insect was red and yellow but changed to green when it sensed danger. It was, George observed, astutely, like a traffic light in reverse.

Some hours later, after staring at various exhibits, all of which were very dead, George wanted a souvenir of his visit so they headed for the shop. He chose a postcard, probably the cheapest item in the shop, but Steven, noting the boy's thoughtful restraint, suggested that they could do better than that.

"Here, isn't this your beetle? Let's buy this set of six. Would you like it?

"Yes, please, thank you very much."

The pack was bought and it was only then that they saw the full name of this very rare insect. It was Insectus Beelus Niger Inter Carpum but its popular name, doubtless used by its friends, was Ibnic. Steven Hassset-Brown remarked that it was " a jolly silly name".

A few days later, after George had been playing on the ground designated for the affordable housing, he announced that he had some "breaking news". He had lost one of his Ibnics. Bravely showing the optimism of a broken Chancellor of the Exchequer, it was, he said, very sad but it only represented a sixth of his collection or just 16.7 per cent.

A few days later, a keen environmentally-minded entomologist, coincidentally, was on holiday in the area. Amongst other claims to fame, he was one of the world's experts on Ibnics, which surely must have been the result of a mis-spent youth. Walking near the site allocated for the new affordable homes, to his astonishment, he believed that he saw an Ibnic. Initially, he approached the little creature with all the grace, poise and balance of a well-trained ballet dancer, but slipped in his haste to see the little creature before it legged it, as Ibnics were wont to do. He crashed to the ground, in a creditable imitation of a footballer trying to deceive the referee that he had been a victim of a severe foul in the penalty area. As he slipped, he caused some considerable disruption to the foliage in the immediate area. Leaves fluttered into the air and landed again without regard for their starting point. Some dry soil had been kicked up and the distraught insect man could not locate the Ibnic. This was profoundly disappointing but at least it confirmed the widely held view that, if the insect detected humans, it vanished as fast as its umpteen little legs could carry it.

It just so happened that the environmentalist was not just any old environmentalist. He was well-known in insect circles and he certainly knew an Ibnic when he saw one, which had only just happened, for the first time in a career already envied by all insect specialists around the world. Sidney Fotheringham-Cunningham was also an influential television presenter and was aware of the law on the matter of insect habitats. The Ibnic was a protected species and SFC lost no time in having the site closed to the various teams of workers who were about to prepare the site for building.

Sir Simon Pugh protested quietly in public, lest he be accused of not wanting to build the affordable homes, but readily admitted that the environment and its wild creatures must be protected, not least for future generations. This remark prompted an invitation to him to join the Business Insects Group, widely known, of course, as BIG, but he declined on the grounds of pressure of work. When nobody was looking, he allowed himself to perform a modest jig around his office. He was too old to perform an immodest jig. Personally, having read all the newspapers on the Ibnic affair, as it was already been called, he did not believe that a very rare beetle did live on the Northfield site but he was grateful for anything that delayed the beginning of the development. He needed a little more time to finalise his own plans. That said he thought how odd it was that a mere insect, albeit a rare one, could stop a project to build houses whilst the wishes of the human population were completely ignored. Still, the Ibnic probably had insect rights enshrined in European Union laws.

Reg had dutifully told his close colleagues in the campaign to ignore any activity, especially at night, in the area, close to the large lake, where the pipeline workers were active. This was some distance from the proposed building site and a long way from the nearest habitation. He could not tell them any more because he did not know any more but he sensed that what was happening would be to the advantage of the village. He and his colleagues were delighted that development work on the building site had ceased, at least for the present, because of the discovery of the Ibnic.

248

Steven, who, had, of course, recently been to the Natural History Museum in London, was, naturally, perceived as an expert on insects, but, when challenged, merely responded that he could understand why there was so much excitement because the insect, as the experts said, was "jolly rare" and the discovery of one had put Woodfield Magna on the entomologists' map of key areas around the globe. Some parts of the specialist media, "devoted to insects and those who care for and love them", had been interested but the main emphasis in the general media was that a beetle had stopped a building development, backed by the authorities and opposed by the local people. Some speculated that, in future, new projects could always be undermined by the discovery of allegedly rare insects, specially bred for such contingencies, but this was ridiculed by the government as a "seriously flawed approach"

Nevertheless, Reg and his chums felt that they could not rely on the beetle indefinitely and planned other tactics which were designed to create a diversion from what the local hill farmers were about to do to some hedges. To PC Swagg's vexation, a number of gardens were subjected to some modest damage. Some potential prize winners, at the forthcoming autumn flower show, would not now be making an appearance. At first, it was thought that some jealous competitors might have perpetrated these "wanton and unwanted outrages" to quote the chair of the awards committee, but later, when a second round of attacks destroyed some of the plants now expected to win occurred, suspicion centred, almost inevitably, on the residents of The Grange. Some locals wondered if this was an example of retribution from those who, so cruelly, had been robbed of their chance of seeing their names in the local paper.

A few days later, irritation turned to anger after it was discovered that the television garden, run by H. Bush-Cook, had been attacked. Again, no great damage was sustained and, ever the imaginative professional, Hilary turned the situation to his advantage. In four special hour-long programmes, to be screened late during the dark winter evenings, when any viewers would not recall what to do in similar circumstances, he showed how to revive a garden that had been damaged by people who failed to appreciate the wonders of gardening.

One week later, all The Grange inmates were spending the weekend at an old stately home, near the coast so that they could enjoy the scenery, relax on the beach and go swimming in the crystal clear waters of Bluesky-on-Sea and bond with their new warden, Ernie Biggs. Whilst they were away, a new outbreak of crime occurred in the village. The thugs, acting under cover of darkness, as the local paper reported dramatically, had stuffed newspapers into at least 10 wheelie bins in the village. This, of course, was a dramatic violation of the rules relating to rubbish. The article went on to say that the bins were then set alight. Apart from the loss of such revered rubbish containers, the smell created lasted into the early morning, prompting many Woodfieldians to wonder if they had been subject to an overnight gas attack. The motive for the attacks was not clear: Rob Swagg, helpfully told by his superior to stop the new crime wave rapidly, knew that some 2,000 such bins were stolen each year, across the country and damage of many millions of pounds had been caused in some urban areas. "We don't want that sort of thing here" he had been warned.

Was this a gesture by the increasingly powerful and articulate group who opposed the use of the W Bin or was it a breakaway, splinter group of those who had vandalised some gardens. What was the motive? Could it have been a court decision to fine someone who had put a small plastic bottle, which should have been inserted in the appropriately-coloured box, in a wheelie bin? The magistrate, imposing the fine of £500 on an old-aged pensioner maintained that it was necessary to avoid "wholesale anarchy on the refuse front going forward".

One victim of the wheelie bin fires was killed when a spark from one had set fire to an adjacent kennel, occupied by an aggressive Alsatian, Bonaparte, whose name indicated what he would like to do to innocent humans. He had a reputation for biting the local postman and was doubtless salivating at the prospect of attacking the thousands of postmen and women whom he had not yet encountered. He was lucky to have survived for so long, despite being proved guilty on a number of occasions, so his departure was not mourned. Indeed, some villagers had felt that his time was up when they had seen notices around Woodfield Magna advertising Dog Trials.

Rob noted that because The Grange inmates had been at the seaside, they could be eliminated from his enquiries and he had a hunch that the horticultural damage and the bin affair was the work of the same group. He had also determined that this "senseless serious series of stupid crimes", as the local paper, in an outburst of alliteration, described it, was the work of local people. Rob wondered what crimes were not stupid but this was no time for diversions into philosophy. His reasoning was that outsiders would hardly have bothered to attack the village in this way when more chaos could have been caused by their "carrying out their nefarious activities in, for example, Archester, where there was much more scope". He also thought that it was easier to commit a crime in the town as it had good fast roads that allowed hooligans to leave speedily. Woodfield, surrounded by narrow lanes and steep hills, was more challenging. His comments were not well received by his colleagues in Archester, where he was to become a sergeant in a few months time.

Rob remained convinced that the chaos had been caused by local people, although, if The Grange inmates had been away, it was difficult to guess who was responsible. As he told his sister, they must be local and intelligent louts. Why had he come to this conclusion?

"Well, it was a well-planned crime and a number of people must have been involved as the bins all, apparently went up at about the same time. But it requires local knowledge to know on which day the bins will be wheeled out for collection. Then, as they are not emptied every week, it needed inside knowledge to work out which week the bin would be put out." "For example", he added, warming to his theme, "different coloured boxes that accompany the WBs, are put out in different weeks. The green box for recyclable material goes out one week, then it's the blue box for waste food, then the black box for cardboard, the purple box for old clothes and finally, the red box for old garage junk. You've got to be bright to know that the wheelie bin goes out only every six weeks and only some of Woodfield's most gifted could have worked out when wheelie bin day was due."

Barbara was impressed but asked how colour-blind people coped. Rob knew. They could ring the Refuse Removal Service offices between 9.45 and 10.15 on the second Tuesday morning in the month and a community support officer (Rubbish removal enforcement) would be despatched immediately to assist.

The oddly-named "Stop Woodfield wheelies now, yes now, (SWWNYN) denied involvement although Rob could not help noticing that they were not very upset at what had happened.

What Rob did not know was that the farmers working on the hills above the designated building site had been busy ploughing but, instead of creating horizontal furrows to encourage rainfall to move sideways, they had drilled vertical channels which cause rainwater to go down the hill where it would be stopped and absorbed by the hedges, or would have been, if the hedges, which had acted as a barrier, for many hundreds of years, had not been thinned out severely and their roots had been loosened. Indeed, some of them, inexplicably, had vanished. Was it possible that the damage to gardens had been done so that, in due course, the removal of the crucial hedges could be blamed on the same gang to divert attention away from those who, inexplicably, had taken such odd action?

Meanwhile, the pipeline employees, enjoying substantial bonuses for working as quietly as possible during the hours of darkness, on a separate project, continued to toil. The site was some way from the village and nobody questioned why so many pipelines were being transported to the site even before the trenches were excavated. The whole area, of course, was divided from the rest of the village by the hills and access was denied to all but those who had been authorised. To achieve such official recognition, personnel had to have passed a new

252

exam, set by the Health and Safety Authority and be approved as a "properly-empowered person" (a PEP) by the newly-created European Union Directorate for Safety, Health and Welfare in domestic, industrial, commercial and agricultural sectors. All this effectively meant that no locals would be allowed on site, even after the Ibnic affair was over, and it was only because Sir Simon Pugh had some university chums on the board of EUDFSHAWIDICAAS, as it was know for long, that his workers were allowed to work at the top of the hill.

Chapter 19

The weather men and women had predicted a wet autumn for the Woodfield area and they were right. The rain tumbled down from leaden skies relentlessly, day after day, night after night with such a remorseless and malevolent force that a few local residents wondered if it was time to develop skills in boat building. The Beckett, hitherto a justly ignored stream, could, surely, soon become a river and even the locals were surprised, because of the sustained ferocity of the rain, that it had not yet changed its character.

The bad weather over so long a period had forced the pipeline men to leave and much of their equipment had been taken away. The company issued a statement to the effect that the conditions were impossible and that, weather permitting, work would begin again as soon as possible. The site, up the hill, had been abandoned and Reg and his campaign colleagues, moving swiftly between downpours, braved the conditions to see what kind of mess had been left by the pipeline men. To their surprise, apart from the ruts in the fields and hills, the area where the pipeline was to be laid, was surprisingly clear. However, as they climbed higher up the hill, they had noticed that some water had gathered in the area designated for the affordable homes. The area had always been relatively dry in the past, even in wet winters, so it was a surprise to see that the rain had effectively carved out a new but modest lake, but the Woodfieldians assumed that it would soon be absorbed into the ground.

Reg and his friends were keen to see the state of the large lake, at the very top of the hill. He assumed that the tons of rain that had fallen would have caused it to have reached a very high level. Obviously, some of any overflow might have kept levels just below the height of the surrounding area but what he and his colleagues saw astonished them. The lake was not full.

After two more days of torrential rain, a puzzled Reg and his cronies wanted to see the state of the lake at the top of the hill. This time, they approached the site from a different angle, some way from the affordable homes site, but were dumbfounded by what they saw. Despite the continuous rain over many days, it was now virtually dry. This ran counter to the fact that rain from the surrounding hills had drained into the lake for many centuries but, now, it was dry. Where had the water gone? Reg and co had already agreed to return to the village via the site for the affordable homes. The ground there had not absorbed the water, as had been expected and it was clear that the hedges, which, for centuries had absorbed some of the rainfall from higher up the hill, had gone. Was their disappearance part of the campaign involving modest garden sabotage and wheelie bin fires, or had they been uprooted by the water?

As the terrain became flatter, near the proposed building site, there was a new feature. It was as if the lake at the top of the hill had been moved close to the building site. The new giant water feature, that would have taken away the breath of Charlie Dimmock, had formed over a sunken area, the base of which, astonishingly, although this was not visible, had been concreted by person or, more probably by persons unknown. A very strong retaining wall, hidden by some newly-planted but mature-looking hedges, had been constructed. It was here that the rain collected from the hills joined earlier gallons in a new home. The area that had been designated for affordable housing, already more than a little damp caused by previous rain, had now become a brand new and impressive lake.

A few days later, after the bad weather had abated, an inquisitive Reg climbed up the hill, past the new lake to see what the old one looked like. It was dry, just as if had been drained and the contents placed in a new lake that now occupied the only land in the immediate area that was suitable for building houses. That was very odd, wasn't it? Reg thought for a few moments, and then smiled. His first task when he got home was to ring his chum Eustace and the two agreed to have a celebratory lunch.

"Where shall we meet?"

"What about Birmingham?"

Reg enjoyed the meal with his new friend and sat back in the car that the noble knight had provided to take him home from Archester station. As he looked out of the side window, near journey's end, he saw a serious wisp of smoke coming from The Grange. As he watched, the smoke was outlined against some vivid flames. The executive car was immediately overtaken by several fire tenders but Reg thought that they would have some problems speeding down the country lanes, especially pasts the tractors that were active at this time of the year and the East European fruit pickers who had left the fields to see what was happening. Fortunately, all the inmates except one were now in the United States on what was described as a study tour. As he watched, the flames curled ever higher, seeking to lick the clouds. The Grange was beyond saving.

"No affordable houses, no executive houses, no half-way house. Woodfield Magna three, central government nil", he muttered, puffing on an expensive cigar.